Deadline Man

Books by Jon Talton

Concrete Desert
Camelback Falls
Dry Heat
Arizona Dreams
Cactus Heart

Other Novels
The Pain Nurse
Deadline Man

Deadline Man

Jon Talton

Poisoned Pen Press

Copyright © 2010 by Jon Talton

First Edition 2010

10 9 8 7 6 5 4 3 2 1

Library of Congress Catalog Card Number: 2009942184

ISBN: 9781590587140   Hardcover
       9781590587232   Trade Paperback

Poisoned Pen Press
6962 E. First Ave., Ste. 103
Scottsdale, AZ 85251
www.poisonedpenpress.com
info@poisonedpenpress.com

Printed in the United States of America

For the true newspapermen and newspaperwomen.
And for Susan.

Chapter One

Thursday, October 14th

In my line of work, it's called an anecdotal lede, a way of beginning a complicated story with a telling human angle. If journalism exactly mirrored life, mine would begin like this:

Troy Hardesty has achieved the paperless office. Not even a Post-it Note profanes his sleek desk. The desktop is ten feet long, made of black marble, framed in platinum, and shaped vaguely like the deck of a supercarrier. It is polished so highly that I can see my face in it. At the desk's precise center are two thin computer screens, facing in at angles, a keyboard, and mouse. The newest Blackberry model sits to the right of the keyboard. Every few seconds the Blackberry chirps: confidential dispatches from the front lines of capitalism. Troy's hedge fund has just invested $75 million into a Silicon Valley startup that will compete against the company that makes Blackberry. Three chairs face the desk, made of the same platinum and dark reddish wood as the superstructure of the desk. They are comfortable, but not too comfortable. After half an hour in one of those chairs your back may start to hurt. Four other chairs of the same design are set at precise stations around a circular conference table ten feet from the desk. It, too, is bare. Two walls are adorned with Picassos and two are all glass, facing the city. His office is expensive and minimalist and it smells like lemons.

A large plasma-screen television hangs on the wall nearest the desk. It has a dark wooden frame that exactly matches the frame of the nearby Picasso. The screen is split into four. CNBC, Fox Business, and some private feed of market numbers are on three of the splits. The fourth is local news, showing a photo of a girl-next-door with straight honey colored hair, parted in the middle, and a peaches-and-cream face with a thousand-watt smile. She's the girl every boy fell in love with in high school. Underneath the screen says, "Megan Nyberg: missing teen." I shake my head: a world of important news out there and people would rather be entertained by the latest pretty white teen in peril. My back is starting to hurt.

I am twenty-six hours from deadline.

Troy glides in, a tall man wearing a sleek black suit and purple shirt, buttoned up to its pinpoint collar, without a tie. It's properly edgy and expensive. For all that, he resembles an Episcopal priest. Father Troy of St. Bigbucks. Except he has that look common to men who make a lot money: expensive haircut, chiseled athletic features, taut skin, chicken lips. He's forty-five and looks it, but in a good way: seasoned, resourceful. He nods and says my name. He quickly pages through the messages on the Blackberry, then makes a show of checking the time on his wristwatch, a silver Breguet with a black band. I saw a story in *Forbes* that said it retails for $275,000.

He then walks with quick strides to the glass doors leading out to the terrace. I stand and follow him outside. He always does this, as if he's paranoid about someone overhearing what he tells me—as if it were that good—or he's supremely proud of his view of downtown, Elliott Bay, and the Olympic Mountains. It's the kind of October day where the long, late West Coast summer lingers in Seattle like a fickle tourist. The temperature is seventy-five, a slight breeze flickers down from the northwest out of a cloudless, nearly cobalt blue sky. A ferry is plowing white froth across the bay from Bainbridge Island. Behind it a massive container ship is beginning the long journey to Asia.

The balcony planters are still wild with colors: red, pink, violet. From twenty stories down, I hear the whine of a siren.

"Is this beautiful or what?" He leans on the balcony railing and I join him. I am not afraid of heights. I am not like Jill. Fear is not hopelessly coded inside me, destined to make me too afraid to leave my loft. It's a disloyal and selfish thought, but then I think about Rachel and figure this is my week for them.

It's a long way down and I make myself study the people-ants scurrying along Fourth Avenue to early lunch. The railing is not quite waist high, but I have long legs.

"Mountain's out." He cocks his head to the south, and sure enough, the giant cone of Mount Rainier has emerged from the foggy muck that often shrouds it.

"So what does the columnist want today?" He gives me an indulgent smile. But his movements are agitated. "You know, I'm still getting grief from that thing you did on me. Don't know why I talk to you."

That "thing I did on him" was a column more than a year ago, discussing the implosion of the hedge-fund industry, but explaining why some players were still making big money. I remember the headline: "Long live the hedge-fund kings." I used Troy as an example—and with his ego whispering in his ear he went along, giving me details right down to his vintage car collection, float plane and getaways to the San Juans. I write as many as 140 columns a year, plus a blog. So it's easy to forget most of them. Writing a newspaper column is like writing in chalk on a sidewalk, an old-timer once told me. But the sources always remember.

So I start with a softball to put him at ease. What's his reaction to increasing regulation of the hedge-fund industry? But he takes it and launches into a lecture about excessive regulation driving capital overseas. There's more than a trillion dollars in hedge funds like the one Troy runs and they long operated outside the rules that govern traditional securities. They're part of the shadow banking system that most people have never heard of, and they've been blamed for helping bring on the big recession, or small depression—depending on how you look at it.

Some of the funds have profited from the repeated federal rescue attempts. Troy's is one. Others have collapsed. A big fund just went down that morning and now is being investigated in New York for pension-fund fraud. I may ask about this later, but for now I just listen as seagulls fly overhead. Troy is probably not a bad guy. But he's a source, not a friend, not an acquaintance. We're here to use each other and I always intend to get the better end of the bargain.

"So how long are you going to stay in the newspaper business?"

It takes my brain a few seconds to process his question because I had tuned out his homily about the sanctity of free markets. My mind is on Pam, in my bed last night. Pam makes a lot of noise when she comes and afterward I read poetry to her as we lie naked and drink shots of single-malt scotch. Robert Frost and Macallan. I let that image go reluctantly and give my stock answer, "Every day I'm employed, I'm pleasantly surprised."

It usually produces a laugh. Troy just leans out, studying the street. I hope nobody cut corners with the construction of the railings. "Journalism is over," he goes on. "Your kind of journalism. Nobody reads anymore. You're too elitist to write about what people want. Celebrities."

"Please."

"The *LA Times* and the *Chicago Tribune* are in bankruptcy. San Francisco may close. The *Rocky Mountain News*, gone. The *P-I*, gone—don't think that'll keep you guys out of the crapper. Ad revenue keeps collapsing by double-digits. Look at all the layoffs…"

For a guy who claims to not care about newspapers, he keeps up pretty well. I am so tired of the newspaper death watch, so tired of arguing, speculating, trying to make people understand all the reasons newspapers have committed suicide. It's the last thing I want to discuss with Troy. I say, "It's all because of greedy bastards like you." Now here I am trying to piss off a source I need for my Sunday column.

"You couldn't get me to invest in a newspaper today!" he sneers. "Mature industry. Declining profit margins. You're all in the buggy whip business after Henry Ford came to town. You ought to do something new, make some money."

"It's not in my nature. I'm a skeptical, ink-stained wretch."

He waits for the sound of a siren to fade, then, "Yeah, and if I was seeing Rachel Summers, I wouldn't worry, either. Daddy will set you up. Hot little daughter with a big trust fund."

I think: *asshole*. I also wonder, how does he know I am seeing Rachel Summers? I say nothing. Most guys like Troy like to operate in the shadows. If they talk to the press at all, it's to the *Wall Street Journal* and *New York Times*. I'm fortunate this particular asshole likes to talk to me. His agendas are mostly benign: to see himself quoted, when he wants to be quoted, and to show the local columnist how smart he is. Me, I want scoops and rarely get them from him easily. Otherwise, I'll settle for an influential hedge-fund manager's insights, or an off the record tip that I can leverage elsewhere. We both have to trust each other. So far, Troy has never burned me. It's a delicate transaction.

"Olympic International," I say. "Hear any takeover rumblings?"

Troy steps back from the railing and rubs his chin. "You're kidding, right? They're a dog."

"But their stock's been doing well. Some of the raw materials prices are rising again."

"They're overvalued," he sniffs. "And don't tell me that demand is going to restart in China. Industrial production is still way down. Look out at the port. How many container ships do you see?" I see one. "Inflation is still a big issue there, it's just that nobody's talking about it. They're stuck with a trillion dollars in U.S. Treasuries—that doesn't make them strong; it makes them weak. Anyway, China has a huge population that's poor out in the countryside. You can forget about the clean energy racket. The Chinese leadership is going to have to do whatever it takes to feed everyone, and that means more dirty industrialization."

This is where Troy is very good: smart and contrarian. A gust of wind streams across the terrace, whipping my tie.

"But," I say, "does the market believe Olympic is overvalued? Private equity outfits are sitting on a lot of cash. What if somebody broke up Olympic and went with the most profitable units."

He looks at me closely. "Are you asking me this or do you know something?" A vein on his forehead is standing out. I think he wants to gossip.

"You know Pete Montgomery is an old friend," he says. "He and I were roommates at Harvard." Montgomery is the chief executive of Olympic, and I have only heard this information a half dozen times from Troy. I nod.

"So are you going to quote me about the SEC thing?"

"You know I don't make promises." I smile. "But I'm sure I can find a home for what you said. You'll sound brilliant as usual."

"Smartass."

"Anyway, everybody's been talking about turning Olympic into a real estate investment trust. That's not the sweet spot of the company." He looks back over the side. "What do you know about eleven-eleven?"

I don't hear him at first, or I don't think I do. But he repeats it: eleven-eleven.

"Some New Age thing involving crystals and Burning Man? I don't have a clue."

He laughs, or I think he does. Then, "Come back in the office and I'll tell you what I know about Olympic. But this is all off the record. I mean it. You can't quote me, even on background."

"Wait. What about eleven-eleven?"

"What do I look like, the newspaper? You want to hear about Olympic or not? I've got another appointment in a few minutes."

Half an hour later I have a good start on my Sunday column. Five or six more phone calls and I'll be done. Oh, there's the writing under deadline pressure part, too. Troy walks me as far as the private side-door to his office, claps me on the shoulder and says, "Think about what I said. Don't take your future for granted." I thank him and head out. I won't be caught napping if one of the city's largest companies is facing a takeover attempt. Once I reach the street, I'll duck into Tully's and make notes.

I didn't want to do it while Troy was talking. It makes some sources nervous.

The elevator is full when it arrives, but everyone is getting off on the top floor. A woman in a gray suit pushes out and crashes against my shoulder with a force that gets my attention. She's tall and pretty with short, blond hair, and doesn't acknowledge the football block she put on my shoulder or look back. Whatever happened to Seattle Nice? I ride down alone, thinking about what Troy had said about newspapers. It might be the end of my world. I know that. Papers have been closing. So many good people I know have been hurt. The survivors have been cutting staffs, dumbing down coverage and acting as lapdogs rather than watchdogs. I am lucky to be at the *Free Press*, which still values serious journalism. It is also a private, family-owned company, a little more immune from the terrible pressures and fads that are bleeding newspapers through a thousand cuts. I don't always make smart choices, but coming back to Seattle five years ago and returning to the *Free Press* was one.

The plaza and street are busy with the lunch crowd. Men in suits with places to go. Young women in skirts and heels with life in their eyes. Tourists studying maps of downtown and carrying Nordstrom bags. Badly dressed Seattle kids in hoodies who think they invented the unbathed, stubble look. Lots of young software engineer-types with windbreakers and computer bags over their shoulders. The usual panhandlers and assorted street rats. Traffic is moving easily along Fourth and every few seconds a green-and-yellow King Metro or blue-and-white Sound Transit bus roars by. Even so, the air smells like it must have smelled the first day the world cooled down and became paradise. I re-crimp the knot of my tie and pull the notebook out of my inside suit pocket. My shoulder still aches where the short-haired woman hit me and I start to rub it when I hear the faintest whistling sound.

The explosion is close, a single sharp boom, concussing and echoing between the skyscrapers. I fall to the plaza concrete and cover my head, a consequence of long-ago training. The concrete is cold and that only makes my heart hammer harder. When I look up, most people are just standing there paralyzed, locked in the second of the detonation, dumb, stunned looks on their faces. I think, of course, terrorism. I stay down, recalling reading how there's often a follow-up car bomb to kill the rescuers. Another part of me thinks: *this is a great story.*

The street is silent for a few seconds, and I can't smell any evidence of an explosion. None of the windows are shattered. There's no blood. As I rise to my feet, people start talking and yelling, moving toward the street. A car alarm erupts. One scream, seismic in its intensity, then a second. Different screamers. I follow the noise and see the wrecked hood of a new black Toyota Camry. The front tires are flat. It's sitting behind a bus on the curb lane, where the building angles away from the plaza and sits hard against the sidewalk. The Toyota's driver is one of the people screaming. Then I see what's left of the body cradled in the collapsed hood of the car. My legs walk toward it, my body drunk on adrenaline. I am amazed by the lack of blood on the corpse. It lies face up. That makes it easy to see that what's left of the man on the Toyota is encased in a sleek black suit and a purple shirt, buttoned at the collar.

Chapter Two

After the anecdotal lede comes what's called the nut graf, the nut-shell paragraph that will summarize the complicated story and put it in a larger, more compelling context for readers. It takes special skill to write an effective nut graf. Editors like nut grafs and I'm good at them. But for my story I'll pass on it for now.

I wait to be interviewed by the police. The sidewalk around the Toyota has been cordoned off with yellow crime-scene tape. They wrap it around the trunks of the trees lining the street. It looks festive. The leaves are starting to turn. The body itself is hidden behind a blue tarp. People leave the plaza to return to work, their lunches ruined. Some are crying. Traffic is awful because of all the police and fire vehicles, and horns echo off the buildings. Seagull cries echo, too, as if they're really vultures. I sit on a cold concrete cube of plaza ornament and try to make notes about my interview with Troy. Not to be a heartless bastard, but there's still a column to write. One of the cops recognizes me.

"Hey, you're the columnist," the plainclothesman says. "I like your stuff," he adds. "I never used to look at the business pages before."

He introduces himself as Sergeant Mazolli. "One Z," he says. Journalists should never stereotype, but he looks like the guy who's owned your favorite Italian restaurant for years: portly, fleshy-faced, stubby cigars for eyebrows and an expression that's friendly as long as you don't push it. I put my notebook away. Mazolli wants to discuss high finance. I stare toward the Toyota.

I remember the view off Troy Hardesty's boastful balcony, dizzy, free-fall, devil nightmare, all the way down to the people-ants along Fourth Avenue. What would you think about on the way down? Would you have enough time to wonder if you'd made a big mistake? Or would it just be one long terror ride to the surface?

"Take the Chinese," Mazolli says. "They're loving these wars. We spend the blood and treasure, and they just keep racking up our debt. What is it? Six-hundred billion a year we borrow from them? And all so we could buy their junk." I nod knowingly. He finally gets down to business.

My hands are shaking. I may or may not have been the last person to see Troy Hardesty alive. Mazolli doesn't say. Something keeps me from wanting to know. So we go through his questions. No, Troy didn't seem despondent when we had talked. No, he didn't say anything about wanting to take a dive off an office building onto the product of the world's largest automaker. I don't know much about Troy's private life. His wife's name is Melissa and he lives on Mercer Island; I've never been to the house. He was a wealthy, influential guy who liked to talk and occasionally he had good information. It wouldn't be the first time money couldn't buy happiness. Hell, maybe he got too close to the railing and slipped. Mazolli wants to know what we talked about but when I tell him he grows bored. "I lost a ton in Olympic stock," he grouses. I wish my hands would stop shaking. Mazolli confers in whispers with another cop and tells me I can go.

I don't get back to the newspaper until nearly three. Now I'm starting to get anxious about the Sunday column, due in twenty-two hours. I can write fast and I never freeze. An editor once nicknamed me "the deadline man" for my poise under pressure. But I still need to gather material and critical time has been lost. Some of the calls I need to make are to New York, where it's nearly six p.m.

The Free Press Building is an art-deco jewel close by the downtown shopping district. If I look outside the window by my desk I can see the blue, vertical Nordstrom sign. It consists of a fourteen-story tower and a five-story addition that mostly holds the presses. The newspaper building was finished in 1931 and has been lovingly preserved, right down to a side door that still says "newsboys only." The main entrance has an eagle, wings spread, and elaborate scrollwork carved into the limestone. Large letters proclaim THE SEATTLE FREE PRESS, and below them is carved DEDICATED TO THE PUBLIC TRUST. A single flagpole hangs out to the street from above the eagle, with the American flag slapping languidly in the October breeze. There's scrollwork, filigree, and other designs above and below the windows, and carved figures inset at the building's corners. One is winged Mercury, another a 1930s working man, yet another vaguely resembles one of the panhandlers down by my place in Pioneer Square. More stern-visaged eagles roost close to the top, poised to fly, then, above them, towering statues emerge from the limestone as the building reaches the roof. These are robed figures: wisdom, truth, philosophy? Obviously they are not most editors. The building attests to a time when the press had great power. Now the company leases much of the building to software firms, game developers, and lawyers.

I walk in the grand entrance, through one of the six brass doors, across the polished marble floor. The lobby was once busy with people placing classified ads. Now it's nearly empty, few people there to see the front pages from 100 years of the *Free Press*, displays holding eight Pulitzer Prizes, and portraits of its publishers. Prominent is the painting of Maggie Forrest Sterling. She looks out on the lobby, frozen at age fifty, at the height of her powers. No matter that she was the grand-daughter of the man who started the paper—she had begun in the newsroom covering cops. I had always imagined her as one of the wise-cracking, tough-as-nails girl reporters from old movies. She had still seemed that way when I knew her, a young eighty, opinion-ated sweet vinegar. She had liked my column and protected me from businesses that didn't care for my take on their troubles. Boeing, Weyerhaeuser, Microsoft, Amazon.com—I don't always make friends. She had died in her top-floor office three years ago. It had been a Friday the thirteenth. I see a very alive publisher near the elevator bank. James Sterling looks like a handsome intellectual, with tortoise-shell glasses, reddish brown hair and beard, and a narrow mouth. He's friendly and has carried on the family traditions with the paper and I don't quite trust him. With him are two men in expensive suits. They look anonymously like bankers or lawyers. Throw them into a convention of either and you'd never pick them back out. I hang back at the security console and let them take the first elevator. A man I knew just dived off a skyscraper. He fell right in front of me. My shoes don't quite connect to the floor and I have a cosmic sinus headache. In a moment, I walk on and push the button for the fifth floor. It takes a moment before I realize someone else is in the car: Karl Zimmer, the head of maintenance. He's a tall, humorless man with an old-fashioned crew cut gone white and a raw-boned face so pale it looks like concrete. He's worked here as long as anyone can remember. I say hello. He grunts. Melinda Stewart jokes that he's a serial killer.

The main newsroom of the *Seattle Free Press* takes up the entire fifth floor of the tower part of the building. When I first started here, it was a low-ceilinged clutter of metal desks and cigarette smoke. I had missed the era of typewriters by just a few years, and IBM Selectrics languished in stacks inside closets. By the time I came back to the paper a few years ago, the ceiling had been opened up, low carpet-wall cubicles had replaced the metal desks, and color-coordinated banners hung over the departments: METRO, NATIONAL, COPY DESK, DESIGN, and more.

Still, you would never mistake it for an insurance office. The cubicles are inevitably cluttered with files, piles of old newspapers and precariously stacked cardboard boxes to hold the overflow from the cubicle file drawers from the Herman Miller designers. Here and there, old timers have thin metal pica poles sticking out of pencil cups—I still have mine, with my name etched in it. From the remains of the old newsroom: waist-high wood cabinets to hold bound editions of various sections or the whole newspaper, and, especially around the cluster of copy editors, shelves contain every kind of reference book. Four large blue recycling containers further destroy the pristine intentions, looking as if they had just been wheeled in from the alley. A *Free Press* newsstand sits beside the metro desk, the day's edition looking out. On the far wall is a large map of the world with six clocks spaced above it: Seattle, New York, London, Moscow, Beijing, Tokyo.

Newsrooms are quiet now. It gives me the creeps. If typewriters and teletypes are long gone, so are most of the loud, profane, eccentric characters that used them, yelled "copy!" to summon the gofer copy boys and girls, and didn't necessarily play well with others, particularly their bosses. The best of them had high-octane talent and taught me much. As a young reporter, I missed deadline by eleven minutes, prompting a screaming tirade from the city editor, who somehow was able to accomplish this bit of mentoring without ever removing the cigar from his mouth. I never missed deadline again. Now shouting is frowned upon, much less smoking. Shout and they'll send you to HR for a talking-to, or maybe they'll Myers-Briggs you, so you know what an inappropriate, extroverted, cynical bastard you really are, and how it's offensive, especially to women.

The room is also quiet because of worry. It hasn't been that long since the *Post-Intelligencer* closed and the *Seattle Times* always seems to have one foot close to bankruptcy court. Not that long ago, Seattle had been the last city outside of New York to have three newspapers. Now it's one of a handful of two-paper towns and the alternative press and blogosphere speculate about it being a no-newspaper town. I don't think that will happen—this is a readers' town—but the *Free Press* news staff is less than half its size in 2000. There's an entire ghost newsroom on the third floor—up until 1957, it was the newsroom for the family's afternoon paper, the *Mirror*. Once that closed, the room was given over to the features department. But with the cuts, features grew so small it could be fit into the extra space up here on five. More cuts could come any day. Everybody's afraid.

The main newsroom is crowded. All the desks and cubicles are taken and reporters, photographers, and editors stand around. Maybe it's a metro meeting. Bad time for a meeting. The daily deadlines are cascading now. Reporters will start filing stories and editors will be under pressure to make the early editions. The 4:00 news meeting will have to be pushed back. Halfway across the room, Melinda Stewart, the national editor, smiles at me, rolls her eyes, and runs a hand against her dark brown wedge of hair. When she smiles wide, it's a goofy sexy grin that can lead you to underestimate her. She complains that I have gotten handsome as she has only gotten older. It's not true—she's as attractive as the first time I saw her twenty years ago. I smile back, then make a hard left and walk down a corridor toward business news, which is off in one of the building's many out-of-the-way spaces. In fact, it sits on top of the presses in the five-story addition.

I pull the mail out of my cubbyhole and glance across the toweringly messy cubicles of ten business writers. Five desks are empty from the hiring freeze. One reporter who left and wasn't replaced had covered Olympic International, and now that company has gone uncovered for three years. The business editor has an enclosed office with a door. I have one, too, but rarely use it. I unlock the door and leaf through my mail. There's a pink envelope and, inside it, a card from Melinda Hines. I smile at my techno-luddite who won't use email and stick the card in my pocket.

"The columnist graces us with his presence," the business editor says. I ask her if she knows about Troy Hardesty.

"The young cops reporter told me," she says, rising from her chair. "Why do all these kids have names like strippers? Amber, Tiffany, Crystal. God, I feel old."

"Amber's a nice name."

"Mmmm. Anyway, newsroom-wide meeting. You're just in time."

"Oh, joy. What do you want to do about Hardesty?"

"Suicide, right?" She seems uninterested as we walk. "Another one bites the dust."

"Maybe his fund is about to crater."

"Just like 1929, huh? Well, good luck finding that. There's probably no disclosure."

"Somebody knows."

"And I wish I had a financial services reporter," she says. "Five reporters down, remember. Chase it if you want."

I think about that. I really want to get ahead on the Olympic International story. But if a fair-sized hedge fund has lost a bunch of money and caused the suicide of its rising-star leader, well, I'd read that one in the newspaper, too. But I don't have time to call in a bunch of favors from the Microsoft millionaires and other assorted gentry, to find out who's lost money in Troy's fund and—harder still—is willing to talk about it. I decide to wait to see if someone calls or files suit. I will stay on Olympic International. If it's bought, thousands of jobs could be cut at the headquarters half a mile away, and a few people will make hundreds of millions of dollars. All those employees, living their lives, paying their mortgages, drawing their paychecks. The company won't tell them the roof is silently crumbling. I will.

The main newsroom is even more crowded now but it's quiet. I see James Sterling standing in the middle of the room, next to the executive editor and the managing editor. They look at the high ceilings, the television monitors of cable news attached to the pillars, the big recycling bin by the metro desk. They don't look at anyone. The executive editor opens the meeting and I am half listening. The rest of me stays back at Troy's obsessively neat office. All that money. All that stuff. Now he's dead, squashed after a twenty-story fall. He knew somebody was stalking Olympic International. It's a big private equity outfit from New York, and the talk is of a leveraged deal. Take on debt, don't use your own money. You'd think after the crash, that kind of thing would have gone out of style.

Sterling starts talking. He has a high voice, naturally soft, and it scratches anytime he tries to project in a room. He's recounting the fiscal year that just ended: the performance of the seven newspapers owned by the company, declining advertising revenue, rising costs of newsprint. Hardesty told me that the leveraged deal would be followed by the breakup of Olympic. Take it private. Strip it down. Sell off the dogs. Go public again with the best parts. Get rich. It's a classic move. Hardesty knew it all and I was amazed he gave it to me.

I had to promise not to name the private equity firm in the first column, otherwise they might know he had told me. Was he in on the action? I asked. He just gave a tight little chicken-lips smile. I can't quote him. I can use the information he gave me to ask others. I can check filings with the Securities and Exchange Commission, short-selling of the stock, insider trading. I can see what relationship the top Olympic executives have with the private equity guys. The golden parachutes will be sweet.

"This is a day we hoped wouldn't come." That's what James Sterling just said.

He repeats it. "This is a day we hoped wouldn't come."

"But we have to live in the real world," he goes on. His professorial face now looks ratlike. A rat in tortoise-shell glasses. So now it will be bad news. No one even coughs or moves a chair. A wave of apprehension rolls silently through the room. Melinda Stewart stares ahead, pale, grim. With her right hand, she silently grasps and releases a stress ball, a handful of sand packaged in a tight rubber wrapping. It's meant to help combat repetitive stress injuries. It silently comes apart in her hand and the sand spills onto her desk. I think: *layoffs.* He keeps talking. Jargon. Filler. He talks about the need to "reinvent the newspaper for the 21st century" and a "difficult journey ahead." He says, "We need to listen to our readers." I watch faces: people I've known for years; younger ones I don't know. I was Maggie Sterling's favorite columnist. I wonder if that means anything now.

"We've hired an investment banking firm to advise us…"

The metro, sports, and lifestyle reporters look blank. Not the business writers. We know what's coming.

"The company will be sold. And if that doesn't eventuate in this media environment, then the *Free Press* and our other papers will be closed in sixty days."

Chapter Three

That night I break up with Rachel. Somehow I don't have enough stress in my life. The newspaper is for sale. It may close. Hell, it will close. Nobody is going to buy the *Free Press* chain. Layoffs are imminent and consultants who know nothing about journalism are studying us. The staff heard that news and then was expected to go put the paper out as always. That's just what they did. They are pros. They did this after a venomous question-and-answer period that James Sterling left as quickly as possible. The top editors were left but it was quickly clear they are nearly as surprised as the rest of us.

Reporters and editors at their desks were typing even as their colleagues were asking what the hell the future held. Phones rang and were answered. They had to move copy. They had to get the paper out. Some of them were crying. We were all sick. I was sick. I backed out of the room and returned to my office, closed the door, and closed the blinds. The computer told me there was no news about Olympic International. All quiet on the Online Journal, Yahoo Finance, Marketwatch. The shares closed down two cents. My scoop was safe. I made eighteen phone calls, left eighteen messages, asking about Olympic. I left my cell phone number. Maybe I would start getting return calls early in the morning. I made two additional calls about Troy Hardesty's fund, just to cover my ass, just in case. I left more messages, then walked down the back stairs five floors without talking to anyone. A drunk was walking up the stairs. He asked if I was the sports columnist. I said no, and called security.

At six minutes after seven, I walked into a bar in Belltown and saw Rachel already at a booth in the back. She had ordered me a martini and was waiting to take her first sip. The place was mercifully empty. There's small talk. The newspaper may close. Easy stuff like that. Then, the hard stuff. I have gotten good at breakups, a master of goodbye. Still, a ball of anxiety and sadness fills my middle. She doesn't cry until I open the door to her taxi. She puts her hand on my arm, promises to keep reading my stuff, "even though it would be hard."

"You're a nice guy," she says, a lie. She is a nice girl, the truth, a brunette with flawless fair skin, abundant and naturally curly hair, and the character to teach middle school in the inner city. Her father is one of the richest men in Seattle. She is a nice girl and that's the problem. She will want marriage and stability, whatever she says, and I can offer neither. It's better for her this way. That's what I tell myself. It's better for me, too, a selfish bastard. I let this one go too far. I broke my rules. Now I have made it right, she can go find a nice boy, and make a nice future, and I feel like shit. The cab glows lurid yellow under the streetlight. The color of the coward. Then she's gone. She's rid of me. I can't hurt her now. A ball of anxiety stays in my middle. It starts raining. Fine, gentle drops. Seattle rain. The sidewalk is wet with Rachel's tears and my face is wet and my footsteps are muffled by the leaves on the sidewalk. It's as if I'm not there at all.

I walk toward my loft in Pioneer Square. I need to pick up my car. I need to be somewhere. As it rains harder, I wish I had done it before meeting Rachel. The wind gusts straight and hard across Elliott Bay, catching me when I cross the streets and lose the cover of the buildings along First Avenue. I button my trench coat tight but I don't have a hat, so my hair is soaked. I deliberately do not look up at the skyline. I do not want to see Troy Hardesty's building. I have to file a column in seventeen hours and I am not prepared. My left eyelid starts to pinch. How could I develop a nervous tick at my age?

By the time I cross Yesler the sidewalks are deserted and it's raining big, frantic drops. My shoes are ruined and my socks are wet. The street is darker and I am surrounded by the 1890s buildings of the old city, built after the great fire. About a third of them have been completely restored. The neighborhood goes through booms and busts and now it's down on its luck. Empty storefronts that a few years ago housed expensive galleries. It can't quite ever escape its old identity as Skid Row: the neon sign of the Bread of Life Mission proclaims "Come Unto Me." A couple of upscale bars look half full, warm, and inviting. I fight the temptation to slip into Elliott Bay Books. The sidewalk tilts at a slight angle toward the street. I can't quite keep from thinking about Rachel.

"Can you spare some cash?"

My heart retreats into my throat as a woman emerges from a doorway. A brown leather miniskirt is visible beneath a distressed coat. She might have been attractive once. Now she resembles a cat that has been drowned, then electrocuted. Her long hair is bunched and wet, and her eyes are two lost marbles. Maybe her nose has freckles on it or maybe she's that filthy.

"Sorry to startle you," she says. I tell her I don't have any cash, which is the truth.

"Is there anything I can do to make some money? I fuck for money."

I shake my head and say I'm sorry.

"I swear I'm eighteen!"

I don't answer. She's so skanky looking she could be seventeen or forty.

Suddenly her gaze sharpens. "I know who you are!" The rain stops. It doesn't turn to sprinkles or drizzle, but stops dead. I turn and walk. I do not want to be this woman's moment of clarity.

"Hey!" she yells and I hear her heels clicking after me. My initial unease returns. Even though I feel as if I can take care of myself, it's been years since I've been in a confrontation, much less a fight. My pulse jumps into triple digits as I walk faster. Then, "Fuck!" She's spilled onto the slick pavement. I laugh out loud. It could be worse: we had a story today about a man who kept a dead prostitute in his apartment for a week.

I look back and she's on the sidewalk, pointing at me.

"Eleven-eleven, motherfucker! You'll pay! Eleven-eleven!"

For a moment I stand frozen, remembering Troy Hardesty's question: *What do you know about eleven-eleven?* My eyelid feels as if it wants to leap off my face and flee down the street. I turn back and stare at her.

"What did you say?"

She backs up against the rough, aged brick of a building, then turns and runs. I run after her, telling her to come back. She trots maybe twenty feet, then slips down an alley. I run faster but when I reach it she's gone. The alley is narrow and hemmed in by old buildings, five and six stories high. A security light hangs in the middle, surrounded by a cage. I step in, walking slowly on the wet cobblestones. A half dozen big trash bags sit against the buildings on either side, part of the city's campaign to eliminate dumpsters. Fifteen steps into the alley and the noise of tires on rainy street is swallowed in silence. I do my best to avoid the puddles as I check the doorways and indentations between the buildings; nothing. She couldn't have run this fast. I can feel the rough, uneven paving stones through my sodden dress shoes. *Eleven-eleven.*

I'm ready for rats, at least I think I am, but nothing prepares me for the size of the thing that skitters out from a doorway, black, fat, and formless. Then I realize it's an empty bag, propelled by the breeze. A jumble of ancient industrial flotsam fills five feet of space between two buildings. Doors proclaim business names and the alarm systems to keep you out. I am directly below the security light. Another few steps and the buildings are empty, the doors replaced with old plywood or iron. Decrepit fire escapes cling to walls and through broken windows and half-covered entrances comes the special darkness of abandoned places. Syringes are scattered every few feet. I walk faster, now not so sure I want to find her after all.

They emerge silently from the blackest part of the alley, all in bulky layers of clothes, all in hoodies. They look like malign

Michelin men. I count five, realizing I can turn around or walk on, neither decision particularly safe. I am thirty feet from where the alley opens out again, but I can see only gloom. The street and park beyond are empty, the buildings dark. Not even a single pair of headlights passes by. I walk on, feeling the medicine ball return to my gut. I look ahead and at nothing, my tough street face on, the one I had learned to use back east. Fifteen more paces and they form up, pretty much closing off the alley. A cigarette end flares. Beyond them, I see a Starbucks sign, turned off, the store closed for the night. The whole street is a dead zone. I keep my pace steady, my face set, and I just walk through the group. Nobody says a thing. I thank God I'm tall, broad-shouldered, and can look tougher than I am.

I turn and walk south again, past darkened galleries, using the windows to discreetly see if anyone is following me. No one is. When I reach the next block there's traffic and pedestrians, noise and neon, as if I have been teleported to a different city. I walk another block to my place. I will have to change clothes.

"Eleven-eleven! Eleven-eleven! Asshole!"

I turn and she is a silhouette, a block away.

She laughs. "You'll get yours."

I shake my head and laugh, too, resigned that she is jabbering and I am imagining connections that don't exist. When I look again, she's gone.

Once an old girlfriend put a hex on me, or so she said. It involved chicken bones and a cup of water on my desk. I just thought it was the leavings of the overnight sports writers, who sometimes camped out there to file their stories. It was only the next day that a photographer walked by, asked if I was all right, and told me of the ceremony that had been performed on my desk, with the girlfriend, Linda, and her shaman, arranging the bones and chanting over them. *The Stranger* found out about the episode and wrote a bit called "Voodoo Economics" about an unnamed business columnist being the victim of a newsroom hex. It was the beginning of the best years of my life.

Chapter Four

Friday, October 15th

I leave Melinda Stewart's house in Capitol Hill a few minutes into the foggy dawn, tossing her newspapers up on the porch and walking across the damp flagstones. She had called me after she had gotten off work at midnight and then she had wanted to go all night long.

Talking, alas.

Our long, on-and-off love affair has cooled, but her friendship is precious. Halfway into a bottle of wine, it became clear that we were reciting all the old lines about the deaths of newspapers: Industry consolidation; impossibly high profit margins promised to Wall Street; groupthink that dumbed down content; monopoly markets that took away competition. How the intellectual capital of the newsroom was only seen as a cost center, and, at paper after paper, the most capable and experienced journalists were pushed out. How the yes-men and yes-women got ahead in management at too many newspapers. How newspapers are the only consumer product that spend almost no money promoting themselves.

Most of all, the problem was a business model that depended on essentially sending out miniskirted sales reps to sell confiscatory ad rates to lecherous old car dealers and appliance-store magnates. With such profit margins, decade after decade, newspaper executives became complacent. Wall Street wouldn't tolerate an innovation unless it promised huge and immediate returns. Then came innovations from outside like Craigslist and the old model collapsed. I'd written about it before, about so many industries: monopolies and cartels always commit suicide.

Trendsetters such as Gannett blamed the newsroom, and "journalism" was degraded into reports about school-lunch menus, entertainment trivia, and missing blond teens. The "experts" blamed new technology. But the heart of the problem was dependence on an unsustainable business model. Giving away our content only made things worse—and then there was no going back, because nearly everybody was giving it away. Nobody wondered just who would be around to produce sustained, sophisticated journalism if people weren't willing to pay for it.

We'd said it all, so many times, over so many bottles of wine. So we got silly after half that bottle was gone. Melinda and I had both started at a little paper in eastern Washington owned by the *Free Press* chain, and we had both started writing obituaries. So we took our turn pretending to write obits for the newspaper industry. The cause of death: suicide. As we laughed, I worked very hard to keep Troy Hardesty out of our magic circle.

We told old newspaper stories—about the time young Melinda got so mad she threw a typewriter at one of her tyrannical editors (he promoted her); the famed "women's page" columnist who had the answers to remove any stain or fix any household emergency; the old courts reporter who would fall asleep in his chair for hours after filing his story for the day and the new assistant city editor (Melinda) who feared he had died that way; Jack Emery, the longtime entertainment writer who would attend press galas so he could stuff his pockets with hors d'oeuvres to eat all week at home; the people who had copulated on the historic conference table of the Governor's Library.

"Not me," I said.

She laughed, "Yeah, sure." Melinda years ago taught me the word "louche." I like it.

We reminisced about all the great scoops the *Free Press* had over the years, all the major news events we covered, when the newspaper enjoyed its greatest prestige and influence throughout the Northwest. At its best, the paper told the people what they needed to know to be informed citizens, told them the things that those in power didn't want them to know.

We screamed together in unison: "It is the mission of the newspaper to report the news and raise hell!"

Next came our one-downsmanship contest—the worst assignments we ever had at the *Free Press*. And notorious corrections. Here the winner was the young features writer years ago, before they started charging for wedding announcements, who wrote up a notice about the nuptials being held in a "pubic ceremony." It ran through 100,000 copies before a night editor caught it.

"And," she said, nearly snorting wine through her nose, "what about Bob McClung?"

Indeed. The legendary sports columnist who spent 55 years at the *Free Press* had asked that his ashes be buried in the building. After his death, the publisher, Maggie Sterling, had arranged for him to be interred in the lobby, under an unassuming plaque. Journalists would bend down and rub the plaque for good luck. No one then could imagine a world without the *Free Press*. What would happen to Bob now if they closed the building?

We stopped laughing. We long knew the mortal danger facing newspapers and the near impossibility of ever finding a news job again, but somehow we thought the *Free Press* might survive. It was privately held, had little debt; readership was stable in print and growing fast online. But the advertising market continues to struggle. I cursed James Sterling, but Melinda was more philosophical.

"He's probably doing the only thing he can," she said. "The heirs control the board. As you probably know, the family covenants allow the board members to call for the sale of the newspaper if earnings fall below a certain level, and they have."

"And nobody on the board wants to keep the paper going?"

"They just want their checks every month. Now they're afraid that not only will that go away but they'll also be on the line for the losses. So they're cutting staff to make the paper more attractive for a buyer. But they're sure as hell not going to sit through months or years of being in the red."

"Bastards."

"I think Sterling would keep the paper if he could. He's not the bad guy. Blame the board. You still have a crush on Maggie Sterling. You never realized how dysfunctional this family is."

I understand dysfunctional families. I don't understand rich people, even though I have spent most of my career writing about the messy business of money. I was careless in picking my parents, didn't get a trust fund, or the gold door-opener from the Ivy League university. All I could ever do was work harder than anybody else. Now even that won't be enough. "Maybe," I said, "I can get a job in the courthouse lobby, the guy at the information desk."

"Yeah," Melinda said, "I can see Mister Big Personality doing a job like that. Sure."

We fell asleep, spooning against each other. But that was it. Me, I'd rather keep tension, unemployment, mortality at bay with sex. Melinda isn't built that way.

Outside it's cool and the air is thick with fog. It takes me a moment to notice the man leaning against my car. He wears a leather jacket and jeans, and as I get closer I can make out his close-cropped brown hair. Seattle is one of the safest large cities but the crime of the season is mentally-ill transients that murder strangers out on the street. I'm on guard but armed only with the warm memory of Melinda's company. But as I get closer he looks pretty normal and well scrubbed, with clean clothes and an expensive brown leather jacket. He has a jock's face. His eyes are very blue under the streetlamp. People in this neighborhood walk their dogs at all hours. He stands and walks away when I approach. He's not walking a dog.

I drive down the hill into downtown, trying to use the wind-shield wipers to wash the seagull attack away. The bay is shrouded in fog and the Space Needle looks like a ghostly alien craft from a 1950s movie. Back home I shower then dress and make a quick run through the *Free Press*, the *Seattle Times* and the *Wall*

Street Journal. It is a good day for the *Free Press*: an exclusive by
our Washington bureau that the FBI had violated the law more
than a thousand times in its domestic surveillance work. We're
proud that our D.C. staff punches above its weight class. Close
to home: another scoop about poor security against terrorism at
the local ports and a story about corruption in the city streets
department. It's a good day to be a journalist. Except for the story
in the *Seattle Times* about the pending sale or closure of the *Free
Press*. It's on the front page. Of course, we wrote about it, too.

The *Seattle Times* has a sidebar about the history of the
paper, including the fabled infighting of the extended Forrest
and Sterling families, the uniting figure of Maggie Sterling, the
seventy-eight heirs to the family fortune who are shareholders of
the company, and even Tyee Island in the San Juans. The private
compound was built by the colorful patriarch, Gov. Eugene
Forrest, and features some grand houses and little cottages built
by some of the leading architects of the 1920s. Family members
are able to reserve a house there one week a year. I think: If they
sold the damned island, it would probably keep the newspaper
going for ten years. But this isn't the way rich people think.

I get a call back from New York, where it's a little after nine. A
good source at Global Insight and he's willing to be quoted. He
doesn't know of an impending deal but he sees how it could work.

"The best part of the company is Olympic Defense Systems,"
he says.

I tell him I've never heard of it.

"That's the way they want it. But it's a very solid unit. They've
done a lot of contracting in Iraq and Afghanistan, avoided the
taint of outfits like KBR. Also a major supplier of night-vision
goggles."

"What about the defense cutbacks?"

"Don't fall for that. Some programs are being cut, but the
budget keeps growing."

I wear my phone headset and make notes on my laptop. I
thank him, shut down the computer, decide to head into the
newsroom and start writing.

Outside on the street, a tall, skeletal young man stops me. He wears a denim jacket adorned with arcane patches and has a silver chain hanging from his pocket. And he is wearing a kilt. I'm wearing a gray suit and one of my favorite ties, sartorial armor for the day ahead. We momentarily stare at each other like members of isolated tribes who suddenly discovered the other. He uncorks the earbuds from his head.

"I read your column yesterday. Why are you always making excuses for big business? The middle class is under siege. Don't you get that?"

I thank him for reading. Long ago I decided to let the columns speak for themselves. I'm not a reporter. As a columnist, I'm paid to have an opinion. How much opinion varies from paper to paper, but at the *Free Press* I have considerable latitude. I try to use it wisely. One day I might take readers into the executive suite, to hear what Steve Ballmer or Howard Schultz has to say. Another day, I connect the dots, backed by twenty years experience as a financial journalist. I'm the one who's paid to see around corners, demystify the news, analyze, and investigate. I start conversations. I start arguments. Three times a week, Sunday, Tuesday and Thursday. Sixteen inches on the weekdays. Twenty-four inches on Sunday—more if I need it. I have the best job in journalism.

This reverie ends when I encounter another man. He's the same one who had been leaning against my car outside Melinda's house. This time he has a friend in a dark suit. They walk toward me.

He calls me by my first name and shows a black wallet with a small badge and credentials. He pockets it after five seconds.

"We need to talk."

I make excuses and ask if I can contact them after deadline. I already talked to Sgt. Mazolli. They stare at me. The man in the suit is more compact than his partner but has one of those ageless, unlined, churchgoing faces. He might be thirty. He might be fifty. I guess that he's older than the first man. His dark hair is thinning, worn unpretentiously, and he looks amiable. But he steps to one side of me, way inside the comfort zone, boxing me in. The first man leans in and smiles at me. His eyes are still supernaturally blue and his skin is flawless. His chin is prominent, nearly overwhelming the rest of his features. He's not a person who looks better when he smiles. He takes my shoulder and steers me toward a black Chevy Suburban.

"We need to talk to you now," he says. I don't like being pushed, but I climb in the truck. They drive south, past King Street Station and the stadiums and the clotted incoming traffic. We're not going to police headquarters on Fifth Avenue or the precinct on Virginia. I say this.

"We're not police. We're federal officers."

The SUV isn't going to the federal building, either.

"What do you want?"

"We want to talk to you."

My heart is pounding to a beat of *why? why? why?* I guess everybody reacts that way. I try to keep my game face cool. I'm unshackled in the back seat of the SUV, both the feds up front. The door is unlocked. It can't be that threatening. I have a small, petty, apprehensive thought: could Rachel have done this? I decide, no.

Eight blocks go by and we're deep in the anonymous warehouse district east of the port. We pull up to a new red-brick building with no windows, where a heavy gate opens. They pull into a small walled-off parking lot, then wait for a garage door to rise. The SUV slides slowly into an immaculate garage area with two other SUVs and three black Crown Victorias. A camera is mounted from one corner of the ceiling. The garage door closes and we step out into cool artificial light. The floor is spotless. We walk toward a wall with four doorways and a larger entrance with a metal door rolled down. We go to the one that has a rectangular metal box attached to the wall on the left. The box is painted the same gray as the rest of the wall and has a glass cover and beneath the glass LED lights emit a reddish glow. The man in the suit looks into the box and there's a solid metal click from the door. They lead me through an empty, blank corridor, painted the same gray. The one in the suit holds open a door and we all step inside.

It looks a lot like an interrogation room.

"Am I under arrest?"

"No, relax."

The first man takes off his leather jacket, revealing a short-sleeved, black polo shirt. He's buff and proud of the muscles in his arms. His knuckles are raw. But I most notice his light-brown leather shoulder holster and in it, the biggest handgun I have ever seen. It's a semi-auto, silver with a black grip and the barrel must be eight inches long. The bore is huge. It hardly looks federal issue. The man in the suit tells me to relax again and pulls out a chair. He sits across the table and opens a leather portfolio with a legal pad. The first man stands to my right, just at the edge of my peripheral vision. They still haven't told me their names.

I look straight ahead at the man in the suit.

The first man leans against the wall and crosses his arms. He says my full name. "You were born in Seattle in 1961. You look younger than you are. Your father died in federal prison. Your sister, Jill, killed herself six years ago. You graduated from the University of Washington and served in the military."

"What the hell is this?" I sit straight in the chair. My feet feel funny.

"You were part of a team that won a Pulitzer Prize eight years ago. As a columnist for the *Seattle Free Press* you make $108,000 a year and your taxes are in order. But your personal finances are a mess, not something I'd want to advertise if I were a business writer. You were married once and divorced. Now you see Rachel Summers, Pamela Moffat, and Melinda Stewart. At the same time. You get around, brother. You have no close friends."

The room is as bare as my mind at that moment. Coffee stains dot the tabletop like meteor strikes. "What do you want?"

"How long have you known Troy Hardesty?"

So that's it. "Seven years," I say. "I met him when he worked for Lehman back East, then we both ended up in Seattle." The man in the suit makes notes in a neat hand on the legal pad. He places his left hand in front to conceal what he's writing.

"What did you talk about yesterday?"

"A column I was working on, among other things. Why are you asking?" I wonder what Troy was into. Securities fraud, insider trading? That's not the kind of thing that gets a journalist picked up outside his building. It had to be something else. They just stare at me.

"Did Troy kill himself?" I ask. "Or do you suspect foul play?"

They actually say it: "We'll ask the questions."

My mind replays those last moments with Troy. He seemed his usual carefree, arrogant self. He let me out the side door, so I didn't know if he met his next appointment or if he ever had one. They demand to know more about our conversation. I had cooperated with the police. After all, a man had just died. Now I start to wonder about First Amendment issues, about telling the confidences of a news source. I tell them I want to talk to the newspaper's lawyers. My mouth is so dry it takes me a moment to finish the sentence.

The man in the suit glances at his partner. The partner pulls over a chair and sits close to my right. I can smell his cologne and it reminds me of something I tried in high school. Brut? Old Spice? He starts nervously shaking his leg. The butt of the big handgun jiggles inside the holster.

"We need to know the details," he says.

"I can't tell you until I talk to our lawyers." I say it in a stronger voice and his leg stops shaking.

"So what do you do in your spare time? What kinds of things does a guy in your position have to read?" The man in the suit smiles at me as if we are just having coffee together. He has shifted the dynamic of the interview, from confrontational to friendly. I should know: I've done it many times myself.

What do I read? How much time do you have? It sounds like a job interview. I give the short list: eight newspapers in print or online, four magazines, ten Web sites, documents from various federal agencies and dozens of companies, and let's not forget those sexy reports from the Federal Reserve Banks.

"What else?"

"That's about it," I say. "Sometimes a novel or a work of history. My eyes get tired at the end of the day."

Writing, writing, writing. The man in the suit makes his notes. I try not to let my leg shake, the leg that knows deadline is coming down on me like a runaway train.

I try to take control. "So what kinds of cases do you guys specialize in?" I direct it to the buff one sitting beside me. He just stares.

"What about the Internet? Do you write a Web log?" This, again, from the man in the suit.

This one is easy to answer. It's public knowledge. I write a short blog entry every day on the newspaper's Web site, on economic and business topics. I tell them that I was one of the first business columnists to start a Web log, more than a decade ago, and that the *Free Press* has one of the nation's busiest newspaper Web sites—something the "you guys are buggy whip makers" critics conveniently overlook. My column and blog are promoted on Twitter, where I have hundreds of followers, and on Facebook. I want to throw them off stride, take some control, find out what they're after. He ignores me.

"Do you keep a personal Web log?"

I shake my head. "No time. Anyway, I do this to get paid, not because I'm a wannabe writer with a site nobody sees."

"Are you interested in conspiracies?"

I watch his eyes for a tell. A skilled interviewer won't let you know when he's asked a question that's vital to his story. This guy's pretty good: his eyes stay steady, his mouth straight and friendly. But he stops writing, even puts down his pen. When I take notes during an interview, I try to put the pad on my leg, beneath the table and out of the view of the subject. I make continual eye contact as I make notes. It only took a few years to learn how to make notes without looking at the notebook.

Am I interested in conspiracies? How the hell does that go with Troy Hardesty's suicide?

I say, "Only if I can prove them. I'm a professional skeptic."

"So what did Troy tell you?" the first man says, circling around behind me. "Specifically."

We're back to Topic A.

"I can't discuss that. There's this little matter called the Constitution and the Washington state shield law." I think: Troy asked about eleven-eleven. And the prostitute screamed it. Eleven-eleven. I would sound like a nut. I keep my mouth shut.

"We've got an amateur lawyer here, Stu," says the round-faced man.

"Let's trade information," I volunteer. "Why are you looking at Troy?"

They look at each other and stay silent.

"C'mon guys, what's up? I keep confidences all over town. Probably some from your bosses."

The room overtakes us with its silence. It's not a nice sound. Nothing penetrates the walls, which means nothing can escape, either. I tamp down the paranoia. Andy Grove of Intel said only the paranoid survive and it's a good credo in one's professional life. But I also have a certain family history.

"We can keep you here," Stu says.

I say, "I want to see your identification again."

The agent starts writing again. He looks up mildly. "We'll give you a ride back. And we'll be in touch."

I decide not to push it. We repeat the path back through downtown. This time I sit in the passenger front seat and the man in the leather jacket sits in the back seat. The digital clock on the dash says 8:30. I have only four-and-a-half hours before deadline. Before the SUV pulls to the curb, the man in the suit turns to face me.

"Rachel, Melinda, and Pamela," he says, staring at me intensely. "A man who has so many compartments in his life makes me suspicious. Have a nice day."

"Can I have your card, in case I think of anything else?"

The window rolls up and the SUV spurts away from the curb into traffic, too fast for me to get its tag number.

Chapter Five

Who.
What.
Where.
When.
Why.

The traditional news story begins with those five Ws. It's intended to get the most critical information at the top of the article where more readers will see it. This pyramid style consigns the less important background material to further down, where it can be cut if space gets short. I'd just as soon cut mine, whether the feds are telling the truth about me or not. I'm old school: I know the first paragraph of a story is spelled l-e-d-e, to differentiate it from the l-e-a-d in an old-time, hot-type Linotype machine, and I don't believe the journalist should become part of the story.

I make a quick stop at my loft. Nobody else has returned my calls or emails yet. You can spend a lot of hours waiting for sources to call back. I don't have those hours now. But I think I have enough to weave tomorrow's column. Troy's background information is critical. Even though we agreed that I couldn't quote him, he told me that someone is accumulating Olympic International stock and is intent on taking it over and breaking it up. When I go on the Securities and Exchange Commission's EDGAR site, I hit pay dirt. A new 13-D filing for Olympic has been made at 9:14 a.m. Eastern time. It's required by law if an investor acquires more than five percent of a company's shares. In fact, 9 percent of Olympic's shares are now held by something called Animal Spirits LLC. My adrenaline washes away all my other worries. This is big.

I have no idea who Animal Spirits LLC is. It sounds like the kind of band that would have played down at the Crocodile in the old days, but I know it was a phrase from John Maynard Keynes. He talked about the role of "animal spirits" in the market. I use Google and Nexis to search for the firm and come up with nothing. Nobody has written about it. LLCs are notoriously murky; they're meant to conceal the identity of their principals. The 13-D tells me nothing more than the name. I guess it's a private equity outfit, still one of the largely unregulated playpens for the very rich to invest their money and reap huge returns, or, sometimes, big losses. Their specialty is "rip, strip, and flip." They buy companies on the cheap, take them private, lay off as many employees as possible, close unprofitable business lines, bolster the profitable sides, strip and sell assets, then take what's left public again. It's big money for the winners. Private equity operates largely in the shadows, parallel to, and in competition with, traditional Wall Street. Even so, many private equity houses have their own Web sites. Not Animal Spirits. This won't stay in the shadows long. Usually a letter to management is made public, saying the company is undervalued and either making an outright takeover or demanding change. That will rock the world of Olympic's chairman and CEO, Pete Montgomery, Troy's old college buddy.

I link into the newspaper's system and write pieces of the column as fast as I can, about its recent performance, speculation on the Street, the SEC filing. Sometimes stories come from press conferences. Everybody gets the news when the company or government allows them to have it. Me, I try to find news as it is becoming. Now I have followed a hunch about an old-line company into a potential exclusive. While I write, I wish more people would call me back so I can write with more confidence.

I don't just want to tell readers about the filing. The *Times* could easily get that, too, if they have a reporter covering the company or an editor watching the SEC. The *Wall Street Journal* can get it. The news may already be online. I type fast and hard. I wear out computer keyboards.

I have to explain what it means and try to look ahead. Here, my source's insights will make a big difference, especially about the defense subsidiary. I sell business intelligence, to shareholders, employees, vendors, competitors—anybody who wants to shell out fifty cents for the *Free Press*. Hell, you can get it online for free. Anybody can be a columnist for two weeks, and then he or she runs out of ideas. Anybody today can be a "columnist" on a blog. But to be a real columnist for a major newspaper, to be one of the most popular destinations at the paper—whether on the dead-trees edition or online—that's one of the hardest gigs to attain and sustain in the working press. A few of us were born to it and nothing else. I'm one.

Finally, I recharge my cell and use the land-line to call in a favor. Once I helped the owner of a parking management company who was being screwed by the city. He knows he owes me big, and after my initial call he gets back to me in twenty minutes with the information I want. I use that twenty minutes to keep writing, and all the while I know that I am losing time, losing time, deadline is coming. I grab my suit coat, a couple of props, and make a fast walk ten blocks.

Olympic International occupies an award-winning glass tower on First Avenue. The lobby has twenty-foot-tall Diego Rivera murals of forests and mountains, and the rough-hewn men who are taking their bounty. They came out of the old headquarters and were commissioned when natural resources were the company's main business. Reinstalling them in the new tower lobby caused consternation among the local environmental crowd, which is sizable. On the other hand, people in Seattle said, Rivera was a socialist so the art provides an ironic critique of rapacious capitalism. And the preservationists were happy to see them saved. But the murals stay because Pete Montgomery wants them to. I walk past the murals to the elevator bank and wait.

Five minutes go by and a pretty Asian woman with a briefcase walks up to one of the elevators for the parking garage. I join her and we step into the elevator. She swipes her card as I hoped she would and the elevator heads for level P-3.

"Thank you," I say.

She smiles and doesn't give it another thought. I'm in a suit, and made sure I am carrying both a cardboard file box, to keep my hands too full to swipe a key card, and my expensive Coach briefcase, to show I am safely in the executive class. The file box is empty. I've attached my *Seattle Free Press* employee ID to my belt; facing inward it looks pretty much like the ones worn by Olympic employees. I'm just the nice fellow management employee who can't get to his card. When the elevator stops I let her go first, then step out and turn in the opposite direction like I know where I'm going. Which I do, thanks to my parking guy. As I was doing sniff work for the column, I looked at the paperwork for an acquisition Olympic had made the previous year for its energy division. That gave me the names of four mergers-and-acquisitions lawyers who worked here at headquarters. Now I am walking toward their assigned parking spaces. I turn a concrete corner and all the spaces are empty. These aren't people who take mass transit. If their BMWs and Benzes aren't there on a weekday, I'd bet they're out of town. Maybe they're already working on a deal to sell the company. It's a small thing, nothing I can use in the paper, but it bolsters my confidence. I take the fire stairs to the street.

On the way up the hill to the newspaper, I call the head flack and get her secretary. Do I care to get her voice mail? You bet. I leave her a detailed message, about the 13-D, about word that the company could be for sale, about sources telling me that their M&A team is already working on a deal. I am giddy with news but keep my voice steady and calm. "This is going to run tomorrow, and I'd sure like the company's perspective." This is the third call I've made to get Olympic's comments. Maybe this will work.

"So is this budget line real about Olympic International?" The business editor stops me in the hallway. It's a sign of the tension in the newsroom that she would ask. I don't write budget lines—the summary of the story or column—that don't work out. I say it is.

"Make sure you make deadline."

I can't tell if she's kidding or not. I say, "Stand back and nobody will get hurt."

The flack never calls back. I wrap up my column, move it along into the CCI system, and call the editor. Then I make a new round of calls to sources, but all I can do is leave messages. Why would the feds be investigating Troy Hardesty's death? One guess would be his hedge fund got into trouble, maybe made a wrong bet on sub-prime mortgages, maybe got into something criminal. But with disclosure for the funds so limited, I can only hope to find a well-heeled client or rival who knows something.

I Google "eleven-eleven." I get a rock band, a real-estate trust, a psychic hotline. It's the date World War I ended. The real-estate trust might be what Troy had asked about and it seems innocently boring.

Next I email the day police reporter, Amber Burke, to see if she knows anything about the investigation into Troy's death. I've seen her byline, but can't place her. The *Free Press* still has more than 200 newsroom employees and I can't claim to know all of them, especially the young ones that often cover the mayhem, er, public safety beats. In a moment, she emails back: "I'm going to pull the police report. Want to come along?"

I'm in a jittery post-deadline mood, so I agree. She says she'll pick me up in ten minutes.

As I wait, I think about those essential five Ws and my encounter with the feds. I'll tell you this much. They're wrong that I don't have close friends. They just happen to be the women I sleep with. They tend to be professional, middle class, attractive but not beautiful, in-between the chapters of their lives. They like sex, and not everyone does. I'm their transitional man, the one they will fondly remember but never admit to once they have returned to the conventional world.

There are a few rules: I don't sleep with sources or fish off the company pier in the newsroom. Technically, Melinda Stewart breaks the second rule, but we go way back. No married women, although Pam has a regular boyfriend who is pleasant and steady, but he bores her in bed. I avoid women with children. No starry-eyed young girls looking for marriage—I broke that with Rachel. Four lovers are about the most I can juggle, although three is best. I try to make it a point not to mix pleasure and love. I married for love once. The sex ended almost immediately and the companionship soon after. I'll never make that mistake again.

I make no claim to be a ladies man. I didn't even lose my virginity until I was twenty-one. Now my lovers appreciate that I like women; I always have liked and related to them, far more than to men—insert family-drama causality here. I'm easy to talk to, good in a crisis, and clean up well for a night at the symphony. I'm discreet. I have the rules so nobody gets hurt, me included. And I know this blissful arrangement of the planets of pleasure can't last forever.

Who, what, where, when, why: The two men in the SUV had left me at the curb outside my place, and I can't answer that basic, critical information about our forty-five minutes together. All I know was that I had been on the other side of a hostile interview. Now I have to shove a growing bundle of dreadful feelings into one of my infamous compartments.

At least one compartment is untouched by my new acquaintances, the feds. They mentioned Melinda Stewart among my lovers. They apparently don't know about Melinda Hines. Hey, I like the name.

Chapter Six

I climb into an old black Jetta and greet Amber Burke. She throws a stack of files from the front passenger seat to make room for me, adding to piles of file folders, reporter's notebooks, and old newspapers in the back seat.

"Why are you all dressed up?" she asks. I get that all the time in Seattle. I want to answer people, "Why are you dressed like hell?" But I don't. I say, "Today it's the rebels that wear suits."

Amber is wearing a black coat, black hoodie, black-and-white striped sweater, distressed denim miniskirt, and gray tights so thick they could be long-johns. Below all this are brown boots that might work well to muck out a stable. It's a classic local look. The ensemble can't quite conceal the attractive young woman inside. She has lush titian red hair, pulled into something like a bun in back. She's probably been complimented on it since she was a baby. Her face is pretty in a deceptively simple way, the kind of face that you'd find growing more in beauty the longer you looked at it. She has a wide mouth. I stop looking.

"Sorry to do this," she says. "My editor wants me to check something out before I can go to the police station. Want to tag along?"

I agree and we drive.

"So, the columnist. I read your stuff. I saw tomorrow's column in the system. That's a great scoop."

"Oh, thanks." Too bad the expression "pshaw" went out with Kerouac. I ask her how long she's been at the paper.

"Six months. Now I'm afraid I might be one of the first laid off."

It's a real risk. But she's a cheap new hire. They'd get their money's worth to get rid of me and a few of the old timers. "I hope not," I say and change the subject. "How do you like Seattle?"

"I love it. Haven't made it through the winter. But I like rain."

"Me, too. It's a nice town. Kind people. Our own pet volcano…"

She has a nice smile. The wide mouth fills her face with happiness. She has great dimples.

We make small talk. She came west from the *Washington Post*. I mention a couple of friends and ask if she knew them. Only their names, she says—she was out in the Montgomery County bureau and came to the *Free Press* to "be a real reporter."

The immediate task is to talk to the former boyfriend of the missing girl, Megan Nyberg.

"The current darling of cable news."

"You're a cynic." She furrows her brow. "I don't disagree. I also don't want to be fired because I get beaten on this story," she says.

"I'm all for beating the *Times*."

"Forget the fucking *Times*. I want to beat the fucking Web."

There I am, sounding like an old fart.

"Rich, cute teenager from Mercer Island disappears. Even a serious economics columnist has to be a little interested."

I hold my fingers up to measure half an inch. She laughs. I'm grateful that the paper still assigns reporters to go out and dig on the cops beat. So many others have taken to just having them rewrite the official statements of the law enforcement public information officers. In other words, getting one side of the story, and the one people in authority want put out.

"Where's the FBI office?"

She looks surprised, then gives me an address on Third Avenue, a good mile from where I had been taken by the two feds. "What about the Secret Service, the DEA?" She names other locations, still different from the low, anonymous building I remember.

The sun breaks up the soft lead in the sky as we reach a street where Capitol Hill meets the Central District. We're blocks beyond the creeping gentrification. Megan's boyfriend is named Ryan Meyers and his apartment is one of the old brick four-story buildings the city has in abundance. This one looks as if the bricks are crumbling, although the columns at the entrance attest to better days. Amber parks on the downhill side of the street and sets the parking brake. Three homeboys deal pharmaceuticals on the corner by a shuttered market and I'm so glad to be the only white guy in a suit on the street.

The lobby is spare, small, and smells like dog pee. There's no elevator, so we climb. Amber tells me that Megan met Ryan at a rave in SoDo and saw him on and off in the months before she disappeared. But while the cops initially suspected him, they never made a case. "Maybe Megan just ran away," Amber says. "Maybe she didn't want to be found by her parents and then got into trouble. That stuff happens all the time."

"Maybe she's not in trouble at all and still doesn't want to be found."

"I just work here, man. Editor says go and I go."

"I bet." She laughs again. She has a loud laugh. I say, "She's how old?"

"Seventeen."

We huff up the third flight of stairs. I ask what do Megan Nyberg's parents do.

"Mom works at Microsoft. Dad owns a yacht brokerage."

"Enough money to raise hell with the cops."

"Exactly."

As we climb, the stairwell becomes even cooler than the outside. We arrive on the fourth floor and pass through the fire door out of the stairwell. The small, wire-mesh-glass window at the upper-center of the fire door is covered with a faded Doors decal. Doors, get it? The bleak corridor carries a heavy smell of cooked cabbage and stale miscellany best not dwelled on. Ryan's apartment is the second door in, and it's partly open. Amber knocks and we listen. Somewhere a Latin tune is playing. A pair of sirens passes outside.

"Ryan?" Amber knocks again, louder. "Hello?"

Nothing. Not a voice, not the creak of footsteps coming to answer. She knocks a third time.

This time the door moves an inch. I see a pair of pale legs on the floor.

"Ryan?" I push the door open and we see it: a thin man with a messy mop of brown hair and a belt around his neck. The belt is hooked to the end of the bed and looped around his neck. His body is turned at an angle. His head is cocked at an angle, as if waiting for an answer. It's not quite as low as his left shoulder and his face, turned down nearly to the floor, is gray, his lips nearly blue. It doesn't look like enough to kill someone, but apparently it was.

"Fuck!" Amber rushes past me, kneels and takes his pulse.

The man wears only a pair of jeans. No shoes or socks. One pants leg has ridden up, exposing part of his right calf. He's lost control of his bowels and the smell assaults us.

"We have to get him down, do CPR."

I stop her. "Amber, he's cold. We need to call 911. We shouldn't even be in here." It's a suicide kind of room, maybe twelve feet square and barely lit by a pair of small, dirty windows that look directly into another old building. Besides the bed, there's a folding chair, a student desk with an iPod in a speaker setup, and a dead plant. It is the kind of plant a girl gives her boyfriend and he forgets to water it. The bathroom looks tiny and part of the floor is covered with plywood. A closet door stands open near the head of the bed. Inside are clothes and plastic storage containers. Another door is on the same wall, on the side of the bed closer to the windows. It's closed. Maybe a kitchen. I bend down to examine a tattoo on his bluish skin.

I'm about to say something to Amber. Something important. I need a witness, if only for my own sanity. But something stops me. I've never had a sixth sense. Jill claimed she did. Yet at that instant I draw a strange breath, feel my scalp leap a millimeter on my skull, and know we aren't alone in the room.

"Oh, fuck…" Amber whispers what seems to be her favorite word as we both see the two dogs.

They stand silently in the open doorway, seeming too short to be much of a menace, their ears perking up playfully. But I take in their heavy dun-colored heads, weight-lifter chests, and piston front legs. Pit bulls. The sudden apocalyptic barking puts an end to any notion that we aren't in deep shit.

"Don't move," I say.

I force back the gusher of panic inside, looking around the sad little room seeking another way out. I only move my head, very slowly. The movement sends jolts of pain into my neck and shoulders. The dogs both stop barking as if on cue and start growling. Their big eyes are black and fixed on us. One bares its teeth, white and sharp. They look the size of a saber-toothed tiger's. They are maybe seven feet away. They are a strong, crazy-bred dog's leap away, and the only thing between us and them is the body of Megan Nyberg's dead boyfriend. They block the door out as well as whatever refuge the bathroom might afford. Amber's cell phone sits useless in her hand. We'll be dogfood before any help arrives. The other door is closer, the kitchen that might even have another door out or at least let us out to a fire escape. We could reach it, maybe. We could keep the bed between us and the dogs, unless they're smart enough to just jump over it. I haven't been too damned smart up to this point.

The door is an eternal six feet away, but I nod to Amber and we both start edging in that direction.

"Down!" I say, mustering my most commanding yet calm voice. "Bad dog!"

The growling grows in intensity. Even the sound of their slobber being inhaled sounds chilling.

Hell. It was worth a try, at least.

The pair follows us, but they're just walking.

Suddenly I grab Amber by the arm; she's so light I pick her off her feet, and bolt to the door. It opens. I throw her inside and follow, slamming the door behind us.

It's another closet. I curse the building's long-dead architect, teasing bastard. But my oaths are drowned out by the dogs. The barking has turned to primal, banshee shrieks. Instantly the door explodes as one or both dogs hit it. The doorknob shakes and jerks. Amber grabs me tightly.

"I have claustrophobia!" she half whispers, half screams. "I can't do this!" She is shaking so hard it transmits to me. "I have to get out!"

"No way." I hold her close as they hit the door again. This time the wood bows in ominously.

"Call nine-one-one," I order, detaching myself from her. She opens her phone, the lighted face somehow reassuring. But at that instant they hit the door again, a bone-jarring sound. One panel starts to split. The splinters shower my hand.

As Amber yells into the phone, I feel for a light-switch, then I feel around in the dark. I pray: *Please be a gun nut, Ryan, please make my day.* I enviously recall the monstrous silver revolver in the holster of the fed. Amber still clings to my arm. The barking outside the door escalates: deep voices roaring and snarling. Then the door explodes and light pours in from a fist-size hole, followed by a snout with teeth. I push us against the far corner of the tiny cell.

Over the barking, I yell, "We can't wait for help here." Mr. Obvious.

Clothes, boots, smelly socks… Then, a baseball bat. I grab it and use it as a spear against the snout, which withdraws without a sound.

In the silence that follows, I give Amber instructions. I use some of Ryan's coats to pad her against dog bites. I zip up her coat. I have her tie a sweater around my left arm, as if the knitting will really cushion against those crushing jaws.

When I open the door the dogs don't spring at us. They are crouched intelligently in front of our only way out. I walk first, slowly advancing on them. When one attacks, he is instantly longer, in the air, his mouth headed to my face. I take a desperate jab of the bat and I can hear its teeth break. In the instant that the dog pauses, I take a savage swing downward on its skull. The dog's scream is high-pitched and short. The second dog backs away, growling. Its muzzle is bleeding. We make it into the hallway and past the fire door into the stairs. I slam it securely. Jim Morrison stares at us soulfully from the small window. Then a sudden slamming explosion from the other side, and Jim's iconic face cracks and crumples.

"Are you okay?" Amber, suddenly calm, puts a hand on my shoulder. She says my name. "You don't look well…"

Okay is a relative term. We're alive and unharmed. But the body back in that apartment had a tattoo on the right calf. It said it in simple blue ink:

Eleven eleven.

Chapter Seven

"You were good back there. Very calm and self-assured. Is that what they teach you in columnist school? I always wanted to end up as a columnist after a long and distinguished career. I don't mean you're washed up or anything. You know what I mean. Anyway, wow. My arm still hurts from where you grabbed me and threw me into the closet. You were so cool. Then you just lost it after we were safe in the stairwell. People are so odd."

I let Amber talk. So I was good at concealing my terror. I don't tell her why I lost it in the stairwell. I have my reasons. Afterward, we spent an hour with the cops. My new friend, Sgt. Mazolli, is less chatty about the financial markets, probably wondering why I keep showing up at suicides. But Amber knows him and he likes her. Who wouldn't? Now I am halfway through my third martini and my calm, self-assured side decides I'd better eat something. I pull over the bar menu and am surprised that "eleven/eleven" isn't printed inside. Hell, I'm seeing it everywhere else.

I'm not going nuts. I almost say it aloud.

"You're like me," Amber continues. "You're a news junkie. You need the rush of something new every day."

"Today was a little too much rush."

"Sorry we didn't get the report on this Hardesty dude. Did you know him well?"

"No, just a source," I say.

"So tell me about you. Are you from Seattle? Not married, or you don't wear a ring and you can be out at a bar after work with a nosy female co-worker. What about your family?"

"I'm an orphan."

She gently elbows me. The bar is crowded so we're standing very close. "Liar. I can tell when people are lying."

"What was that about back there?" I interrupt early into her life story.

"The boyfriend? Suicide. You heard the cops say he left a note on top of his desk. Hey, I wish he had written a note saying he'd killed Megan…"

"That's just it," I say. "I didn't see anything on the top of his desk but the iPod and the speakers. Nothing else. Not a note. Not a computer. Whoever heard of somebody his age without a computer?"

Amber looks at me straight on and curses under her breath. "I think you might be right. I didn't see a note, either."

"Did you see the tattoo on his calf?"

"No." She frowned into her drink. "Why would the cops be lying? Not that they need a reason to lie to the press."

A cup of chowder arrives. I ignore it. "And the dogs. The cops couldn't find them. I didn't see any evidence Ryan owned dogs. No bowls on the floor. The place was tiny."

"Yeah, but in a neighborhood like that? They're the favorite pets of gang-bangers. So maybe these were strays looking for dinner. What are you saying?"

I make myself eat a spoonful. Everything right that moment lacks taste except the liquor. I say, "What if somebody wanted us out of that apartment or worse?"

Amber studies me and lays a hand on my arm. "Maybe that's a little paranoid."

Chapter Eight

I am outside, just to walk the night streets, watching the rain dance against the pavement. Loud bars around Pioneer Square give way to bleak streets of empty buildings on the edge of the International District. The news racks are empty. Those piles of debris every few yards are really homeless people who couldn't find a doorway for shelter. What am I doing about it? The homeless had been a big cause for Jill. So were prisoners. She was also convinced one of them would kill her. If I am a little paranoid, I come by it honestly.

Now that the crisis has passed I can't stop thinking about the young man hanging from the bed frame, looking impossibly fragile in death. His skin blue and thin as parchment. The dogs, snarling and lunging. I keep looking behind me, as if they will be there on the sidewalk, as if we're still in the hallway and can't quite make it to the stairs. The feelings almost, but can't quite, mute the sound of Troy Hardesty falling into the street right in front of me. The sense of menace from the federal agents who staked out my lover's house and followed me. And all the feelings, all the events, flow into the big bay of "eleven/eleven." Don't they? Then I am on a dark street I've never walked down, then I am down looking up. I sense the figure looming over me, then I see it and I hear my scream before I am conscious of screaming.

"Baby, it's all right."

The figure sheds its fedora and trench coat and slides into my bed next to me. She is warm and soft-skinned, and almost nude.

"I didn't mean to scare you," Pam says.

The game is called "the Phantom." Pam likes to dress up in a trench coat, stockings, garter belt, and nothing else, then drive to my loft late at night, let herself in, and have her way with me. The idea of driving around town that way is part of the turn-on for her. Then, an hour or four hours later, she puts back on the coat and wordlessly leaves me naked in bed. Pam most enjoys the Phantom when no words at all are exchanged.

Pamela is an executive with one of the biggest non-profits in Seattle. She wears tailored suits and her straight blond hair is cut in a sensible bob. I love the way it sweeps back and forth against her shoulders when she moves her head. She reads copiously, even buying the *Weekly World News*; my column was a great icebreaker when she first walked up to me at an otherwise boring party. I find her incredibly sexy, and fortunately for me, I am the one she has chosen to work out her wantonness with.

I had forgotten this was a Phantom night. Now she wants to comfort me and talk about my nightmare, she's that kind of person, but in a few minutes I persuade her to go back outside and let herself in again. The trench coat falls off. Her warm, wet mouth finds mine. And I lose myself in the sounds we make without corrupting them into words.

After Pam leaves and I hear the door lock, I fall into a deep and dreamless sleep. But it doesn't last. I am bolt upright awake and the clock says three. I walk to the window and lose myself for a few minutes by watching the street. The window is cracked open and I smell the cool, wet air coming in. A man walks by quickly. Somewhere I can hear another man's voice yelling profanities, probably at nothing.

Then I see him, walking north with a lurching gait, another Michelin man with the heavy padding of his layers of clothes, all brown under the streetlights. Every few steps he turns and engages in his profane soliloquy, turning in to face a doorway, then turning out to face the street. Individual cars go by every few minutes. I hear the fire department roar out of the big station nearby, their sirens fading slowly, then replaced by a train whistle. Then,

"Wooooooooooooooooeeeeeeeeeeeeeeeeeeeeeeee…"

It's a funny sound but it makes my flesh crawl. Maybe it's the pitch of the woman's voice making it, high and wailing and terrible.

"Wooooooooooooooooooooeeeeeeeeeeeeeeeeeee…"

I can't see where it's coming from. It's like a banshee on the moor. I think about the woman on the street, "eleven-eleven," and the tattoo on the dead kid's leg, "eleven-eleven." I listen for the banshee but she's gone. Eleven-eleven. How creepy is that, especially after the national nightmare of 9/11. But maybe it's just me. I had a sister who believed she saw bugs crawling on blank sheets of paper. Sometimes a cigar is just a cigar. There are coincidences. I went my whole life never personally knowing anyone named Mary Beth. Then one year I dated three of them. One claimed she loved me. I crank the window shut and go in the other room.

At my desk, I open the laptop, sending white light into the room. I can link to the CCI system and actually see my column as it will appear on the front of the Sunday business section tomorrow. "Is Olympic stumbling toward a takeover?" the headline reads. Not bad. Civilians think the writers do their own headlines, and often the headline can misstate the totality of the story. We get the angry phone calls and emails from people who only read headlines. Headlines are powerful. I surf over to the *Seattle Times*—so far, they're clueless. They didn't even pick up the 13-D filing. Their economy columnist writes some esoteric blah-blah-blah on the credit markets. It's actually not bad. But he doesn't have news. I do. The *Wall Street Journal* and *New York Times* also don't have it. Again I Google the name "Animal Spirits LLC" and get nothing. I am just about to get sleepy again when I Google "Olympic International" and "takeover." I get one hit. My pulse rate doubles.

"Shit."

It takes me to a site called Conspiracy Grrl. I've never heard of it. I read the post:

The takeover boys are at it again, going after Olympic International. Don't yawn yet. The company is known for its mining and timber businesses, but Conspiracy Grrl has found that it also has a tasty little defense subsidiary that makes, among other things, night-vision goggles that don't work. Hey, Support the Troops! Oly got $120 million for this no-bid contract and the Government Accountability Office found that the goggles had a huge failure rate—not a good thing on the battlefield. Where was the fine? Turns out the CEO is a big contributor to both parties, and so far no action is being taken. More contracts just keep coming. So now Oly is takeover bait because the wars will just keep adding to the profits of this little-known subsidiary. Look for the top executives to get golden parachutes while the workers get screwed. Who else benefits here? Stay tuned. If you wonder about the conspiracy that is the Military-Industrial Complex, watch this one. Has this been reported? No. That's why you can't trust the corporate media.

I sit back in the chair and let out a long sigh. The post came out a week before my column. I've been scooped by a Grrl.

It's a bare-bones site. The kind you can get with a ready-made template. Most of it is devoted to conspiracy debunking. The tale that most passengers on the 9/11 airplanes could possibly have used cell phones to call is questioned. Speculation that the World Trade Center was deliberately demolished is persuasively deflated. In another post, she writes about the vice-president's secret energy task force and higher oil prices. She links to documents showing the players—big oil companies—that attended the closely guarded meetings, and how Iraq's oilfields were divided among them. This all before the United States invaded Iraq. Another has a report on the safety standards for microbiology labs.

It's not a nut site. There's some real journalism here. It makes me crazy.

I click on the link "about me." There's a piece of clip art, a young woman in a trench coat and fedora. I think of Pam and smile. But there's no real name. Her location is listed "somewhere in the United States."

I can't help myself from clicking the link to her "Passion Page," a separate part of the blog where she writes about her love life. It's basically a diary of her musings on past and present love affairs, and, brother, she gets around. It seems out of place on a Web site devoted to furthering or debunking conspiracies, but maybe this is what gets the eyeballs. If I were after pornographic writing this would be a great find. Now she has a new man in her life, Mr. EU. The new man is attractive but mysterious. Conspiracy Grrl is not looking for a father figure, but older men are attractive. Still, who knows if the romance will happen? He is shy and distracted. I think, wake up, Mr. EU. It is a global economy. Why am I wishing her well?

Chapter Nine

Monday, October 18th

The phone wakes me at ten minutes after eight. It's James Sterling's secretary, Holly, asking if I can meet with the publisher at nine. *Of course, Holly.* What other answer am I going to give? I hurriedly shower and dress, toss the newspapers inside the door, and walk up to the office in the light rain, wondering what's going on. Like most Seattleites, I don't use an umbrella. I drape my Burberry trench coat over my shoulders. At nine I am in the ornate publisher's office on the top floor. James Sterling sits before me, his triangular face partly hidden by tented hands.

"That's quite a column you had Sunday morning."

I don't think it's a compliment, so I say nothing. It's been three years since I have been in this office. That was when his mother was publisher. She would laze back on the leather sofa, eat Ritz crackers with peanut butter, and gossip about Seattle business. Since her death, her son has exercised the correct separation between the business side of the newspaper and the editorial side. Either that, or he has been disinterested. Now I don't think he wants to gossip.

"You're sure everything is correct?"

I run through the documents I have. My voice is pleasant and respectful. Nowhere will I show the tangle of my emotional guts. *You're selling the paper, you jerk? Your family's legacy? You might close it down?* I mention my sources but I don't give Troy's name. The tent remains in front of his mouth. He doesn't make eye contact.

"And why didn't Olympic talk to us?"

"It's not unusual," I say. "If they're facing a takeover they'll want to lawyer every statement. I asked them to comment repeatedly."

He gives a noncommittal "Hmmmm." He stares out the window.

This is not a happy conversation for me. Why is the publisher involved? I don't know James Sterling well enough to drop the mask and ask outright, what's the real agenda? I could have done that with his mother. But, then, she never had a hidden agenda. I always knew where she stood. I can guess what prompted today's call. It's not unusual for bigwigs to complain directly to the heads of newspapers. CEOs are modern royalty and they only want to communicate with each other. Many would never deign to complain to a mere business editor, much less a columnist. So I am assuming Sterling heard from Pete Montgomery.

"Pete Montgomery and I are old friends," he says, folding his arms across his chest. His body looks as if it hasn't stretched in a decade. "I'm sure he'd talk to you at the right time."

I don't know what to say. I'm not going to lecture the publisher about the need to get information out the door. If we sit on it, there should be a good reason. Hell, Conspiracy Grrl had it a week ago. But she doesn't have my readership. I hope. So I just tell him I think the column is solid and I hope Montgomery will talk. That we scooped all the competition, including the *Wall Street Journal,* doesn't seem to interest him. Readers will often say, "You guys just want to sell newspapers." I wish it were so. At the big chains, they want a hefty profit margin—if they can get it by cutting circulation, fine. At the *Free Press*—the family just wants its money, and the publisher doesn't want to be harassed by his buddies at the Rainier Club.

My body is rigid in the chair. I don't want to be here. Maybe he's called me up to give me my pink slip in person and the column will just be the excuse. I never thought I would believe that about a publisher of the *Free Press*. Publisher meddling is commonplace at other papers, bad papers—hands off the advertisers, give a puff piece to this department store. But not at the *Free Press*.

Still not looking at me, Sterling talks about the uncertainty of the market, how we have to be careful what we write because it can move a stock price. I nod but I am half listening. The rhythms of daily newspapering have ruled my adult life. The Tuesday column is due at one p.m. My job may be gone well before that, but all I really know is that I am taking a fresh breath and a column is due. In the morning you're on the front page, but by the evening you're on the bottom of the birdcage. The machine must be constantly fed. I am thinking of the next column.

"It's a very delicate time in the life of this newspaper," he says, propping his hands in front of his face again. His voice quavers. Nerves? Maybe he is about to fire me.

I wonder what he's trying to tell me. Back off? Do more? He doesn't say.

"I'll try to get an interview with Pete Montgomery," I say. In a minute the tent comes down and the meeting ends.

The newsroom oozes a paranoid, bitter, sad vibe. People look up from their desks and look away. Some huddle in groups and gossip quietly. Gossip is usually a newsroom delight. Now it's all bleak. It's a hell of a time to be looking for work in the news-paper business. I think about telling the business editor about my audience with the publisher, but, no. I don't want her to start looking over her shoulder. An Olympic follow-up column needs to be written soon. I open up my little office and the red message light glows merrily on the phone. The first message is the nearly hysterical voice of Heidi Benson, the director of cor-porate communications at Olympic. Her voice is little changed when I get her in person.

"I've never read such an irresponsible piece of reporting! This is full of errors! I just can't even believe you write on the business page, you are so anti-business. It's no wonder you people are going out of business."

Some flacks are helpful to journalists. Others see us as The Enemy, particularly if we fail to be cheerleaders, ask embarrassing questions, or discover unpleasant information. Anyone who questions the company line is little better than a child molester. Heidi Benson is definitely in this latter category. As I listen to her, I write readers thank-you notes for their emails—I call it constituent service. Everybody who writes me gets a reply, even the nuts.

"Well?" she demands.

"Why didn't you return my calls?" I crook the receiver on my shoulder and check in on the Web. My column is one of the most-viewed items today on the *Free Press* site. And Olympic shares are up five percent. I look at my emails: concern from friends about the *Free Press*: its sale or demise is at the top of the media news report from Romenesko. In the same report, a professor says "this is the best time ever for the media." Maybe if you have tenure and are not a working journalist trying to find a job. A reader emails: "I've always said YOU'RE A SOCIALIST MORON! You don't have readers because you are all SOCIALISTS. The *Free Press* is a dead horse that needs to be put down!!!" I close my eyes and listen to the voice on the phone.

"I thought it would be clear we didn't choose to participate in the story." Heidi lectures with the finesse of an old lawn mower.

"That's a pity," I say.

"This should never have appeared. What will our shareholders think? What will our employees think?"

Maybe they will think they're getting some real information about the future of their company, instead of the tomb-like silence that has emanated from the executive suite for the past several months.

"So walk me through the errors," I say. "I'll be happy to make a correction." I'm not too worried. I know it's nailed down, and indeed she wants to argue about things like the headline and "the tone."

"It draws the wrong conclusions!" she sputters. "This is all speculation!"

I remind her that part of what I do is to speculate, based on facts and analysis: I'm a columnist. This sends her into a long silence.

"Heidi?"

The phone line is empty, then, "I'm just trying to make you understand how unacceptable this is. How one-sided." I can almost hear her teeth grinding.

"I want it to be more complete. An interview with Pete Montgomery would be a great start."

"That's not going to happen."

"Is he in town?"

Again, silence. I just cradle the phone and run through my emails. I set one aside to read again.

"So talk to me about ODS, Olympic Defense Systems." I start a fresh page of Microsoft Word just in case.

"Are you crazy?" she nearly screams it.

"Let's start off on the right foot again. I know the paper hasn't had a reporter cover your company for a long time, so maybe we can have lunch?"

"After this? After what you've done to me?"

God, I want a drink. I say, "ODS looks very interesting. I had never even heard of it before." Conspiracy Grrl knew about it. I pull up her post on the Internet and read about the faulty night-vision goggles. I don't mention this. "I see it's headquartered in D.C. I'd like to go back there and meet people."

"What right do you have to do this?"

"You're a public company, for one thing. And you're making news. The 13-D filing is real. What about this Animal Spirits LLC?"

"What about it?"

"They've taken a stake in your company. Who are they? What do they want? What are you going to tell your shareholders?"

When her voice comes back it's trembling with rage. "We have no comment! I've never seen such shoddy, yellow journalism in my life! We have a great story to tell!"

"So talk to me."

"Never. I intend to call your publisher to complain."

I'm tempted to tell her that her boss has beaten her to it. But I give her Sterling's extension. I offer to transfer her, but she's gone. With the new phones, you can't hear them slam down like in the old days.

The business editor breezes by with a "Good column. They said nice things about you in the ten o'clock." That would be the morning news meeting, where the editors sit around and critique the paper. I go back to my email and open one with no name on the sender slot, just a subject line: "About Olympic International." I open it and read: "You made a good start. But you're missing the big story. Dig deeper."

I hit reply and type: "Tell me more."

It immediately bounces back from Yahoo. "Undeliverable."

Chapter Ten

Friday, October 22nd

Friday morning I am in the newsroom early, working on the Sunday column. Sunday is the biggest circulation day. The job cuts have begun. The film critic is taking early retirement. He's one of the most respected in the country and he won't be replaced—we'll use wire copy. The reporter covering transportation was pink slipped on Wednesday. She left the building in tears. She is my age. The top editors spend hours in meetings in the fish bowl, the glassed-in conference room on the fifth floor. We walk by and pretend not to notice. Rumors and gossip flood the newsroom.

There's much to write about in the world: the continuing banking fiasco, more layoffs at Boeing, the potential for a new rise in energy prices, a classic Seattle fight over declaring an old Denny's a historic landmark. I decide to focus again on Olympic International. James Sterling's old buddy Pete Montgomery has not returned my call. But my cell phone rings as the system is booting up and I am brought back to the lethal centrality of my recent days.

"I hear you were meeting with Troy the morning he died."

I might ask how he heard such a thing, but the voice belongs to one of the richest men in the city, in the world in fact, and of course he has myriad ways of knowing. He'd make a hell of a reporter if he were willing to take the pay cut and the aggravation. I tell him I was there.

"That must have been a shock. I never would have seen Troy killing himself, but I guess you never really know, do you?"

"I guess not."

So much I'd normally want to ask about his business or philanthropy ventures. So often I would let the conversation find its way into the real reason he has called. But I'm on deadline, so I just blunder ahead, seeking an easy payoff.

"Were you in his hedge fund?"

"No," he says.

"Was his fund in trouble."

"No way," he says. "Troy was one of those guys who made money in the bubble, and then he made money from the rubble." He doesn't laugh. "Troy was quick to see the equation had changed. For years borrowing costs were so low and asset appreciation so high that everybody looked like a genius. Now it's going the other way. Lots of hedge funds and private equity suffered. Not Troy."

I usually have trouble getting good cell reception when I'm deep in the newspaper building, but his voice is sitting-right-next-to-me clear. I ask if he had invested with Troy.

He just laughs. Then, "There's a lot of uncertainty right now. Lot of bad bets. I just thought the columnist knew everything."

I laugh briefly. He can command the top research in the world, so he doesn't need me. Unless he wants to know what Troy and I talked about that morning. I leave that alone. I ask if there's any reason the feds might be interested in Troy.

"Why do you ask?"

"Because you know everything."

"Huh. Interesting question. I'll see what I hear."

"Any of your friends invested with Troy who might talk?"

"Craig Summers."

Great.

"Ever hear of an outfit called Animal Spirits?"

"No. Great name. Wish I'd have named a program after it."

It's a strange phone call and afterward I have a quick debate with myself about chasing Troy's death and the status of his hedge fund. But the time calculus is against me: I don't have time to call a bunch of rich people on spec and hope that someone calls back, much less that they were investors. I don't have time to deal with the surly federal beat reporter, to see if anyone in the U.S. Attorney's office would talk about why those agents were so interested in my conversation with Troy Hardesty. I don't have time.

Next week I'll start looking for lawsuits or enforcement actions against Troy's hedge fund. For now, the better target is the Olympic follow-up. I go to the corporate Web site. It has elaborate pages on each of its business units, with top executives, plant locations, statistics, and history, and this is a company with a lot of history. But when I use the pulldown menu and go to Olympic Defense Systems, a bare bones page pops up with little of that information. I read, "ODS serves America's war fighters at the front lines…" Then the computer screen goes black. I do all the things the technologically semi-literate do: hit the return key, run the mouse around. The screen stays as black as annihilation. The little green light on the computer stays on. I call tech support, tell them I'm on deadline, and in ten minutes one of the systems people comes down. She's a luscious little wren with dark hair and oval, black-rimmed glasses named Faith. She's helped me before.

"What did you do?" She always asks that.

She fiddles with the big box under the desk and in a minute the screen revives, at least a blank, blue sea of screen. She fiddles some more and folders start to appear. It's all magic.

"Try to be good," Faith says, tossing her hair without artifice, and walking out. Too bad about my "no fishing off the company pier" rule. But the ones her age are rarely interested in me. Back on the Olympic Web page, I learn little about the defense unit. Yahoo finance has a bit more: in addition to making night-vision goggles for the Army, ODS is a subcontractor on a new information services program for the Air Force, and provides "protection services," whatever that means.

The newspaper morgue is all online now. Unfortunately, the last major article in the *Free Press* on Olympic International was three years ago. Nothing has ever appeared in this newspaper about the defense business. A Nexis search shows a *Washington Post* story about Olympic's defense subsidiary making a $100 million settlement with the government last spring for selling defective night-vision goggles to the Army. We never ran it. Even Conspiracy Grrl knew. Not us. I take it personally. How did that fall through the cracks?

Hell with it. I open my filing cabinet and pull out paper files, and quickly scan the annual report, a couple years' worth of 10-K and 8-K filings. The unit has been the fastest-growing subsidiary, thanks to the wars. It has "dig deeper" written all over it.

I send Heidi Benson an email asking again if I can interview Pete Montgomery. I send the business editor an email asking to travel to D.C. Better use the travel money before it's cut off. Then I get a call back from an analyst in New York, returning my call from two days before. I put on my headset and take notes on the computer while he spends fifteen minutes filling in some gaps. He sends me a file with a PowerPoint presentation to analysts from earlier this year by the head of ODS, James Martindale. He suggests I contact a friend of his in D.C., who works at a defense think tank. I make the call and she picks up on the first ring. The newspaper gods are with me. I make more notes.

It's noon and I'm starving but there's no choice but to write. The column is due at one. I'm one of the few people who can write a publishable first draft. I can write fast. I can write like hell. I joke, if you can't write well, write fast. I can do both. I'd like to outline and carefully plan every column. I'd like to walk through the evocative streets of the city and read Mencken or Liebling on a park bench, thinking great thoughts about the dying craft of columnist. Some days it's not possible. Now I have to stand and deliver. The truth is that I never know if I can produce another column. The big white page on the computer just sits there, taunting. I wonder about the day I will freeze, the day I will have nothing more to say. So far it hasn't happened.

What I need is a lede. That's always the hardest thing. Some reporters fail because they can't write decent ledes. Editors fool with them, piss on them, sometimes make them better and often don't. I walk to the Coke machine, feed in a dollar, pop the can, take a swig, walk back. I am aware of how silently hyper I am, how inside I am insane with deadline, with the gathering and the writing and dangers of error or libel or readers just tossing you aside. I am insane with deadline. It's a fever inside. But I walk with my usual easy stride. I nod to friends. Pretty soon I am reminded of why I like to work from home. In addition to the noise of a dozen conversations in the newsroom, people drift by to talk. One of the metro columnists wants to speculate on how the layoffs will turn out. Somehow I think she'll be fine. She trucks in easy emotionalizing and any outrage directed against her is short-lived. Me, I've pissed off some of the biggest executives in town and not a few advertisers. But I can't think about that now. I gracefully break away and close the door to my office. I stare out at the street and figure out the next step. Now I know how I will start the column. Everything else will just flow.

By four-thirty, my column is through the copy editor and the slot. "Slot" is old newspaper slang, usually meaning a senior copy editor who checks headlines and copy one last time. Lots of eyes see these stories before they go in print or online. It's amazing we can still make mistakes and nobody catches them. The copy desk is not as good as it once was, when it was populated by unsociable gnomes, the greybeards who had memorized stylebooks and dictionaries, who would question minute word use—"nobody knows what 'recondite' means"—and drive you crazy. But they would also save you from yourself and your errors. That's why I hang around this afternoon. I want to make sure this column is absolutely accurate. Obviously the publisher is watching. On the CCI computer system, I can see it laid out on Sunday's business front, in the usual spot, the left-hand column, with the five-year-old mugshot of me looking serious. The headline says, "Olympic's quiet defense profit machine."

I answer the phone on the second ring. It's Rachel's father.

I used to work for an editor who advised: unless you're expecting a return call from a source on deadline, never answer the phone. It won't be the Pulitzer committee calling to say they made a mistake and you actually won this year. It will be the angry reader, the special pleader, granny demanding bigger type for the obscure stock listing you haven't carried for four years anyway. Somebody needs to talk to them, but that's what editors are for. Otherwise it's needless brain damage.

Rachel's father tells me to meet him in thirty minutes.

Craig Summers grew up in hardscrabble British Columbia before immigrating to Seattle to work on the docks. He put himself through the University of Washington and then went east, studying and teaching at MIT. In the early '90s, he started a company that made software to track shipping worldwide. He sold it a decade ago for $75 million, started another company and sold that one for close to a billion. Then he quit to devote his life to philanthropy. My job involves dealing with liars, truth spinners, and phonies, among them rapacious executives that want the world to see them otherwise. But Summers is real. He's a good guy. Too bad I have to brace for the worst.

I walk through the end-of-day crowds to Pike Place Market. Stalls are shutting down and discarded ice is melting on the cobblestones. Tourists take photos. It's overcast, cool, and blustery. There's a crowd in the Starbucks when I walk in. I see him instantly, he's wearing a blazer and blue jeans, wearing the eyes that his daughter makes lovely. Once he sees me, he walks over quickly. He doesn't extend his hand.

"I'm surprised you came, you're such a coward, the way you treat people."

His voice is not low, and the tourists and other patrons at this famous Starbucks location turn to watch us. I meet his angry glare. "Look…" My mouth is almost too dry to form the word.

"You think that normal rules of behavior don't apply to you."

He shakes his head slowly, the cords bulging in his neck. "I know your type, selfish prick. But you can't get away with it when my daughter is involved!"

I came prepared to be contrite and conciliatory but I am starting to get angry. Then I wonder, like a selfish prick, if Rachel is pregnant. He doesn't give me a chance to think about it. He advances on me, seizes me by the lapels and gives me several hard shakes, pulling my coat halfway down my arms. Then he gives me a sharp hand to the chest.

I manage a weak, "Now, wait…"

"You're a real son of a bitch!" He yells it, then pushes me back into a display of coffee mugs, rubs a hand across his hair, and turns away. "A real son of a bitch!" he repeats, waving a hand backwards toward me, just in case anyone missed the target of his venom.

I watch him walk out, conscious of the eyes on me. My face is burning. None of the mugs break.

"Wasn't that Craig Summers?" This from a woman in a lumberjack shirt and jeans. Then, "Hey, aren't you the columnist?"

It's way past time to leave.

Chapter Eleven

Rachel might have saved me. I might have saved her. But I'm not sure I wanted to be saved. The price might have been too high, the gain desperately fragile. It wasn't until our second date that I even knew about her father, so no one could say I was after her money. I was only her second lover. I didn't know that when I let things go too far. Let's take our time, I said. I want you to really get to know me. She laughed at me, gently joking that "maybe we'd never have sex." But of course we did.

Outside I cross the rough old bricks of the street and slip into an arcade, searching for anonymity. I stop in a deserted alcove and fix my collar, readjust my assaulted suit coat. That's when I feel the envelope in my inside coat pocket. I pull it out. Inside is a piece of off-white stationary with Rachel's loopy half-print, half-script handwriting.

Hello, Writerman. This note isn't what you think it is, although I miss you terribly and am convinced you made a big mistake. You aren't the only one with secrets. My Dad has them, too. A whole other life I never told you about. He's a good man, but he knows bad ones. Long story short: you're in trouble, even if you don't realize it. You have to take my word for this and trust me for once. I always wanted to protect you, but this note will have to do. Even writing it could put us in danger. Leave 11/11

<u>alone</u>. Please. <u>Drop it</u>. <u>Back away from it</u>. <u>Tell no one</u>.
And please take good care. I love you.

Rachel

p.s., Dad doesn't really hate you, but the scene was the best
way to make sure you got this note in a timely manner
and still protect us. Please destroy this note and don't try
to contact me. No joke.

I replace the note in the envelope and put it back in my pocket.
My heart hammers against my sternum. I walk outside again,
dazed, crashing into a guitar case just outside the door. The musi-
cian curses me until I drop a five-dollar-bill in his hat. But when
I hear his thanks I am already half a block away. I duck behind
a building into a deserted courtyard where I sit at a table and
re-read Rachel's letter. Then I read it a third time. I pull off my
suit coat. My skin feels as if it is radiating heat on a forty-degree
day. Sweat is visible on my dress shirt. I let the cool wind whip
into me, chilling me. By that time I am feeling a landscape of
vulnerability, from the shop windows behind me to the buildings
hanging above on the hillside. It's time to get moving.

When I was an investigative reporter I once worked on a story
so sensitive that the cops suggested I get a gun. I did. But that
was only about drugs and organized crime, horrible but tangible
things. What am I to make of Rachel's letter? It was delivered
in a way that gave Summers perfect cover for being seen with
me, but ensuring that I got the note. And of course it's about
eleven/eleven. At this point, I actually pause on the street and
pinch the skin on my forearm hard. The pain is a wonderful
confirmation that this is real. I'm not going nuts.

Eleven/eleven, or as Rachel wrote it, "11/11." The prostitute
had yelled it at me. Ryan's tattoo said "eleven/eleven." Now
Rachel had written it as a date, rather than some obscure piece
of numerology. But a date for what? A terrorist attack? No,
Rachel would have urged me to go to the police. Maybe it's a
formula, a code, a password—but for what? What 11/11 could

be so dangerously potent as to make Craig Summers afraid, and cause him to go to such extremes to warn me? I know this much: this is an unlucky number, with two dead and a crazed crack whore to show for it. And November 11th is only twenty days away. That's a big story.

It's time to talk to an editor.

First, I stop at home. My card key unlocks the small lobby door and it relocks with a heavy, safe metal sound. But I wait just out of view, against the outside wall but away from the door, just to see if anyone might be following me. It's dusk and soon Seattle will enter the season of short days and early dark. People walk by quickly, huddled into their coats. The neon starts coming on up and down the street. After five minutes, I take the restored old elevator up to my floor. The ambient city light is enough to see by, so I don't turn on lights. I sit on the ledge by the tall windows and read Rachel's note again, and yet again, speaking it aloud in a low unfamiliar voice. In the kitchen, I pull out an ashtray that stayed when a smoker lover left. I fold the note and place it in the glass bowl of the ashtray. In another drawer, I find matches and strike one, its light unnervingly bright. I move it to the edge of the paper and hesitate. The journalist in me knows this is critical documentation. I stare at Rachel's handwriting and the match burns my fingers. I strike another match and put it to the paper, watching the ashtray flare into a bright little pyre. Then I dump the ashes into the sink and wash them away. I owe Rachel this much.

I go back out in the car. It crawls along in the downtown traffic as I retrace the route the federal SUV took the other day, carrying me to the anonymous building. It sits in the low-slung industrial area south of downtown called SoDo, not because it's south of downtown but because it is south of the old King Dome, long since demolished. I am very aware of my rear-view mirrors, but it doesn't look like anyone is following me as I turn off Fourth Avenue South. Rain starts to lazily fall onto the windshield. The skyscrapers soar into the clouds and fade under raindrops.

The streets around the building have less traffic and I cruise slowly around the block. The building is a new, windowless brick and concrete rectangle, bracketed on each end with small parking lots surrounded by high walls topped by curved iron bars. Through the gates I can see SUVs like the one that carried me, and one large white unmarked van with emergency lights. The only door to the street is protected by a heavy black gate. I slow and pull the car over. Saplings are planted between the building and the sidewalk. Video cameras hang off each end of the roof. It has no address. I write down the cross streets in my notebook. A building with no name, no address, where I was taken by federal agents who didn't want to give me their names or leave their cards. They asked about Troy Hardesty, who had asked what I knew about eleven eleven. Now the memory of Rachel's note is so real I can almost feel it in my pocket, like a phantom limb. Pieces are connecting even if I don't fully understand them.

A guard appears within seconds and walks quickly toward the car. He is uniformed and armed, but there are no patches on his arms. He glares at me and approaches the passenger side. I drive away and he writes down my license tag.

Chapter Twelve

It's full dark by the time I get back to the newsroom. The light is still on in the managing editor's office but the door is closed. I see Amber's red hair in one of the chairs facing away from the glass wall. She has it down this time and it falls just below her shoulders. She hasn't taken off her coat. The M.E. is talking and gesturing. He nods and studiously rubs his beard, something he does when he's uncomfortable or delivering bad news. Behind him is a poster showing a reporter in a fedora, telephone to his ear, with a cartoon bubble showing the words, "Get me rewrite." I sit in an empty cubicle nearby and wait. Most sections of the paper are finished, "gone" we would say, "put to bed." Lifestyle, entertainment, and business are composed and waiting for the presses. What's left is for the nightside crew: the main news section, the metro B section, and sports. The big room is quiet and tense as reporters finish their stories, work that will move to the originating editors, the night copy desk and the designers. The temperamental lead city hall reporter faces her computer terminal like it's a creature from hell that must be subdued in mortal combat. Two metro editors lean over a reporter's back, reading the top of his story. They make faces, comedy and tragedy. I don't see Melinda Stewart.

The door opens and Amber stalks out. She hesitates when she sees me. Her eyes are red.

"You okay?"

"No. Come have a drink with me."

Now I hesitate, until the M.E. closes his door and starts a phone call.

"Let's go."

◇◇◇

We end up at a dark, expensive bar several blocks away, far from where we might run into *Free Press* people. It has edgy, angular furniture, not particularly comfortable. It's packed, but we find a table.

"Things are changing already. The paper's not the same. Can you feel it?" Amber peels off her full coat. I take in the nicely tailored black dress she has underneath, her feet in peek-toe pumps. She looks like a million dollars untouched by inflation.

"They want to send me to the East Side. It's bullshit. I don't want to cover boring suburbs. I've done good stuff. I've paid dues. I came here to cover real news."

I smile inside at her wounded passion, recalling myself from years before, when I didn't even know what I didn't know. Maybe I still don't. The waitress brings martinis and I take a deep pull, trying to slow my heart, which is still pounding, heavy and insistent. I absently reach inside my jacket, where Rachel's note sat before I burned it. I alternate between the liquor and a glass of ice water, trying to get the sandpaper taste out of my mouth.

"Assholes. Fuckers." She takes a full swig. "Have you met with the fucking consultants, yet?" I shake my head. "You're in for a treat. Anyway, this isn't even the worst. Something is going on with the cops. I went to pull the report on your guy, Troy Hardesty, and they wouldn't release it. Then the same thing with Megan's boyfriend. Nada. So I go to the M.E. to get the lawyers on it. This is freedom of information. This was their big story, the little missing blonde teen. Now they're not interested."

"What do you mean they're not interested?"

"Just what I said." Her voice rises. "He said I could hand it off to Kathy." She's another, more experienced cops reporter. "He said we'd had too much on the story lately and readers are getting tired of it. 'There's nothing new.' Can you believe that? Ryan's suicide is new as hell! Nobody has it. Television doesn't have it. We could have a national scoop. Anyway, that's when he tells me I'm going to the 'burbs. Should I quit?"

"Wait, wait." I ask her again about the police reports. "How often do they withhold this kind of thing?"

"Never. And my good sources among the detectives clammed up. One did tell me that Troy had put his wallet and wedding ring in a plastic bag when he took the big dive."

I tell her Troy never wore a wedding ring.

She exhales hard. "This is a big deal."

"So what did the M.E. say?"

"He said it was 'premature' to do anything." Her face contorts at the word. "Can you believe that? The *Free Press* has always been aggressive on freedom of information. These are public records. Suddenly they're chickenshits."

Amber keeps talking and I nod sympathetically. Inside, I am making "eleven/eleven" connections, warranted or not. Sealed reports concealing what? That these supposed suicides are really homicides? I can't decide whether to involve her, tell her about the note from Rachel. Maybe I should pay for our drinks and let her go to the suburbs and live a happy life. Maybe she's in as much potential danger as me.

"I want to work downtown," she says earnestly. "I want to work with the great journalists. I can learn so much from you." She reaches across and takes my hand. She's a toucher.

I interrupt her. "I need your advice, Amber. What would you think if I said the words…"

A group of businesswomen walks by and I feel one lingering by the table. It's Pam, wearing a chic navy outfit with a tight skirt. The Phantom's trench coat rests innocently over her arm. I smile. She doesn't.

She says my name and curtly nods toward Amber. "She's a little young for you, isn't she?"

I laugh the laugh of the clueless and start to introduce Amber when I feel the cold water cascade off the top of my head. Pam pours it with the slowness of a performance artist. It sluices off my shirt, down my tie, into my crotch. Ice cubes rattle off my chest onto the table. A black straw rests momentarily on my left ear before falling into my shirt pocket. One of her friends giggles.

Pam glares at me for a long time. Then, in a low voice, "You are a monster."

Her blond hair flies behind her like a contrail of wheat as she hurries out the door.

I say nothing as I stand, releasing more ice cubes from my clothes. My hair and shirt are downpour wet. At least I'm not hot anymore.

"Excuse me for a minute."

In the restroom I tear out paper towels to clean up the mess. Pam is the last person I would have expected to be jealous. Not only does she have a fiancé, but she gets off on sex talk, including about other women in my life. She's the only one who knows details of the two Melindas. Rachel, I didn't talk about. Now Pam is suddenly jealous. I guess it makes sense in a way I will understand when I am not so damp. Thoughts of 11/11 are temporarily tabled.

The door latch sounds and I am about to say something when I see Amber. She comes in and locks the door.

"It says unisex bathroom." She dabs at my shirt and coat with paper towels. Her very fair, freckled hand strokes at my tie, then she uses it to pull me to her. She is tall. The kiss evolves over long seconds and her tongue lightly probes inside my mouth.

When we finally stop, she says, "If you're doing the time, may as well do the crime."

"Amber…"

She kisses me again, and my resistance, not much to begin with, vanishes.

The door jiggles and I stop. She pulls me back to her and says "mm, mmm, mmm," in a low voice. With my hands on her slender waist, she hoists herself onto the vanity. Again using the tie, she pulls me close. Then I feel her hands on my crotch, on my zipper. She reaches into my boxers and I feel skin on skin.

"My, my, you're a big one."

I didn't know if that is true, but if so it is the only good thing I ever inherited from my old man. The thing I do know is how good her hand feels.

"Let's go to my place," I say.

She laughs. "Right here. Right now."

Her skirt has already ridden over her hips, revealing that her sheer black stockings are thigh-highs. She pulls aside a black thong—she is a natural redhead—and guides me inside. I try to go slow. She pushes against me and gasps. We move at an easy rhythm.

"You're fuckin' me." Her face carries an angelic smile.

My breath comes faster as we buck against each other. From the mirror, I can see myself impaling her. I have my own smile. I lean forward to kiss her and stroke her soft hair. When I raise up she starts rocking faster, pulling me into her with her lovely legs. Her face is turned to the side and her eyes are shut tight as her moans coalesce into a sharp, percussive scream. I'm… right…there…too.

Chapter Thirteen

Monday, October 25th

The first sign of my personal train wreck is not when my kinky, even-tempered Pamela pours cold water on our relationship. After all, I lose Pam but gain this luminous young Amber. I am back to three lovers; economists might consider that a manageable equilibrium. The first sign is not when I break one of my cardinal rules of romance: I shalt not bed co-workers. I even turn aside from one of my inclinations. I tend to avoid women in their twenties; they have rarely been attracted to me, even when I was that age, and now I find most of them boring and unformed. She might be young enough to be my daughter. But a night with Amber has washed away these reservations and I am feeling way too proud of myself. Later I may begin the cycle of regret over losing Pam. What if Pam had been The One? I don't even believe in The One. Maybe Amber is The One, instead.

"You are a monster."

Later I may wonder why I broke the rules that had served me so well. Was it that I was deeply attracted to this young woman, that I loved her sudden, impulsive seduction in a public place, that I was insane with worry on many fronts and needed the mysterious escape of chemistry and flesh? All that, and who the hell knows. "All men are dogs," Jill used to say, with some fondness. "There's no logic when they're thinking with their little head."

Nor does the sign of impending ruin even manifest itself in the warning from Rachel, delivered by her father using what can only be described as *tradecraft*. Somehow the intensity of my night with Amber lets me set that aside for the week ahead. It's too big, too unknown, like living under a nuclear showdown. You get used to it. You lie alone Sunday morning on sheets that still smell of Amber and read the newspaper. You read your column and it has no typos. You've told the world things it didn't know about Olympic Defense Systems. The ashes of the note are down the drain. Only as the day goes on does it come back to me. I can recite it from memory.

"You're in trouble, even if you don't realize it..."

No, the first sign of my personal train wreck is forgetting the breakfast speech I am scheduled to give this morning to the Lake Union Kiwanis Club. It is the first time in my many years on the rubber-chicken circuit that I have forgotten a commitment. I tell a lie, feeling guiltier than if I had fibbed about my schedule with one girlfriend in order to spend the weekend with another. There is no excuse. My calendar was neatly laid out on my computer just as my loft reflects a Sunday night spent obsessively ordering and reordering my files.

Now it's Monday morning and a new column is due in less than four hours. I have done no research on anything this weekend. I am way too thrilled at having bedded Amber and that the Sunday column was the second most read article and top emailed one on the newspaper's Web site. And yet the goddamned machine must be fed. I will have to pull out an evergreen—how is port traffic doing? What's the latest report out of Brookings? When you write three times a week, forty-eight weeks a year, not every column will be a Pulitzer contender. I bargain with myself, in an odd paralyzed change-the-subject daydream, even as the train is tumbling off the tracks, the delicate physics of moving wheels on steel rails fatally violated, motion and gravity becoming destiny, only I don't know it yet.

A column is due in less than four hours but I sit on the sofa and recite Rachel's note again from memory. Stay away from

11/11? I wanted nothing to do with it. It keeps trailing me like a bad reputation. Twenty years of journalism have taught me to be skeptical of everything. If your mother says she loves you, check it out. So could the situation really be as dire as Rachel writes? I don't even know what the situation is. Is she trying to get me to chase a foolish non-story, maybe get payback by seeing me humiliate myself in print with a "what's 11/11?" column? But there's nothing vengeful in Rachel. Is it a warning that matters cosmically—a calamity on the way—or just personally, maybe an embarrassing financial imbroglio that involves her father? No, it is written with coiled violence in the background. I recite, "He's a good man, but he knows bad ones. Long story short: you're in trouble, even if you don't realize it."

I don't know what to do. Now even my determination to talk to the M.E. and explain the 11/11 weirdness evaporates. Doing so might endanger Rachel. Look what happened to Troy Hardesty and Ryan Meyers. Both had an 11/11 connection, whatever that means. They may have been murdered. The police have sealed their death records. So why not go to the police? And tell them what? Eleven/eleven makes me sound like a paranoid, like a lunatic. Like my sister. No wonder I told Amber nothing about it in our time together. I need to call Rachel, and yet I don't dare. It puts me into a neat loop of paralysis. I think about Amber as I knot my tie.

I walk back into the living room as the front door flies open, pieces of doorknob and lock skittering across the floor. The sound is like a bomb has just gone off in front of my face.

I stand there feeling nothing but terror and timelessness as figures move quickly toward me. Two men aim guns into my face, the barrels looking impossibly large. They are the feds from the anonymous office. Before my brain can react they turn me and one drives a foot behind my right knee, dropping me hard on the floor. A bundle of nerves in my kneecap sends an urgent message to my scrambled brain. The pain shoves me suddenly, excruciatingly, into the moment.

"You can't..." It's the first words I can manage.

"Shut the fuck up, asshole." The barrel of the long silver handgun sits cold against my ear. Stu holsters his gun and pats me down, digging his hands into my pockets. He spends long minutes looking through my wallet. He tosses it on the floor.

"Get up."

With no similar help from them in rising, I pull myself up. I'm afraid to even touch my aching knee. They push me into a chair at the dining table. Stu is wearing a suit today. The guy who looks like a kindly preacher—I still don't know his name.

"Fathers and sons, they never stray too far apart." He pulls out a chair and sits opposite me. He leans close. His face is pleasant, self-satisfied. He speaks softly, like a high-school counselor talking to the kid who can hope for nothing more than to drive a delivery truck. "You can't outrun your DNA. Your father was a criminal. You're headed that way, too. All your compartments."

"He was a nutty tax protester. Fuck you! Why couldn't you knock?" I feel my temples throb with useless anger.

"You're potentially dangerous. You were Army Intelligence," Stu says, leaning against a counter.

"Are you nuts? I was an Army journalist."

His lips go pale in a small smile. "Right."

"You can't just break into my home!"

"We can do whatever we need to do in a terrorist investigation." Stu gives the briefest predator smile. A glacier flows suddenly into my lower legs.

"Terrorist?" They've said that magic word. I've read enough of our own reporting to be irrationally afraid, as if they have thrown me into a fairy tale where one word can bring destruction.

Stu leans toward me, fists on the table. "How long did you know Ryan Meyers?"

I tell the truth. They demand to know why we went to his apartment, how we discovered the body. I tell the truth again. This goes on for an hour as they try to catch me in any discrepancy. Neither one makes notes. They don't mention Hardesty, their previous obsession. This is not about a hedge fund. It is about eleven/eleven. Stu wanders, opening cabinets, tossing books off their shelves. He has a heavy, wide-legged walk. He sits at my desk, opens my laptop, dumps a pile of files on the floor. Next he goes into the bedroom and I hear the closet doors slide. He's out of my view for a moment, then I see him again, digging his hands into the pockets of my pants, suits, and coat. Drawers come out of the dresser and their contents are dumped on the floor. He looks underneath the drawers, as if expecting to find something hidden there. He lingers at my bed, pulling back the comforter, looking at the sheets that still smell of sex and young woman. The safe retreat of my Seattle loft feels forever violated.

Slowly, my body recovers from the shock. I watch Stu nervously play with his tie, his collar. He doesn't like the suit. They are really lousy interviewers, doing nothing to build rapport. The other one reaches into his coat and retrieves an envelope. He slides it across the table. I open it and see the letterhead: U.S. Department of Justice, Federal Bureau of Investigation. Stamped above that is the word "SECRET." I scan it: Below my name, address and a salutation ("Dear…"—how quaint), are dense paragraphs that look as if they were produced on a typewriter. "Under the authority of executive order 12333…" I am ordered to produce all my notes, tapes, e-mails, and research, for all dates, on Troy Hardesty and his hedge fund. I am ordered to produce the same for Ryan Meyers and Megan Nyberg. And there's a new name: Heather Brady, no one I know.

"This is a national security letter, friend." I barely can get through the legalese when the agent reaches across and pulls it back. I can't even see who signed it. "That means you are prohibited from discussing this request with anyone, on penalty of law."

"Nice how that works." I reach back to rub my sore neck and they both tense. I slowly put my hands back on the table. "You're assuming there's a connection between Troy and this missing girl…"

"Don't play games," Stu says. So there is a connection. These two aren't so smart. I am about to tease them into discussing 11/11, then I think better of it. I try to take the letter but the other agent keeps his hand on it.

"I can't keep it?"

"It's a classified document."

"What judge approved this?"

"You read the papers," Stu says. "We don't need a judge."

"Just like the way you could seal the death reports," I say.

"What a genius. No wonder you write a newspaper column."
He studies my face. "You have quite the nervous tick, columnist."
My eyelid is pinching madly.

"We're going to want all your notes. And the names of your
sources."

"That's not going to happen, but I'll be happy to pass your
request along to the newspaper's lawyers."

The preacher pulls out a hardpack of Camels, unwraps the
plastic and tosses it on the floor. He pulls out a cigarette and
lights it, blowing a long plume into my direction. It seems out
of character with his clean-living face.

Stu says, "He doesn't get it, Bill."

"No, he doesn't." Another long, almost lewd drag on the
cigarette. The end burns brightly. I have another new friend:
Bill is his name. Preacher Bill. He laughs, his hands on his hips.
"No, he sure doesn't."

I just keep staring at the table. I don't want my face to give
anything away. I need them to get out of here so I can get some
help.

Suddenly Stu has his hands locked around my wrists. I try
to pull back but it's no use. He holds them tightly to the tabletop. I can't help the testosterone rush of humiliation, that I am
weaker than this guy.

"Look asshole," he says, "we own you and nobody will help
you. You will produce this material by tomorrow." He keeps my
wrists tightly in his grip, pulling my hands forward, palms down.

Bill speaks softly, dropping ash on the floor. "We have so
many ways we can hurt you. Who knows what terrorist correspondence might be found on your computer? We know where
you go online. We know who you call. You might disappear."

"Snatch and grab," Stu says.

Bill's voice drops. "And you know what? You have no rights." I make sullen eye contact with him. He has dark flecks in the whites of his eyes. "People like you," he says, "people in the media. You hate America. You're traitors."

Before I can argue, my right hand convulses with pain. His cigarette hovers a millimeter above the seared skin. A whiff of burned flesh hits my nostrils. He lowers the cigarette again. I know what's going to happen now, but can't stop it. I twist and pull my body, dig my feet into the floor and push back, but still he holds my hands tightly to the table. The burning tip disappears into the same wound. I surprise myself by letting out a scream.

"We have so many ways to hurt you. Remember that."

They leave me at the table with a blank business card, a handwritten phone number on it. That, and a second-degree burn on the top of my hand.

Chapter Fourteen

The managing editor is rubbing his beard. His long, painterly face seems even longer. He has tragic eyes, tilted slightly as if to keep the tears from flowing down his long, patrician nose. He used to have a great laugh, a fat man's laugh, even though he's a triathlete. I haven't heard that laugh much since he took this job. Even so, he's good at what he does, good at managing the egos and feuds endemic to any newsroom, even one with relatively little political knife work or hidden agendas such as ours. Often he sits back in meetings like a Zen master, saying nothing, letting the good people he's hired work things out. Now I've told him everything but the eleven/eleven connection. I wish I could call Rachel. I wish the top of my hand didn't feel like it was still on fire.

"And they didn't let you keep this national security letter?"

I shake my head.

"And they didn't identify their agency?"

"No." I slide the card across the desk and he examines it.

I have a pair of reporters' notebooks and several file folders from interviews with Troy Hardesty. I have my laptop in my briefcase. Nothing is safe at home. Yet while I'm shaken up and hyper, I feel safer now. My notes and sources are safe. I'm in the newsroom.

The M.E. shakes his head. "But you're the business columnist. What problem could you stir up?"

My ego is briefly stung but I let it go. "Apparently I have." I run through what I've found about Troy's hedge fund, which isn't much. It seems in good shape, delivering a good return to well-heeled clients for several years. I tell him there's no obvious connection between Troy and the missing girl. Of course the key may be what I'm not saying: eleven/eleven.

"That one Amber Burke is hot to solve," he says. "She's a pistol, but she's got a lot to learn. She wants to play cop."

"You shouldn't send her to the suburbs."

The sad eyes in the long face perk up. "What? Are you fucking her, too?"

I hesitate just long enough. "I just tried to help her on this story." Amber. I haven't seen her in the newsroom and worry what the two federal goons might have done. I have already left three messages on her cell phone.

He says, "I bet you're a big help."

"You ought to be more concerned about her safety. These guys are out of control. Where is she?" He shrugs.

I feel my eyelid start to twitch. "So we're writing about this for tomorrow, right."

He leans back and studies me.

"Have you filed your column?"

I nod. I found a new report from the Bureau of Economic Analysis that showed strong per-capita income growth in Washington state. He seems pleased. Sometimes it's amazing what will make editors happy.

"I'm glad you're giving Olympic a break."

"We broke that story. The *Times* is following us now. We ought to have a reporter on it. But I'm talking about the national security letter. I can't remember reading about one being presented to a newspaper reporter."

"I think that's the point."

"So let's do a story."

Then he rubs his beard again. "I want to talk to Kathryn." That's the executive editor, who spends much of her time traveling to attend panels of distinguished editors. "And probably to the publisher."

My hand stings like hell. "Are you kidding me? This is prior restraint. This violates the First Amendment, and that's just for starters…"

"Look." He says my first name. "There's a lot going on right now. It's not easy letting people go." His voice is soft and professorial.

I interrupt. "The paper for sale. Consultants. Layoffs. So?"

"So I need to talk to Kathryn and…"

"I know, the publisher. I can't believe you're backing down. This is the *Seattle Free Press*, not some Gannett info-mercial. What's the goddamned I-Team working on right now? Give them to me and we'll get to the bottom of this."

I know I am too worked up, but I don't stop. "So they're going to sell the paper? Let's at least go down swinging. You have a staffer facing a national security letter! I'd say that's news. This is a major First Amendment issue. I've never known you to back down."

Wham. His hand slaps the desk and he bends forward like a striking snake. "You've never been very smart about some things. That's why you're a columnist instead of running a major newspaper, which you could have done. And you don't have the market cornered on being the incorruptible journalist. This newspaper has been very good to you."

"No question."

"There's a big story running tomorrow, out of the Washington bureau." His voice is back to humanities professor level. "It's an exclusive on a report about how badly the CIA screwed the pooch in the lead-up to 9/11." Hearing the date makes me wince. "It's got incredible detail, stuff nobody has had. The Obama administration is trying to suppress it—just like back in the days of W. So I've had to go to the mat for this story, been in meetings all week. The bureau is terrified they're going to get scooped by the *Washington Post*."

He leans back in his chair. "I didn't have any choice. The CIA director has been demanding that Sterling not run this story, saying it would be a grave threat to national security."

There were those words again.

"Good," I say. "Our bureau was the only major news organization that challenged the intelligence on the run-up to the war. We reported first on the lack of body armor. We've beaten the *New York Times* over and over."

"And it's made us some very highly placed enemies."

I can't believe I'm hearing this.

"Don't forget that Jim Sterling is a sometime hunting buddy with the former vice president." He sighs, "There are going to be big changes. There's a lot up in the air. I need to discuss this with the head shed, and until I do I want you to do nothing, say nothing.

"What about my notes, my sources? They're demanding them."

"Tell them to wait."

"They used a damned cigarette on me." I hold up the back of my hand. "I want to call the cops. Call the lawyers. This is assault. Police brutality."

"I understand." He looks at his Blackberry, showing me how busy he is. "Wait. And don't tell your little fuckbuddy Amber anything. I mean it."

I walk back through the newsroom and one of the assistant city editors tells me that Amber is covering a news conference at the Ferry Terminal. At my office, I find a vase of red roses on my desk, with a note from Amber. Curious reporters stop by to ask and I smile for the first time in hours. A woman has never sent me flowers. I could end up in a cell at Gitmo, but I think about sex. Sex with Amber.

I pen a note of apology to the Kiwanis Club. Then the business editor tells me I am supposed to meet with the consultants. This goes badly. They ask why a newspaper needs columnists in an age when everyone has a blog and readers would prefer to see their own opinions in print. It's true that many people think they can be columnists, and they can, for a couple of weeks. Few people can keep a column fresh week after week, year after year, not to mention doing it with graceful or compelling writing. Most blogs, meanwhile, are boring, and the bloggers would have little to talk about without real journalists breaking news. And few people anywhere can do what I do, as a business columnist. Of course, so-called citizen-journalists are cheaper than real journalists, but you get what you pay for.

I say all this. The consultants grimly make notes. They talk about the Web, stickiness, page views, and eyeballs. I talk about the need for quality journalism, however it is delivered. It's more difficult to take a laptop into the bathroom to read, I say. They don't smile. Good journalists are the antithesis of the corporate mammal. They don't see the world as a salesman does, and everyone in America today seems to be selling something.

Back at my office, the roses seem a little faded. My hand throbs and all of me wonders what the hell to do. But there's a column deadline at one p.m. Wednesday and I need to push ahead. Dig deeper. I slide the chair to the computer and start filling out Freedom of Information Requests to the Defense Department on Olympic Defense Systems. The new administration has been better on FOIAs than its predecessor, so this is definitely worth a shot. Then I go on Lexis/Nexis and start downloading every document I can find on ODS. If I can't write about Hardesty or 11/11, at least I can keep ahead of the competition on the story I broke. Olympic International shares closed today up another five percent.

I learn more about the defense subsidiary from Securities and Exchange Commission filings, research reports, and the lawsuit over night-vision goggles. I make a few calls to West Coast analysts—New York has long gone home. I am ingratiating, charming, persistent, skeptical. ODS has benefited by several no-bid contracts in Iraq and Afghanistan. As Conspiracy Grrl reported, Olympic International's top executives have also been a big donor to both parties. The defense unit is clearly a cash cow. No wonder the private equity boys would love to buy Olympic and break it up.

I check Conspiracy Grrl and am relieved that she has nothing else on Olympic. She writes about electronic voting and election fraud. I am tempted to click on the Passion Page and find out what's new with her and Mr. EU. But I fear it might bring the IT and human resources Nazis down on me.

After the third phone call, Heidi Benson comes on the line and refuses to let me speak to any executives. Last Sunday's column was, she says, "beyond the pale." I warn her that I will keep writing on this with or without her help. She screams at me and hangs up.

In between my column work, I brood about my pals from the government. Now I know they call each other Stu and Bill. And somehow Troy Hardesty and Megan Nyberg are connected. Not only that, but there's another strand, Heather Brady. Who the hell is Heather Brady? I run her through the newspaper's computerized morgue, but only get a teenage soccer player from Shoreline. I go down to the street and walk to Pioneer Square, using a pay phone to call the number on the business card: it rings once then beeps, nothing more. I walk back to the newsroom, waiting for a call from the ME. He doesn't call. I resist the temptation to check on my Hardesty files.

Chapter Fifteen

Monday night, I meet Amber in a tavern called the Siren, which sits on a homely stretch between port and the railroad yards. I used to catch up a source from the Longshoremen's union here, and it is enough out of my usual routine to provide a measure of safety. Even so, it's not that far from the unmarked brick building. I take a circuitous path, on obscure streets up and down hills, through the warehouse districts; no headlights follow me. Movies stoke my worries: what exotic devices have they planted on me, so that my every sigh can be recorded from geosynchronous orbit? They promise to hurt me if I don't hand over my notes, and there's no way I am going to comply.

There's an old adage for young reporters: it's not the big investigative story that gets you sued, but the police blotter brief that misidentifies a suspect. So the routine, the banal, matters. Even so, I can't figure out their obsession with my reporting on Hardesty. I went through my notes and there are no dramatic revelations, no obvious connections with Megan Nyberg or Ryan Meyers. Still, I didn't feel safe with them sitting in my files in the newsroom or at home.

I checked out a box on the wall in the business news department. It's connected to the old pneumatic tube system. Years ago, it was used to send typewritten pages to editors or the printers in the old back shop. The process is all computerized now, the printers long retired. The old tube system remains. But the dusty old box with pipes coming into it is too small for the files. Maybe I could put them in one of the empty desks. No, that won't do, either. Who knows when the building services people will start carting away cubicles at a newspaper likely to close.

The cubicles were still intact on the third floor, where I emerged from the stairs minutes later. This was the old *Mirror* newsroom, then the features department before it was decimated by cuts and moved upstairs. Only one row of overhead lights illuminated the room. Almost all of the third floor had been redone in the big remodel, too, with one exception: the Governor's Library. It's a rectangular room with a high ceiling, entirely lined with mahogany bookshelves. In the middle is a thick wooden conference table with red leather chairs around it. At one time it was the personal library of the newspaper's founder, Eugene Forrest, who also served as Washington governor. He had it built specifically by the newsroom—he wanted to be close to his reporters, and he rarely used the executive suites on the top floor. It's still sometimes used as a backup location for news meetings, although it has had its share of newsroom romantic assignations. I have never used it that way, but I walked back through the shadowy old newsroom and into the Governor's Library.

The room was empty but the lights were on. The chairs were disheveled at all different angles. On the far wall was the door to the governor's private, hideaway office. The door has a darkened window in its top half. The office is preserved as it was on the day he died, and the family only opens it to the public—mostly employees—once a year. Even his smoking jacket is hanging on a coat rack. I scanned the library. Five shelves down and too high for most people to easily reach, I found a row of books by Churchill, their jackets yellowed and tops dusty. I slid the files behind them and pondered some of my history at this newspaper. It was only when I emerged back into the barely lit big room that I started to feel creepy chills up my back, like a kid who's afraid to look behind him. Without waiting for the elevator, I walked quickly to the stairs.

◇◇◇

The tavern is dark and blue collar. On the bar rest large hands that forge, repair, manufacture, haul, and fish. Scratch the surface deep enough, and this is still a blue-collar town, a seaport. I find Amber at the far end of the bar, and for a long time, we hang on each other like teenagers. She is long-limbed, a thoroughbred. I wonder what she sees in me. God, I need to feel her close against me.

In between kisses, she asks, "Why are you trembling?"

I just lean down and kiss her again and she melts into me. We stand out and pay no attention. Finally, I order a double Maker's Mark and steer her to a booth in the back.

"So shall we swap life stories?" she asks merrily. "You first."

"I was raised by wolves and ran away with the circus."

She smiles at me until her eyes light on the tabletop. "What's wrong with your hand?"

Somehow in the dim light she has still spied the button-sized burn on the back of my hand. The skin has the look of clotted blood and ruined skin trying to make a scab. She takes my hand and examines it.

"It's a long story."

"I have time, Mister Life of Secrets."

I smile for the second time that day. I ask if she's all right.

"Why wouldn't I be?"

Right at that moment I need someone to talk to more than I need the drink, which is a hell of a lot. Not just someone to tell about the feds and the National Security Letter, but the whole damned thing, the note from Rachel, the mystery about her dad, the growing web that I don't understand. I need to talk about eleven/eleven. But it's a lethal number and Amber is just a rookie. She gently kisses my hand.

"What do you know about eleven/eleven?" I just ask it as bar conversation. Come here often? What's your sign? What do you know about eleven/eleven? Columnist walks into a bar...

She looks at me blankly and draws her mouth into a half smile, then shrugs.

"It was tattooed on Ryan's calf," I say.

"His birthday?"

"The day Hardesty jumped to his death, he asked me what I knew about eleven/eleven."

Her hand lessened its pressure on mine.

"What does that mean?"

I shook my head.

"Coincidence? What could Hardesty and Ryan have in common. He was a poor kid. Your buddy was a rich guy."

"A homeless woman screamed it me the other night."

"Eleven-eleven?"

"She said it and then said 'you'll get yours, asshole.'"

"Maybe she was somebody you used to date, like your girl-friend with the water glass?"

"Come on. I'm serious."

She is unzipping my pants. She disappears under the table and takes me in her mouth. My breath comes quicker and I see the faces at the bar watching us impassively. They've seen worse. Then the bartender looks our way and raises the gate on the bar. I gently pull her back up. He lowers the gate. Amber smiles demurely at him. She keeps her hands under the table.

"Is it a date? In a month the world comes to an end?"

I half-shake my head. "Maybe it's a bank account in the Caymans. But how does that tie into a pair of teenagers from Seattle?"

Her face assumes a thoughtful beauty. "Maybe it's just a meme, started on the Internet by a sixteen year old. Maybe it's like Y2K, and it sounds scary but nothing happens in the end."

I sip the drink and tell her about the feds and the cigarette burn, but not about Rachel's note or the National Security Letter. Her shoulders hunch in agitation.

"Feds?"

"FBI, I guess."

She bites her wide lower lip. "So you told the bosses? You're going to press charges? The paper's going to fight?"

I shrug. "I hope so. But the M.E. said he had to talk to Kathryn."

"Fuck! They're so spineless."

"I'm trying to see their side."

"Fuck their side. Corporate journalism is on the way. We'll be left running stories about Paris Hilton and dog-washing services." She continues to fondle me under the table. Her expression is serious.

I'm inhaling in shorter bursts, trying to stay focused. It's not easy. "What about this Heather Brady they mentioned? Friend of Megan's?"

"I've never heard of her. I can check before they send me to suburban hell. You could put in a good word for me." I tell her I did.

She says, "You're not giving up those notes on any conditions. You've got the story of your life there."

"Uh, huh."

"You like that, huh? Take me home, now."

I tell her I can't. I have to figure out what to do tomorrow, when my notes are due on pain of God-knows-what.

"What if we're followed? You could be in danger…"

"Let them watch. Let them listen. We'll give them a thrill." Her hand gropes and strokes. I start to speak, but my attention span has compressed. I am about to start moaning right there in the tavern. So I slug down the rest of the bourbon and we leave.

Chapter Sixteen

Tuesday, October 26th

Amber leaves before sunup, the darkness, sweet aches, and the scent of sex on me making the previous day's events seem unreal. I make a cup of coffee and again check the new lock on the door. It looks undisturbed. I sit at the desk and go through my email, seeing a response from a FOIA coordinator at the Department of Defense: my requests related to contracts with Olympic Defense Systems have been received and will be reviewed, blah, blah. It's a form response but at least the request is moving ahead. We'll see how committed the new administration is to transparency.

I am less interested in the Olympic story now. It could be a great tale: get inside the head of Pete Montgomery, reveal the private equity players working to do the deal, peel the bark off of Heidi Benson's press releases once an acquisition becomes public. Winners and losers. Stakes. It's the stuff of a great column. But my mind returns to the piece of paper with the Department of Justice letterhead. Troy Hardesty. Megan Nyberg. Heather Brady. Ryan Meyers. Half of them dead. Maybe more. Maybe I'm "just the business columnist," but I am still curious. And the paper, for the first time in my career, doesn't have my back. I am not looking forward to the day. I sip hot, bitter coffee.

Back to the screen. My personal email inbox holds a note from Pam, sent Monday night:

I'm sorry about the ice water. Yes, I was a jealous bitch.
So come over Tuesday night and make me territorial and
horny with all the gory details about the underage redhead. You know what your problem is? You want flings,
but women fall in love with you. Some day that's going
to get you in real trouble.

P

I would have missed Pam more than most if she went away.
But now there's Amber. The thrill of complications makes me
shake my legs. To distract myself I go to Conspiracy Grrl. She
has a post about the sale or closing of the *Seattle Free Press* and
a rant about consolidation of the corporate media. Grrl notes
how our Washington bureau has been aggressive in challenging
lies about the war and uncovering scandals in the government.
"They've pissed off a lot of powerful people. No wonder there's
an interest in this newspaper company going away." She also has
a link to my Sunday column about Olympic Defense Systems.
It's nice to be noticed. What the hell: I click the passion page
and see that she has consummated her relationship with Mister
EU. But it's a short entry. She promises more details to come.
I've never been a voyeur, but I'm interested.

Chapter Seventeen

Wednesday, October 27th

I wake up with a headache. Like my forehead collided with an anvil. Maybe it's the price to pay for the bottle of red wine I shared with Pam the night before, or the release from having a calmer day Tuesday. Cooler heads prevailed. That's one of those clichés that good writers avoid and editors remove. Clichés like "police remained tight-lipped" and "bright and early." Trite and overused expressions bore readers. Good editors also add a layer of skepticism that reporters and columnists might miss, being too close to a story. So the day after Amber took me home from the Siren and gave me a working over, the M.E. called me in and settled me down. What proof did I have that the two thugs are federal agents? Anyone can buy badges. Anyone can fake a letter that is conveniently snatched away before it can be verified. It sounded more like a hoax. They had talked to the newspaper's security people and the police, and I could have protection if I wanted it.

I wasn't so easily convinced: there's eleven/eleven, the unexplained (and apparently uninvestigated) deaths, and Rachel's pleading letter, delivered dramatically by her father. Unfortunately I couldn't say all this without bringing Rachel into it. I also noticed that the story about CIA missteps didn't appear in Tuesday's paper. Instead, there was a very un-*Free Press*-like feature on Page One about fall leaves.

Amber has the sentimentality of the idealistic. It's not as if the *Free Press* hasn't done its share of stories that bored me, and we have more than a few lazy reporters and editors breathing the air, people who had long ago abandoned any curiosity or passion about what I consider a calling. Ones who, in a superior tone of voice, shoot down any story idea by saying, "We've already done that" or "I don't see the story there." They're rigid and they dither. It's just a job to them, and if any higher-ups call them on it, they'll raise a stink with the Guild or threaten a lawsuit. Still, our staff is better than most papers. We are still a destination newspaper—a place people aspire to reach and spend their careers. Or they once could. And we didn't do stupid weather stories—"it's sunny today!"—or feel compelled to put a weak mom feature on page one for Mother's Day.

Yet Amber is right. The paper is changing already.

But on my personal troubles, the M.E. promised to talk to the U.S. Attorney and ask about the supposed national security letter. If it proved to be a fake, as it almost certainly would, then we could file an assault complaint against the two "agents." And so, cooler heads…well, sanity makes a welcome reappearance in my life. I ignored Stu and Bill's deadline and nothing happened. I even kept my job for another day.

Now it's sunny outside, I am supine on soft sheets, my head hurts, and my ears are buzzing. I quickly shut my eyes. Pam's bedroom has big windows on three sides and the light floods in joyously. I have overslept and a column is due today, yet somehow I don't care. I can feel Pam asleep next to me. My high-functioning executive is usually out the door before sunrise. Amber had wanted to come over last night, but I had put her off. "Must be the blonde who poured water on you," she said.

Before I can even decide whether to lie, she added, "Give her a goodbye fuck and come back to me," and gave me a long, lewd kiss.

And so I had spent the night at Pam's, something about which I am careful. There's the boyfriend. I brought the red wine and she intended to make dinner, except we devoured each other at the front door, eventually made it to the bedroom, and the wine seemed enough to keep us going. At one point, she wanted me to tie her hands to the headboard and blindfold her while I took her roughly. She likes to use my neckties for this purpose. Then we made love missionary style, eyes meeting, bodies comfortable with each other's pleasure, and it was as sweet as life gets.

But as my head clears now, the buzzing and the quality of light make me panic. The buzzing is Pam's alarm and she hasn't shut it off. She hasn't gotten me out the door at five a.m. as she promised, so she could be prepared when her boyfriend, Ron, came by at seven for coffee. Something is terribly wrong. My hand reaches toward Pam's shoulder to shake her, but her arm is raised toward the headboard and she's very cold. My hand follows her arm up and her wrist is tightly bound with fabric. None of this makes sense. I had untied her long before and we had fallen asleep, her back to my front, my arm around her, the way she likes it.

I hear myself shouting her name even before my brain processes what my eyes see. Her face is gone, half of her face, replaced by a pulpy crater of blood, brains, and pillow feathers. Skin tatters at the edges. The wound looks like a meteor strike. Blood is spattered onto the wrought iron of the headboard and the tastefully painted wall beyond. My hands are fluttering uselessly over her, not knowing what to do, she is so hopelessly gone…her lovely face…she worried about the wrinkles around her eyes…my hands cupping what's left of my beautiful Pamela's skull, halfway preparing for a hopeless resuscitation and then I am on the floor, flat on my back, having fallen straight backwards out of the bed and all around us is the damnable sunlight.

I stand. In the silence I hear myself mumbling and crying.

She lies on her back, totally nude, her hands tied to the headboard and her legs partly open. The sun illuminates her obscenely. A gun is sitting on the bedclothes where I had been lying. It's a black semi-automatic, but small, like a .22. I've never seen it before. I back away, spin around, look for her phone. *Help me…help us.* I trip across something heavy and immovable, fall across it and barely get my arms out to avoid hitting the hardwood floor face-first. The floor is very cold.

When I look over my shoulder, I see a man lying on the floor. He wears jeans and a flannel shirt. His head is turned at an angle and he's staring at me. I am on my feet before I am even conscious of the movement. It's Ron and he has a hole in his chest. It's about the size of a quarter, dark red, and singed. Under his back is a plume of darkening blood. He stares to the side with wide doll eyes. The torrent from inside my stomach is already flying up my esophagus.

Then I am outside, fully clothed. The autumn light has never been more beautiful. It makes the trees look like golden and orange mushroom clouds. Loose leaves swing around in the light breeze coming up from the bay and the sidewalks are comfortably broken and old, grass hopefully poking up. I don't know how my legs walk on them, but they do.

Chapter Eighteen

The black fender glides alongside me suddenly and quietly, unnoticed, like death.

"Get in," Amber commands.

Then we are driving toward the water down the extreme slope of Queen Anne Avenue. My already woozy stomach does an upward loop. I keep swallowing. We are right behind an electric-powered bus, its black rooftop tentacles gathering power from overhead wires, and it blocks my view. I am startled when a Seattle Police cruiser slams past with lights and siren, speeding in the opposite direction. Its engine roars insistently as it heads uphill. Five seconds later another cruiser whooshes by. The police cars are the color of the ocean in summer and their sirens make me feel as if someone is jamming knitting needles in my ear.

"They're going to Pam's house." My voice is a harsh whisper.

"Your hands are shaking." These are the first words Amber has spoken since I climbed into the car.

She's right. I put them between my legs.

"What were you…?" I leave the sentence incomplete. Words aren't coming easily. She had found me a block from Pam's house on a quiet side street.

"I was spying on you," she said simply. "What happened back there?"

"Spying? Why?"

"Because you're my boyfriend and I'm a jealous bitch. And don't ask how I found her address. I'm a reporter, remember? Oh my God!"

She swerves into a parking space a block beyond the Lower Queen Anne business district, unhooks her seat belt and leans over toward me. "You're hurt." She says my name, which sounds soothing in her voice, and she gingerly tilts my face toward her. "You're bloody. How did you get bloody?" She examines my cheek and hairline. "I don't see a cut. What happened back there? Did she take a frying pan to you?"

Amber's dimples appear, but something in my expression erases it in an instant. I am feeling far away, living in the land of a giant headache. I know the symptoms of shock. When I was a Boy Scout, they said to elevate the victim's legs. My legs look far away on the floor of the car, with more blood smudged on my slacks. I touch my face with an unfamiliar hand, feeling the fine grainy texture of dried blood.

"What happened back there?" she repeats softly.

I am the master of the white lie. It's essential to protect sources, keep editors off my back, and manage my time with different women. Yet I say, "They killed Pam."

"What? Who?"

"The feds."

"What?"

"They said they'd hurt me." I hear a slow monotone voice, mine. "They shot her in the face. I woke up and she was next to me, but she was dead and her face was gone. The gun was in the bed, right there." I try to talk through a mouth as dry as a desert. "On the floor, her boyfriend, shot in the chest. She was cold. She was so cold. I couldn't warm her up." I am only vaguely aware of the tears cascading down my cheeks.

Amber leans close and hugs me tightly, my eyes covered by a curtain of her red hair. I am sobbing and shaking.

I say, "We've got to go back there. Tell the police."

"No."

"That's where those cops were going, to Pam's house. We have to go back."

"No." Amber sits back, pulls the seatbelt across her long, slim frame, and drives back into traffic. "They'll think you did it. You were with her last night and I bet you didn't wear a condom. She tossed a glass of water on you in front of witnesses. I bet her girlfriends know she was doing you. That's motive. You knew that instinctively or you would have called 911 and waited for the cops. Did you call 911?"

I say that I didn't.

"Well, somebody did. Maybe you were meant to be caught there, still passed out. Don't worry. The cops'll come to see you soon enough."

I slowly come to, as if I am awakening from the kind of afternoon nap that presages a nasty head cold. Amber turns onto Denny Way and then slides south again on Second Avenue. The Jetta's white speedometer needle stays fixed on thirty-five.

"What did you do with the gun?" she asks.

I tell her that I left it on the bed. After I had wiped it down with my T-shirt. After I rinsed my bloody hands off in the sink, not even noticing Pam's blood on my face.

She says nothing as we pass through the condo canyons of Belltown and head into the central business district. I know what she's thinking: Why did you have the presence of mind to do that? Did you really kill them both in, as they say in the newspaper, a jealous rage?

I talk as we crawl along a street clogged with cars and roaring buses and crosswalks crowded with pedestrians in coats. I feel hemmed in and vulnerable, scan the sidewalks for Stu and Bill. My neck hurts from looking behind us. "I knew they were going to try to frame me. I knew they had put my fingerprints on the gun." I am more awake now, finally feeling the chill of the morning. "After that, I didn't know whether to stay or go. Call 911 or go. I don't know. Then I was just out on the street, walking."

"You sound drugged."

I ask her what she means. Why would Pam slip me a mickey?

"Whoever killed her could have use a cloth with chloroform. Or injected you with valium, something like that. There's lots of ways. They drugged you before they shot her."

And with Ron thrown in as a bonus. Pam's boyfriend must have let himself into the house as they were finishing up and they killed him. A colder thought comes through: They waited for him, hoping to frame me for both killings with the everyday motive of a love triangle gone bad. "You're right. They intended for the cops to find me with the bodies…"

"Who is 'they'?" she demands.

I don't know how to answer. I hear my voice: "Her face was just gone…"

"That's an exit wound." Amber sounds clinical, detached.

"But it was such a small gun, like a .22."

"Soft-point bullets," she says. "They expand on impact. Nasty. Assassination issue. You have blood spatter on your face. They would have shot her in the back of her head. Probably used a pillow as a silencer."

"How do you know these things?"

By that time we are at my apartment. She finds a parallel parking space a block away and expertly slides in.

"What time is it?" I ask.

"Nine-fifteen."

I curse. I have a column due at one. "Maybe I'll call in sick."

"No." She turns off the car and jams up the parking brake. "You have to act normal. Like nothing happened. Let's go."

Inside my loft, she helps me out of my clothes. I am sitting naked on the bed as she momentarily cups my crotch in her warm hand. But it's only for a moment, a half-smile on her face. "You are trouble. Get in the shower, now. And clean under your nails really well."

I do, even though I feel every individual spray of water as if it's an electrical charge hitting my skin. I scrub hard everywhere, washing off Pam. Pam who is dead and I'm to blame. When I watch the water swirling down the drain, I start to feel nauseous again. I imagine gallons of blood spilling down, circling counter-clockwise in a dark red vortex. But it's only water. The familiar shower is brightly lit and white tiled but it feels like a cell. When I step out and towel off, Amber is putting my clothes and shoes into a plastic garbage bag. She walks over and kisses me, then holds my face tightly, aiming eyes to eyes.

"What's the last thing you remember?"

She might as well have asked me to give the GDP price deflator for Bolivia in 1998. I search my scrambled brain. The wine bottle empty. In bed with Pam, starting to fall asleep. Nothing out of place. The house locked.

"What time?"

After a second, I remember. "Before I put my head down, I actually looked over at the digital clock on her night table. It was 11:11."

"Are you kidding me?"

"I thought how weird that was, but it said 11:11. Then I went to sleep next to her."

"That's the last you remember? Are you sure?"

I nod. But the memory of the clock brings back more. How looking up and seeing those numbers chilled me with dread. How I cradled my arms around Pamela, already sleeping, held her in the tight embrace of mortality, her skin soft and arousing even after an hour of lovemaking. Her soft hair close to my face as sleep overtook me. I keep all this to myself.

Amber lets go and takes a step back. Her voice is businesslike. "Act like nothing happened. If the police ask, tell the truth like you just did. But you left her house after midnight to come be with me. Got it? You woke up with me this morning, here. And you damned well better be a good actor when the cops tell you she's dead. They'll watch how you react." She raises a strawberry blond eyebrow. "Just pretend you're lying to one of the women in your life. We'll sort the rest of this out later. I've got to be in Bellevue in an hour."

She slips on her coat and starts to go, carrying the trash bag.

"What are you going to do with that?" I ask.

"Dump it far away," she calls over her shoulder.

"Wait."

She stands in the doorway.

"Why are you doing this?

She tilts her head, tossing her red mane, and examining me as if from a far distance. Her expression is neutral. "Maybe you have potential."

Chapter Nineteen

After trying four times, I knot my tie correctly, a dimple in the middle. I had started to reach for a favorite Ben Silver, but realized that it was one Pam had given me. My hand withdrew as if it were a snake. So I settle for a burgundy tie with no history. The cops will take my tie and belt so I can't kill myself. I slip on my suit coat and walk out the door on rubbery legs.

Just act normal. Easy enough, when I am expecting to be intercepted by a SWAT team when the elevator doors open, or when I step out onto the street. Yet everything outside is normal, from the homeless guy sitting on his scuffed plastic crate selling *Real Change*—probably a failed business columnist himself—to the hoodie-clad techies streaming into the software company three doors down. I become aware of the coolness of the day, the brilliant reds and forlorn faded greens of the leaves on the trees. Soon Pioneer Square will be without its shade canopy. I should have worn a coat, but the chill steadies me and in ten minutes I step off the elevator into the newsroom.

It is 10:16 a.m. and I have no idea what I am going to write.

"I've been looking for you." It's the business editor, and she should be in the ten o'clock news meeting, and yet she's looking for me. I get a sour wave in my stomach. The detectives are here. Act normal. Act surprised that Pam is dead. I can barely breathe.

"I know this is late notice, but you've seen the market today..."

I nod. I haven't a clue, but it's probably down again, maybe big time. That's been the story for months, years.

"Can you set aside what you've got going for tomorrow and write a market explainer?" She is tense, out of breath. All my muscles relax by fifty degrees. "I know we're all kind of burned out and there's not much new to say. But the head-shed wants it." She nods toward the fishbowl, the glassed-in conference room where the news meetings are held.

"Sure," I say. She pats my arm, thanks me, and strides back to the meeting. I lean against the wall for a moment, feeling my chest expand with air, studying my hands, fingers, and fingernails for any traces of Pam's blood.

Then I am on deadline.

I am saved by the news. Once I left the Army, every day of my working life I have wondered if I could sit before a blank computer screen and produce a story or a column. I know that I am a fraud, whatever readers might think or however many awards I have won. When will I be found out? What day will I have nothing fresh to write? What moment on deadline will I finally freeze? That's really one of the determining characteristics of the ones who succeed in newspapering: they never freeze. I don't freeze today. I create a new file. It is named like all the others over the years, with my name and "col" and the publication date, all rammed together, a cabalistic computer tag for editors and designers. We still call this a "slug," one of the many holdovers in our tribal patois from the days of hot type and Linotype machines. Then I start to write.

For months I have been wanting to write this: We have entered a period of discontinuity. Anyone looking for the market to return to what we used to call normal is on a fool's errand. The next thirty years won't be a replay of the past thirty. Too much is different: peak oil, a hollowed-out economy, too many bets made on financial products that turned out to be swindles, global warming. The easy days are gone. It's too blunt for the careful *Seattle Free Press*. But I write it today and to hell with it.

Discontinuity. Nothing will be the same again. The clean white bedclothes are fatally stained red.

I write like a maniac, banging the keyboard. I am in the crazy zone of time telescoping in on me. At four minutes before one o'clock, I hit the key that sends the column into the editing queue. I check to see that it is there, the button on the CCI menu glowing a festive green. Outside my window, even this high in the building, the fall leaves blow up and linger before flying away forever. The column is filed. Only then do I push the chair back, walk to the door, close it, turn away to my desk again, sit, and bury my face in my hands, weeping.

The rap on the door is sharp. I wipe my face off, swivel my chair and turn the knob. The managing editor stands in the threshold, rubbing his beard. It is newly trimmed, looking like a mowed lawn of dead winter grass. He's nearly as tall as me, but reedy like a runner, and he has terrible posture. His body can't avoid a slump for long, and he tips himself against the wall.

"Let's talk."

"Sure."

He slides past me and drops into the single chair that my little office will accommodate. He closes the door. Obviously the police are here. I'm surprised he didn't bring them along—surprised they didn't insist. Obviously they are waiting downstairs. He will lead me down the elevator, one last favor, helping me avoid the humiliation of being taken out of the newsroom in handcuffs.

"Are you okay?"

He coughs nervously, and then studies me with those tragic eyes through the lenses of his fashionable glasses. Usually he wears contacts. Everybody who works in the newsroom ends up with glasses or contacts. Somehow I have managed to keep twenty-twenty vision. A sniffle I can't avoid, however. My eyes are red. He only saw me cry once before, when my ex-wife left me. I pull myself up in the chair and say I'm fine.

"We need your files."

I stare at him, my emotions quickly shifting to anger. The wave of emotions rumbling inside me has only partly to do with freedom of the press. I say nothing.

"I know what you're going to say." He wags a finger at me. "But this is the way it has to be. I talked to Kathryn and Mr. Sterling…"

"So we're going to turn them over?"

He removes his glasses and wearily rubs the bridge of his nose. "Apparently the National Security Letter is real. Our compliance is mandatory."

"What do our lawyers say?"

"This is what they say. We have to produce your notes and emails."

"Are we going to write about this?"

He looks away, out my window toward the Nordstrom sign, then checks his wristwatch. I keep talking. "Aren't you curious about what they're after?"

"I need your notes."

"The First Amendment…"

"Just stop." He says it quietly, yet it carries more force than if he had slapped the desktop. I study his face, which looks drawn, gaunt. He looks as if he's been crying. "Bring them to my office. I've got a two-thirty meeting. Please have them on my desk before I get back."

He stands quickly and opens the door, then pauses. "For what it's worth, I think this is shit. I tried. I really did." Then he's gone.

I sit for a long moment considering options. I have so many. There's that nice flat in Paris where I could fly this afternoon, hide out, reinvent myself, drink wine, and write novels—all that, except I chose the wrong parents and the wrong career and there's no flat in Paris.

I return to the Governor's Library and fish out the files, half wishing that some of the building's infamous rats had eaten them. Then I take the fire stairs down to advertising.

A couple of years ago I dated one of the classified sales reps. Carrie. I used to thank her for ensuring my paycheck; now, thanks to Craigslist and the shortsightedness of newspaper publishers, classified advertising has crashed. Carrie and I ended badly. Don't fish off the company pier. But I need a copy machine that's not in full view of the newsroom, and Carrie's cubicle is on the other side of the room. At least I didn't get her killed. She should come thank me. For the next twenty minutes I copy everything: handwritten notes, printed out email messages, story drafts, SEC documents. It looks boring as hell to me. Troy Hardesty was not that great a source.

We have so many ways to hurt you.

As the machine whirs and paper spits out the side, I try to make connections. The agents obviously killed Pam and her boyfriend. I was going to take the fall. If I had dozed a few moments longer, I'd already be in jail. Pam floats across my consciousness, without a face, without a pulse. I grip the sides of the machine. Cause and effect, damn it: They warned me. But I wasn't writing about Troy. I sure wasn't writing about Megan Nyberg. But I never called the number they gave me. I kept the notes and they killed Pam. And now the paper is giving up the notes, too. What is in there worth killing for? Apparently something connected to eleven eleven. Rachel warned me I was in danger. I study the scar congealing over the top of my hand.

We have so many ways to hurt you...

I return to the third floor using the fire stairs and take the back hallway into the business news department. There I wrap a rubber band around the copied records and slide them into a manila folder. Nobody said I couldn't keep copies. They didn't give me enough of a chance to read the National Security Letter to know if it's a violation of executive order whatever-the-hell. I could ask the M.E. But I don't. I slip the file into my briefcase. It's a handsome Coach, black-leather job, and it was a Christmas gift last year from Pam. I latch it and walk out, carrying the original files under my arm, feeling nauseous.

I can count the strides it takes me to round the hallway and cross the main newsroom to reach the managing editor's office. Thirty-five. Every one of them feels heavy and painful in my feet. I ease myself down into a chair at an empty cubicle and stare into the empty office. I am waiting for a reprieve that won't come. The digital clock on his credenza reads 2:28 p.m. in red. The chiseled face of the reporter on the poster still calls for rewrite.

The chair creaks as I lean back and look over the newsroom. The air is heavy and overly warm like so many interior spaces in Seattle this time of year. I watch the clocks on the far wall, above the mural-sized world map. Reporters and editors walk past; others huddle over their keyboards, heads low in concentration, or lean back in chairs with telephone receivers cocked between their ears and shoulders. Most of them are my age or older. Every cubicle is decorated. Flags, awards, maps, bumper stickers, ancient *Shoe* comic strips, a Che Guevara T-shirt, coffee mugs of all provenances, badly dressed people with large, delicate egos and, sometimes, awesome talent. One copy editor has a large sign: "The only difference between this place and the Titanic is that the Titanic had a band." Three dozen conversations going at once. And most of them are about the news. The excited energy flies around, ricocheting off the walls.

The newsroom at its best is a place of magic and conflict and profanity. It's a room where Pulitzer-prize winning stories have been brainstormed, reported, written, and edited. Where a few of the best-known writers in America passed through on their way up. Where, every day, new news originates and goes out to the Northwest and the world, on paper and on the Internet. Read by nearly a million people every day.

And yet, at the moment, it suddenly all looks dead to me, as if I am looking back through time at a long-ago era, and hearing the sounds of ghosts. Suddenly everything is bathed in a sepia-toned sadness. The reporters and editors wear masks of sadness, their movements lethargic, the usual noise of the room replaced by a subdued haze. As I look around the room, I run my hands across the day's edition, sitting there for me atop the otherwise empty desk, feeling the fine fiber of the paper. I suddenly know, a tactile premonition. It's all gone. As gone as the reporter on the managing editor's poster, with his press card stuck in the band of his fedora.

I stand, nod to the M.E.'s secretary, and leave the package of original files with her. Then I return to the Governor's Library. A meeting of features editors is going on. I silently curse all the damage endless meetings have done to newspapers as I go to my office to wait, the briefcase with the files on my lap like a heavy tumor, the stress of the day about to twist my head off. I try again in half an hour and the room is empty. I slide the briefcase behind the Churchill books and walk quickly to the door, turning out the lights.

My cell phone rings as I step out into the lobby. It's a producer at one of the radio stations. Can I be on the five o'clock show to talk about the market? Sure. If I'm not in jail. I scan the big room, looking for detectives walking my way from the elevators. I only see a young woman in a black-and-red checked miniskirt, her hair swaying lushly as she walks by. I smile at her. I hear Pam: *You are a monster.*

Chapter Twenty

After the radio show, I walk outside into the gathering gloom. I don't know where the day has gone. The sidewalks are thick with people leaving their offices, rushing to catch the bus, and the weather has changed. A cold wind gusts off the bay. Soon daylight savings time will be gone and Seattle will slip into the winter months when night comes early. It's suicide season and the time of year when distracted drivers run down black-clad pedestrians and people complain about the dark and the rain. I like it.

The police have not come for me, not even to talk. I couldn't bring myself to check the online site of the *Free Press* to see if there's news about Pam. My cell phone says it is 5:30 and it shows five missed calls and one voice message. I had muted it while writing on deadline. All the missed calls and the message are from Melinda Stewart. I didn't see her in the newsroom today and I don't want to talk. But I step into an alley and call her.

"Where have you been?"

"Bad day," I say.

"Tell me about it." She speaks slowly, her voice odd. "They called me at home. Did they get you?"

My stomach tightens. Everyone I know could be in danger. But I ask her what she's talking about.

"I'm out."

"They fired you?"

A long pause, and then: "No. They demoted me to night news editor and laid off Jennifer Campbell." Jennifer had been in that job. "They're killing the national desk, closing the Washington bureau." The cell towers carry the sound of her choked-back sobs.

"Oh, Melinda, I'm so sorry." Against the street noise I ask how they could do this. That she was the best editor in the newsroom. And closing the Washington bureau—along with Knight Ridder, it had been one of the few news organizations to challenge the Bush administration's claims over weapons of mass destruction and al Qaeda links in the run-up to the war. How could they? "What?" I lean against the wall, disbelief shaking my abdomen.

"That goddamn James Sterling," I nearly yell. "He never had the guts his mother had. She would never do this. She would have kept the family in line, and she never would have closed the bureau."

"I thought she was a shrew," Melinda says. "But you were her boy. To me, Jim has been a better publisher. He's fought against the family. They would have sold years ago. Now they'd just close the place without him. He's at least trying to find a buyer."

"What, you're on familiar terms with the asshole? I can't believe you'd defend him, especially after what they've done to you."

"I'm not defending him." Her voice changes. "Are you okay?"

"I'm still employed, I guess."

"They're laying off 125, I hear. Most are older staff. Mark May is gone. Susie McDonald. Who's going to cover federal courts? I can't believe it. I get having to cut staff to make a sale happen, but why do it to the top talent?"

"Maybe they don't know what the hell they're doing," I say.

She talks over me. "You'd better be prepared. You're a high-cost employee, babe. Not to mention how many people you've pissed off over the years."

"I know."

"Are you hearing me? Maggie Sterling is dead. You don't have your protector any more. What are you going to do if you get cut? Have you been thinking about this? They might close the whole paper."

I lean away from the street noise. "I've been kind of preoccupied."

"Aren't you worried?"

"I'm scared to death." My brain kicks out statistics: twenty percent of newspaper jobs lost between 2005 and 2008 alone— good jobs—what the hell happened to all those people? But that's not my biggest concern at the moment.

Melinda's voice hikes up half an octave. "These greedy, short-sighted sons-of-bitches have destroyed our profession." Her voice changes, melts. "I don't know what I'm going to do." Now she's holding back sobs. "What am I going to do?"

Her reaction is understandable. She had one of the plum editing assignments in the paper. But at least she's employed. Me? Even if I had the temperament, I can't go to work for some PR shop selling stories to newspapers, because there aren't going to be any newspapers.

After a long pause, I just say her name again.

"Would you get a bottle of gin and be with me?"

I want to. Every instinct wants to fly to her side. We've been this way for almost twenty years—it staggers me to think about all that time flown by, so fast, so fast. We've seen each other through failed marriages, career troubles, and the verities of the newspaper business. Sometimes sex is involved. In many ways, she is my best and oldest friend. But Pam is hovering over me. Death is in my bloodstream. I'm amazed I can't smell it seeping through my skin. I'm not healthy for my lovers or friends right now. I tell her no.

"Why not?"

"I just can't."

"Break the date. I don't ask you for much."

"I know you don't. I can't."

"You're fucking somebody new, aren't you?"

I search the faces walking by, the fast-walking Asian woman with a computer case, the plump man in a too-small jacket, a homeless guy sitting on the sidewalk with a violin case open for cash but no violin. None are hard-eyed law-enforcement faces. Melinda pauses only momentarily.

"It's the little redhead, right? She's young enough to be your daughter, for God's sake."

"I'm not fucking Amber," I say. "It's not about anything like that."

"You are fucking her! I can tell by the way you say a woman's name if you're fucking her." I hear her blow her nose. "I need you. Amber doesn't. She'll throw you away in a heartbeat. She's a little bitch."

"She's a good reporter." I want to throw the cell phone in the empty violin case and be done with it, but I keep talking. "Why did they send her to the East Side?"

"I don't know. The M.E. did it."

"And did he stop the coverage of Megan Nyberg?"

"As a matter of fact, he did. Why do you care? You hate that kind of trivial shit. 'The economy's in the biggest crisis since the Depression, and we're playing tabloid.' That's what you'd say. The M.E. said readers are bored with it. You're trying to distract me."

"It's been all over television," I say. "Why would we not cover it?"

"It's not on TV lately, either. This is not my problem. I haven't supervised metro in five years."

"So tell me about the national desk, then. What happened to the big exposé that was supposed to run last weekend? The one from the Washington bureau on the CIA?"

"Kathryn herself stopped it. Said it needed more work. She actually flew back to town from whatever journalism shindig she was attending, called us all in, and held the story. We'd already lawyered it—every source and every fact was nailed tight. She had signed off on it the previous week. Then she changed her mind."

"And the reason was…?"

"She didn't give one."

I could tell my own First Amendment sob story and it would be a doozy. But I may have already put her in danger, just by being her lover. I didn't need any more proof that they could hurt me. I didn't need more bodies on my conscience. My voice is sandpaper. "This is very strange stuff. We've never backed down before. And this Nyberg girl. What if she were more than just the missing blond teen of the week? What's going on?"

She doesn't answer.

"Has anyone been to see you, asking about me?"

"What are you talking about?"

"Have they?"

"No!"

"Have you heard the term eleven-eleven?"

"I lost my job today!" she yells, so loud I hold the phone away. After a long pause, Melinda says my name. "Please come be with me."

"I can't."

After another long silence, her voice is strong and final. "You're a real son of a bitch."

I walk around the block of my building, absently touching the 120-year-old stonework that frames the first floor. The rough, damp texture is somehow comforting. Everything appears normal. The small lobby is empty, the elevator door open. On the second pass, I enter through the alley door. It takes a key to get in and I quickly close it behind me. Residents use it to take down their recycling. I climb the stairs up to my loft, lock the door, and leave the lights off. The city lights fill the living room with a diffuse blue glow.

I own 850 square feet on the corner of the building, with three rectangular windows facing First Avenue and one window that overlooks King Street. The ceilings are twelve feet high and the windows are nearly tall enough for me to stand in. I have a large living room, a pocket kitchen, and a sleeping loft up three steps and surrounded by a low wall that separates it from the living area. Tall IKEA bookshelves line the walls opposite the windows. I got the place for a steal during the last recession. It was the only smart money move I had made in my life. I love my place, but tonight it smells musty and unlived-in. The wood floors were reinforced against earthquakes when the building was redone, so they don't creak. Still, I walk carefully to the big front windows and look out. I keep my body against the wall.

A steady flow of people pulses along First Avenue, none looking up toward me. I'm attached to this place partly because there's always action going on. You can always look out the windows, day or middle-of-the-night, and see something happening down below. Melinda Hines told me it was the ideal Seattle pad, that a person was less likely to feel depressed on dark, rainy days if there was something to see out the windows besides another house. The Melinda my federal agents didn't know about. The lights are on at Cowgirls, beckoning drinkers. An employee locks up a pricey rug store. No black SUV is parked at the curb. Yet the trees aren't bare enough for me to see far beyond the middle of the block. I leave the lights off.

When the door knock comes it's like a kick in my middle. It's a hard rap: one, two, three. Like a cop knocking. I let it be until the knock comes again, harder and faster. *Just act normal.* I'm still in my suit. I set my face, cross the room, and unlock the door.

Amber stands in the hallway. She is wearing a gray knit cap, leather jacket, black sweater, denim miniskirt with a wide, grommet belt, black tights, gray leg warmers, and off-white tennis shoes. She has a plastic bag in her hand.

"Do you like to sit in the dark?"

I tell her I just got home and invite her in. But I stop her from turning on the lights.

"Kinky," she says, shedding the coat. "I brought Thai."

"Thank you. Do you still have a job?"

"I do, but four other reporters were escorted out today. Sucks."

She finds a candle in the kitchen and lights it. I don't object. We sit in the living room, drinking beer, and using the takeout joint's cheap chopsticks to eat out of the containers, sharing them back and forth. One is pad Thai and the other is a dish with pineapple, rice, and pork. I realize I haven't eaten all day as my stomach growls loudly.

I tell her everything. This time, I hold nothing back, including the note from Rachel. Hearing my voice, I realize how incredible it sounds. "In-credible"—lacking the one thing a journalist carries like gold: credibility. Your former girlfriend's note sounds intriguing—where is it? You were served a National Security Letter—may I see your copy? Yet Amber has lived some of this: the dog attack in Ryan's apartment, his lifeless body hanging from the bed frame. Unfortunately, she didn't see the tattoo on his leg. Nobody has screamed "eleven-eleven" at her on a darkened street. I just try to tell it straight, chronologically, keeping the doubt out of my voice. I know it's real. Amber says nothing. She sits so close that our bodies meld together. Her warmth comforts me as we hold communion with containers of noodles and rice. I broach eleven eleven, cautiously, watching her green eyes. She nods sympathetically.

"Do you think I'm crazy?"

"No."

I reach for the briefcase to show her the documents but she pushes me back firmly on the sofa, shoves away the food, and starts to undress me.

"Will you ever tell me your life story?"

"No." Her wide mouth parts in a smile. "Maybe. Boring, fucked up family."

"Bet I can top you."

"Shhhhhhhhh."

My suit is soon in a pile on the floor. She kicks it away. It has to go to the cleaners anyway. She strips off her black tights and gray turtleneck, tosses aside a black bra, steps out of skimpy black panties. She must be the only woman of her age in Seattle without a tattoo. My body reacts inevitably as she climbs onto my lap. I am unfaithful to my loss, to Pam. Amber sits astraddle me wearing only her knit cap, which I pull off to free her lush hair. Tonight she's wearing it straight, parted in the middle.

I cup her face in my hands and kiss her, lightly at first, then more deeply. She gently bites my tongue. My fingers are daredevil divers, making slow-motion plunges down her soft waterfall of hair, which assumes the color of buffed copper in the ambient light from the street. They land on the smooth skin of her back and slowly find their way to her hips. Her breasts are small and perfectly formed, topped by prominent nipples. She orders me to suck them harder as she throws back her head and moans. When she leans forward, her hair falls around me, blocking out everything.

The world is gone for now. Death is outside the force field of her hair. She reaches down and readjusts, gasps and begins to ride me. Between the urgency of kisses, I whisper for her to slow down. She ignores me, moaning, and bucking against me. She sounds close to hyperventilating. Her hands and arms grip me more tightly and she whispers obscenities in my ear, over and over, then… Her orgasm is a long, loud eruption: sudden, lingering, rising and falling and soaring again, a seismic wave, finally giving way to sobs. She cries a long time as I hold her, feeling her tears pool on my bare shoulder.

I am swimming in very deep waters with this Amber. As I have told myself so many times before, I will mourn later, later.

Chapter Twenty-one

Amber is naming people who were laid off today. She lies on the sofa now, only her head visible under the blanket I brought in from the bedroom, funereal disbelief in her voice. The room smells of sex.

"I thought the *Free Press* was one of the stronger companies. I know everybody's in trouble, but this just came out of nowhere."

"The heirs want their money," I say. "Greed is a powerful thing, maybe especially in a recession." I am standing beside the window, staring into the street.

"Do you think someone will buy the paper?"

I say no.

"I don't know what I'll do if I get laid off."

"That's silly," My tone is too abrupt. "You're so young, you can do anything."

"I'm not as young as you think. And the only thing I ever wanted to be was a reporter for a great newspaper." Her voice is fierce.

"I'm sorry. I'm the one who's fucked, unless I end up in prison."

"Mmmm. You are fucked, and you will be again." The wide, sunburst smile. "You'll be fine. Everybody reads your column."

"That may not matter." Out on the street, a woman is leaning against the door of a gray Ford with four doors. The car looks unsettlingly official. She has short, pale blond hair, pale skin, and high cheekbones. She's looking in my direction. The wind is still blowing strongly. I can hear a wind chime from somewhere, and every few seconds the woman brushes the hair out of her eyes.

I hear Amber's voice.

"Maybe it's all over."

"The newspaper might close. I get that."

"No. I mean, you gave up your notes. The newspaper cooperated. I hate that. But this was what they were after, so now maybe they'll leave you alone."

She goes on, "I saw the Web site this afternoon. I don't know if you looked. I probably wouldn't have if I were you. Anyway, the story said your friend died in a murder-suicide. The cops blamed her boyfriend. Case closed. You're okay." When she sees me lean forward, my hand on the wall and my head sagging, she adds in a soft tone, "I'm sorry about your friend."

I am watching the blonde. She wears an olive raincoat that accentuates the pale color of her hair and skin. It flaps in every gust of wind. "They meant for me to be asleep or barely awake when the cops arrived at Pam's house. They're not going to be satisfied until I'm..." I let it hang. I don't know who the hell they are or what they really want.

"I mean, what if it really matters?" I return to the sofa and Amber raises up so I can cradle her head in my lap. I stroke her face and hair. My hand shakes and my eyelid twitches. "What if something in Troy's world is connected to the disappearance of these girls? What if they're dead? What if they're kidnapped? What if eleven-eleven is when somebody blows up the Space Needle?"

She says, "Do you think these guys who said they were FBI agents are working on that?"

"And it's important enough to kill an innocent woman?" I hear my voice crack and I swallow hard. "There's something so wrong here. Even what you used to read about the abuses in the Bush years, rendition, holding people without charges, even American citizens. I never read anything like this."

"Maybe it needs to be written now."

I can't tell what Amber thinks. Should I leave it alone or not? Can I leave it alone if it won't leave me alone?

"I think somebody is watching my place."

Ten minutes later we climb into Amber's car and she drives east at an easy pace. It's five minutes before eight and the weeknight traffic is light. I can't tell if she's trying to calm my paranoia or if she's curious about the blonde, too. Maybe both. We drive in silence as she turns on Fourth Avenue and again on Spring Street. Then we're stuck at the light on the incline leading out of downtown to Interstate Five.

"Gray Ford?"

"Mmm-hmmm."

"She's made every turn we have. Sure it's not an old girlfriend stalking you?"

"I'm sure."

"Oh, you remember them." Her lips curl into a smile.

The light changes and we gradually climb over the freeway and into First Hill. Amber turns again at the hospital and makes another onto Madison going east. She's driving the speed limit. The wind gusts buffet the Jetta.

"Sill there?"

She squints into the rear-view mirror. "Yep. She's a few cars back but still with us."

The vise that has held my stomach all day tightens again.

"Could she be a cop?"

"I never saw a homicide detective who looked like her," Amber said. "Back in the wonderful days before I was exiled to Bellevue. Let's have some fun."

Amber punches the accelerator and I am pushed against the back of the seat. She closes an empty two-block gap to the truck ahead of us in seconds, then swings left onto Broadway, headed to Capitol Hill. She's quickly jammed in traffic. Broadway is two lanes, running through the heart of the hip business district. Even with the wind, the sidewalks are crowded. Couples, neo-grungers, the ever-present homeless. It's mostly young people. They're so thin.

Amber moves into the left-turn lane, signaling. Suddenly she shoots ahead and slides back onto Broadway, three cars beyond where she started. Somebody honks. She laughs and swings into a side street, gunning it around a traffic circle and going left. It's so dark that it's hard to see pedestrians, who dart across in the distance as mere shapes. From the side mirror, I see another pair of headlights take the circle and come toward us, fast.

"She's very persistent."

In a minute we turn back onto Broadway and crawl along with the traffic, hitting every light red. A crowd stands in front of the order window at Dick's, craving burgers. Amber signals again, but this time she makes the turn and we slide into the drive-in parking lot. I can see the gray Ford brightly illuminated in the streetlights, waiting on Broadway to follow us in. Then we catch a break. A Mini Cooper backs out of a space behind us, blocking the Ford's way into the lot.

Amber guns it again and shoots into an alley. We bump hard across a side street—I don't even think she looked for oncoming traffic—and wind around couple of blocks and into another alley. We speed past the backs of buildings and dumpsters. A homeless guy with a shopping cart curses us. She has turned the lights off. The lots are small and the buildings uneven. After driving half a block she pulls the parking brake and turns into a dark niche. She stops the car with the parking brake. No red brake light betrays our presence. We're in the loading area of a business, but concealed by the longer building on our right. A white delivery van is on the left. We're six feet farther in from the front of the van. Amber turns off the engine, grabs my hand and pulls me down. We're face to face below the gearshift and my side and back ache from the position. Amber giggles.

"This is fun."

I hear the crunching of car tires, see a flash of lights, then hear a swoosh going down the alley. We just may have lost the blonde.

Amber tentatively raises up, then starts the car and tears out after her.

"What are you doing?"

"Aren't you curious to see who's pissed off at you?"

I readjust my seatbelt and sit back. "How did you learn to drive like that? Journalism school?"

"I was a history major," she says. "I have brothers and I've watched a lot of action movies."

Now we're three cars behind the Ford as she turns onto Denny Way and descends out of Capitol Hill. She winds her way through the streets to get on Interstate Five. Amber confidently follows, keeping a distance of maybe two hundred yards. The task is made easier by the Ford's brake-light malfunction: only one works. So every time the blonde taps the brake, she signals her position.

"Can you make out her tag?"

I can. She tosses a reporter's notebook at me and I write it down. Just an ordinary Washington state tag.

The freeway traffic runs fast and thick, and the Ford accelerates quickly, changing lanes. Amber doesn't match lane change for lane change, but keeps the same distance.

"She's going for I-90."

"Got it." Amber moves to one of the lanes that will merge into the freeway headed east. Sure enough, the Ford takes the exit. We follow and drop into the noisy tunnel that carries traffic out of downtown and under the Mount Baker neighborhood. It's a long, narrow run, not a time to be worrying about earthquakes, and not for the claustrophobic. Amber seems unperturbed. She hides beside an eighteen wheeler in the middle lane while the Ford takes the fast lane.

Then we blast out of the tunnel onto the floating bridge over Lake Washington. The water is dark and at eye-level, churning white caps in the wind. The Ford is gone.

"Do you see her?"

"Fuck." Amber keeps her speed constant. Ahead is an anonymous stream of red tail lights. A wave crests over the concrete barrier, splashing my door. Amber runs the wiper.

"There," she says. Perhaps other waves caused traffic to slow down—the one-side brake light flashes half a mile ahead. The

Jetta rattles for a moment then responds, jumping up to 80 to close the gap.

"I'm getting creeped out driving back toward the 'burbs," Amber says.

We're almost to Mercer Island, and as the lighted exit looms the Ford signals.

Darkness is the primary matter here. The road is narrow and serpentine. On both sides, huge trees rise up to block out even the marginal light of the moonless sky. The big houses sit mostly far back, behind trees, hedges and gates, invisible except for a fleeting window or security light, but none powerful enough to penetrate far into the gloom. The water is everywhere nearby, but you'd think you were far from shore in forest primeval. Even the wind has surrendered to the overpowering blackness. The road is treacherous. As it winds around, a sharp drop-off would put a careless or unlucky driver through the roof of houses just below the grade, as the island falls off to the priciest lots near the water. The Ford drives the speed limit. Amber drives with her lights off.

I don't even bother to ask if that's a good idea. She seems fine. We've come this far. Now we're on the Rock, the Alcatraz for the rich in the Puget Sound region, which doesn't lack for affluent enclaves. The isolation would drive me nuts—even though it's minutes from downtown Seattle, if the traffic is light. No wonder Megan Nyberg took every opportunity to get the hell out. I watch the substantial homes pass by and wonder which one was hers. Yet their lights are barely visible in the overwhelming darkness. I half expect Megan's ghost to step out in front of us. My mind is beyond addled.

"Check it out…"

The Ford's reliable bum brake light burns and the car slows. Amber uses the handbrake and lower gears to reduce her speed. We're a quarter mile behind. From the other side of the road, I see one quick flash of headlights. Another vehicle parked off to the side, facing our way. There's actually a shoulder there, and beyond it a large house nearer to the road. The Ford angles over and illuminates an SUV. It parks front bumper to front bumper, and the blonde leaves her headlights on.

We're still on the road and I'm praying nobody comes flying up behind us. We'll be like one of those teenage road tragedy movies they used to show in high school drivers' ed. Amber slowly eases over to the left. I can't see if the shoulder extends this far or whether we'll hit the side of a hill or go into a gully. When the tires finally crunch on gravel I take a breath. The handbrake cranks noisily in our little cockpit.

"Are those your guys?"

I look ahead and my heartbeat triples. It's them. The two are wearing suits, standing in front of the SUV, learning in toward the blonde. She's talking. I study her face, her features. Stu slams his hand down on the hood of the SUV and shakes his head. Why do I get the impression I am the subject of this conversation. They stand this way for maybe five minutes. Then they turn off their car lights and darkness reclaims the environment.

"They don't look like Feds to me," Amber whispers.

"Why not?"

"The way the big one slouches. The woman looks way too glam."

If they are walking toward us with guns we'd never know it. The only sound in the car is our breathing. Next I feel my hand on the door latch. The mechanism responds with a metallic click and the door opens. My legs start to swing out, the only sentience in my body is blind rage. My hands are palsied with anger.

"What are you doing?"

"Pam." It's all I can manage. The ground scrunches under my shoes.

"If you get out of the car, they'll kill you, too." Amber roughly grabs my arm and I reluctantly slide back into the seat and ease the door shut. "Thank god, the dome light is broken," she says. I know she's thinking it's a display of macho. Insanity is more like it. I climb back inside my body, breathing heavily.

Flashlights flare. They swing like three lightning bugs, out into the road but then away from us. They move up toward the big house. It's completely dark, not even a porch light. I can see a piece of the blonde's coat lighted for just a second, then they're gone.

Amber starts the car and slowly glides toward the other vehicles. In less than thirty seconds we're past, with no sign of the agents. The house is tasteful and must have commanding views of the water. It also has enough of a window of light through the trees that I can make out a for-sale sign in front.

Another quarter mile in darkness, then Amber lights up the Jetta and takes off on the windy road to the freeway. Before we get there, she pulls into a Shell station parking lot and stops the car.

"What were you going to do back there?"

"I don't know," I say. "Get revenge." I am still feeling shaky from the primal instinct that took over my body.

"Don't be stupid." She stares ahead, then unfastens her seatbelt and turns to face me.

"If you want to get back at them, do it on your terms, not theirs."

"You said maybe it was over. I should let it go."

"I never said let it go," she says.

I don't know what to do. I can't go to the police. I can't get help from the newspaper. Maybe I'm not safe on the street or in my own bed. I just say slowly, "They won't let it go. And Pam is dead and those motherfuckers are still taking up oxygen."

"Help me work my story then. They're somehow involved with the disappearance of Megan Nyberg. Now they're connected to the murder of your friend. If I can break this story…"

"The paper doesn't want it."

"They don't know what they want," she says vehemently. "They're running scared and making bad decisions. If I—if we—can bring in this story it's going to be a lot more than a tabloid missing-girl thing. It'll get me out of the suburban bureau. If the paper closes, it will get me a job somewhere else. If the whole industry is dying, at least let's go down swinging! Let's go down with some integrity!"

I stare into the night. "It might get you killed."

"Journalists are killed every day in the world. It doesn't stop them. Fuck, I need this story!" She nearly shouts the last words. Then I feel her hand in mine. She has long fingers. She speaks quietly. "I remember as a college student walking into the *Chicago Tribune's* headquarters on a cold winter afternoon. No appointment, no meeting upstairs, just a wannabe gazing in solemnity at the walls around me. All that hushed cold smell of marble, the feel of history. For me, it was a little like a visit to a historic cathedral. Even then the *Tribune* wasn't the paper it once had been, but for a kid from a small town, it represented everything I held in professional reverence. I bought a reporter's notebook that day somewhere, a real one, and just carried it around, maybe like a talisman."

I squeeze her hand and can't risk trying to speak. I've cried enough today.

"Help me. I need a veteran as a partner. You haven't lost your fire like so many of the people your age."

"I don't know what to do."

"You can't freeze!"

I study her face, flushed with passion. Then, quietly, "I never freeze."

It's craziness. It surrounds me. I fall back on curiosity and pull out my phone.

"Why don't you use mine."

I look over at her, but her eyes are on the road.

"Maybe they've tapped your phone, your computer, too. Use mine." She slips me a sleek new iPhone. I use it to call an old source. He also happens to be the name of the Realtor on the for-sale sign outside the dark house on Mercer Island.

Ron Pohlmeir is one of the top residential real estate agents in Seattle. He calls himself "Nine Day Ron" for the speed with which he can sell a house, although since the bubble burst he might be Ninety Day Ron. He answers his home phone on the fourth ring.

"To what do I owe the honor of the columnist calling so late?" He sounds a little aggravated and a lot lit. I ask about the listing.

"What, you've gotten a big book advance?" he says. "Anyway, I thought you were an urban type."

"Who's the seller?"

"I'm not really comfortable getting into that."

I needle and cajole—he's been a helpful real-estate source, but he's also gotten plenty of publicity by appearing in my column. When he finally gives it up, I almost can't speak.

"You there?"

"Yeah, just swallowed wrong. Troy Hardesty?"

Amber gives me a sharp look.

"It's been on the market for three months, and he was really on my back to find a buyer."

"Why? Did he seem like he needed the money?"

"Don't know," Nine Day Ron says. "But that's why his suicide shocked me so much. I got the sense he was really going to try something new. A new lifestyle, whatever."

"What do you mean?"

"He said, 'I want to be on the other side of the Cascades by the second week of November.'"

"What does that mean?"

"I don't know. Said it that way, and said it more than once."

I repeat what Ron says. I want Amber to hear every word. I feel the need for a witness now, as we speed back to the glittering city very much on this side of the Cascades.

Chapter Twenty-two

Thursday, October 28th

Amber and I make plans. We will use only paper—paper documents, paper files. We will do it old school, the way it was done when I was a young reporter. We will have to find a safe place to keep the work—maybe rent a storage locker somewhere. Some place.

She is from the digital generation but apparently not of it. She doesn't trust electronic files. Maybe part of that is her native messiness—a look at the stacks of reporter's notebooks, files, and newspapers in the back seat of the Jetta confirms that. But she claims she has been burned by too many computer crashes, and now she believes I'm being tracked—online and on the phone.

I have been accused of being a neat freak. Maybe that's true, but I know I'm lazy. I want to touch a piece of paper one time and be done with it. I love my emails, search engines, and electronic files. I love being able to research a corporation's records online through Edgar, rather than waiting for Fedex to deliver paper 10-Ks and 13-Ds from the SEC in Washington like in the days when I was a young business writer. But my digital world is suddenly toxic.

Amber drops me off at the newspaper. The wind has eased and the sidewalk is empty. I decide to go in, using the side employee entrance, showing my ID to the security guard. I can hear the distant rumble of the presses. It is midnight. When the elevator door opens, I am visibly startled. Karl Zimmer, the old maintenance guy, is standing there, his tool belt hanging like a gun belt. I nod. He doesn't speak. He stares at me hard. Lots of people outside the news department hold us in quiet contempt. We think we're better than they are—that's the sense, wrong to my mind. I always speak to the pressmen, janitors, phone operators, dispatch runners, advertising people, if only to dispel this little unspoken class war in the building. My background is probably as blue-collar as Karl's. But like many in the building, he's probably not unhappy to see the snots with their college degrees get theirs. He stays on the elevator when I get off.

The newsroom is empty except for a skeleton crew of a couple of copy editors, an assistant city editor and a cops reporter. The paper has been put to bed and will only be remade if there's major news. I feel exhaustion overtaking me, but I want to make one last check.

Back in my office, I spend the next hour going through my files, both in the computer and the filing cabinets. I meticulously go through my electronic address book. I go through stacks of business cards. No Nybergs. Nothing that would involve Ryan Meyers. No connections. The only thing that stands out is the last quarter of a notebook from a year earlier.

Newspaper writers use all sorts of notebooks: yellow legal pads, steno pads and a long, narrow sheaf of paper called the reporter's notebook. I use reporter's notebooks. They're about eight inches long, three inches wide, with thin cardboard on each end and held together by spiral wire. I usually use one for all sorts of interviews, then put it in the files when it's full, marking it by dates. I'm too lazy to write every story it was used for on the cover, unless it's highly sensitive. In that case, it goes in a file box along with the other documents related to that story. I haven't needed to do that since I was an investigative reporter, and the danger of being sued or challenged was ever-present.

The notebook that catches my attention looks like all the others. But when I see its dates, I decide to thumb through it. Sure enough, the last quarter of it is notes I took for a column on

Troy Hardesty a year ago. My idea had been to look at the local money men who had survived the big crash. But for whatever reason, Troy had been especially forthcoming and other column topics were backing up. So I used a cheap columnist's trick, took a shortcut, and just profiled Hardesty. Now I hold those notes and involuntarily check behind me, making sure nobody is around. These are Troy Hardesty notes that never made it to the Feds. I slip the notebook in my pocket. Then I send an email to Faith at the IT help desk and log out for the night.

I leave the way I came in and walk along the Seneca Street side of the building. Soon I am illuminated from the bright lights flowing out of four-story-tall glass windows. It's the best show in this part of town and it happens every night. It's been too long since I've seen it.

Through the glass, the giant printing presses are running at top speed, turning rolls of blank newsprint into today's *Seattle Free Press*, my column included. They make the sound of a distant thunderstorm. The paper shoots up and down through the gears, drums, and rollers of the towering machines as ink imprints stories, photos, and graphics. Finished papers are automatically cut, folded, collated, and set onto fast-moving conveyors that will take them to the loading docks. Pressmen in blue uniforms monitor control lights and panels on the sides of the presses. A couple of them stand scrutinizing the finished editions, page by page. They're all my age and older. Unlike the old days, they wear fancy ear protection.

In the newsroom, the paper is put together with the latest computer programs. Page designers do everything and more that the old printers used to handle in the back shop, the last of whom were bought out eight years ago. But the printing presses remain, the muscular manufacturing process that puts news on paper. When I started, the pressroom was grimy, the presses old, noisy as hell. It looked exactly like something out of the black-and-white movie *Deadline USA*, where Humphrey Bogart as fearless editor defies a threatening mob boss. Now it's surgical-suite clean and high tech, with stainless steel catwalks surrounding Goss Uniliners that can print 80,000 copies per hour in full color. They're still loud. I can hear them—feel them—through the glass.

The *Free Press* is one of the last major metros that still prints downtown, rather than using a satellite plant out in the suburbs. I sit on the metal bench on the sidewalk and watch in a wonder that has never diminished. The company installed the bench several years ago, facing toward the big windows, with metal arms every few feet so the bums don't sleep there. A statue of a 1930s newsboy stands next to it, his mouth frozen in a call of "Extra! Extra!"

How many times have I been here, in all weather, all hours, and stages of life, often sporting a glow of liquor from the nearby Puget Embassy. We all called it the Putrid Embassy, or just the Putrid. It was the last newspaper bar in Seattle. The place was long and narrow, smoky and dear. The booths were ancient and the walls were decorated with notable *Free Press* front pages. It was run by an old Greek, who would run us out at two a.m. exclaiming in his wonderful accent, "got to go, got to go!" When I qualified to run a bar tab, I knew I had become a real newspaperman. The bar had closed four years ago, replaced by a Starbucks. But the presses still thunder.

In less than sixty days, all this may be gone. That was the press, baby. Still, the presses center me. I won't freeze. I turn away, aware that this time last night I was with Pam. She was still joyously alive.

But another realization pushes all this away. I stand on the empty sidewalk. *Free Press* trucks crowd along the street waiting to pick up papers, their tailpipes blowing fog into the night air. One has a billboard on its side advertising my column. I ignore all this. After one of the worst days of my life, my brain finally reconnects.

I know that blonde.

I've seen her before.

The blonde who was watching my place. I've seen her before. She gave me the shoulder block that day by the elevator, the day I was leaving Troy Hardesty's office. She must have been headed in.

Chapter Twenty-three

Years ago, I was part of a team of investigative reporters sent to Texas, to look into a rash of unsolved drug killings. In some cases, they were classified as suicides, such as the man who lay naked in his bathtub and shot himself three times with a pump-action shotgun. Law enforcement was compromised. Big drug money will do that. Only the Texas Rangers and a few local cops were trustworthy. They suggested that we be armed at all times. Our ethical qualms went away once we found that the dealers had contracts out on us. This in the days before lawyers and HR people had castrated newsrooms. We didn't bother to tell the bosses.

I did my job with a gun in a shoulder holster and a rock in my gut. There was the ever-present knowledge that a bomb could be under the car; that guys with submachine guns could appear out of the night. I learned about the Columbian Necktie and how many bodies are sitting in oil drums in the Gulf of Mexico. We moved around a lot, stayed in small-town motels. I was glad to leave. The fear stayed with me a long time after I left Texas and our stories were winning awards and putting people in jail.

I have that rock in my stomach again. I also still have the gun, a Smith & Wesson .357 short-barrel Combat Magnum in blue carbon steel with custom grips. I am a good shot. It feels heavy and comforting in my hand, and I think hard about carrying it. I decide against it.

It's twilight as I step aboard one of the Third Avenue buses and ride up to Brasa, a restaurant that was very chic a few years ago. But the money and madness of a few years ago are gone, replaced by worry and waiting. The bar is half deserted. I sit at a table by the window, facing in. Twenty minutes later, Wendy Chan walks in, sees me, waves, and walks over.

I haven't seen Wendy in three years and she's cut her hair. From lush and straight touching her shoulders, it's now very short and no doubt chic. It still strikes me as a cancer-survivor 'do, but she is radiant as always, a smile briefly playing across her delicate features.

"I shouldn't be doing this," she says as we sit. "You know that I got married. I'm really happy."

I tell her I'm glad about it.

"Don't get me wrong, we had fun. But it's over." The server arrives, takes our orders, and goes away.

"I just wanted to talk," I say. She looks at me suspiciously. Her lawyer look, I used to call it, back when Wendy worked for the U.S. Attorney's office. From her LinkedIn page, I found that she had moved to the Securities and Exchange Commission. That would have been an impediment to our relationship back then. Now I hoped it might help me.

"What about you? Are you holding up? I read about the newspaper. How it might even close. Awful. You'll be okay, of course. Are you still rescuing birds with broken wings and then letting them fly away?" She smiles. "Am I still on your account at Megan Mary's flowers?"

"I have a real girlfriend now." I don't know why I say this, but I do.

She looks relieved and I begin a slow seduction of another sort, interrupted briefly as our drinks arrive. Wendy makes the common protestations about talking to the press.

"I keep secrets all over town," I say. "Cheers. I don't want to quote you. I just want some guidance before I go off half-cocked."

She studies her white wine for a couple of minutes after taking the first sip. For several seconds I worry that she will just get up and walk out. Then she sighs and cocks her head slightly, a mannerism I still find sexy when she does it.

"Shoot."

"Troy Hardesty."

She looks relieved. "He's as clean as they come in a dirty industry. Was. What a horrible thing."

"I was there. We had just had a meeting. I was down on the street."

She says my name in a way that makes me miss her. I ask her if she knew anything about him.

"Only what I read, mostly. He was a man who seemed to have everything to live for: pretty wife, private airplane, the big house over on Mercer Island. I went to a party there once with Chad." Her husband. "This was about a year ago."

"Those cozy regulators."

"Stop it. He wasn't under investigation, and Chad was doing some IT work for one of Troy's friends. Anyway, no expense was spared. I could get a real taste for beluga caviar…"

"So nothing wrong with his hedge fund…"

"That I knew of," she says. "I don't mean to sound cold, but the suicide of a big investor isn't exactly a surprise nowadays. But was he a Bernie Madoff or Allen Stanford? If he was, it sure hasn't come to our attention."

"Was he faithful to his wife?"

"The columnist digs for dirt. How would I know that?"

"No taste for young girls?"

She laughs loudly. Wendy has a great laugh. "We don't have a morals division at the SEC."

"So why would the FBI be investigating him?"

She eyes me warily, as if she's afraid I am going to drag her into some bureaucratic swamp. She holds up her hands. "I just can't tell you. I mean, I don't know."

I let it go. Something ties Hardesty to Megan Nyberg. I let the conversation drift and she's telling me about their ski trips to Whistler last year, about fixing up their house in Magnolia. It all sounds very domestic and predictable and I am happy for her. When the drinks are drained, I pay the bill and ask her about eleven-eleven. She shrugs and smiles, says, "I'm pretty out of it when it comes to pop culture," and we step out into the night.

It's starting to rain a very fine mist and the street is turned dark black.

"I can't believe October is almost over," she says.

"Do you know what a national security letter looks like?"

She hesitates, bites her lip. Finally, "You know I can't even go there."

"But you know what one looks like. Just hypothetically."

"Just hypothetically."

I stand there letting the mist gather on my forehead. She raises the hood of her coat.

"Just hypothetically," she says, "it would have a Justice Department letterhead. It would have some officialese up there, like, 'In reply, refer to file number' blah, blah."

"How would it be worded?"

"Very legalese. 'Under the authority of Executive Order…' 'In accordance with…,' that kind of thing."

So far, it sounds very much like the piece of paper I saw on my table the other morning. "And it would be signed?"

"Of course."

My letter didn't have a signature.

"Would a person who received a National Security Letter be allowed to keep it?"

"Of course," she says. She pulls back the hood and looks at me. "Are you in trouble?"

"I don't know."

We hug. It's a hug that lasts exactly three seconds too long and I remember exactly the way we used to fit together. Wendy had a fondness for Billy Collins poems and foot massages. Her girlfriends didn't like me.

Now she walks to a silver Lexus and drives away. I stand in the rain. So many pieces of me are left in so many places. Some times it's a good feeling and every once in a while it hurts like hell.

◇◇◇

I am losing time. The Sunday column is due in less than seventeen hours, but I can dig into the evergreen file. A column idea squirreled away for a slow news day. The bosses are so distracted they won't notice. In fact, they seem to prefer it now when I don't write about controversial topics—another change from the old days when the *Free Press* had real balls. But I'm not getting results where it counts. Wendy was my hope for a home run. Troy was under investigation for a massive investment fraud? Maybe that would have made him a target for suicide—or maybe assisted suicide if he made powerful enemies. The only trouble is, it's apparently not true. Not only did Wendy say he was clean, but I haven't received one tip about trouble in Troy's hedge fund. I am further than ever from connecting him to Megan Nyberg, Ryan Meyers, and Heather Brady—kids who should be far out of the orbit of Troy's lavish life.

I ride back toward Pioneer Square on a quiet, electric Third Avenue bus. As night has arrived, the clientele has changed. I look like the only person aboard who makes more than $25,000 a year. A woman with a long, scraggly beard sits across from me. Parts of downtown are dark and seedy looking, new empty storefronts added just since the last time I was along this way. A long recession will do that.

I pull out my Blackberry, wanting to call Amber. I am missing her. I am missing Pam and Rachel and the two Melindas. I put it away. It's untrustworthy for much more than calling to order a pizza. Why am I really surprised? It was well-reported, including by our soon-to-be-dead Washington bureau, that the National Security Agency had spied on reporters during the Bush years. I thought most of that was all in the past. And why would anyone be listening in on a business columnist at a paper in Seattle?

That had been Faith's question to me that afternoon, a quizzical half-smile on her face—after thirty minutes spent fiddling with my computer.

"Has it been slow lately?" she asked, running an anti-virus program while I sat on my desk watching. I told her it had been, and had crashed a couple of times. She nodded and opened different menus. "No obvious viruses," she said. "I see from the AV program that you've been rebooting every day. That's when we install new anti-virus patches. You wouldn't get it if you didn't…"

I nodded cooperatively.

"Sit down here." I followed her instructions and sat at the keyboard. She got on her knees and swept her black hair out of her face as she watched the CPU on the floor. Her hair fell in a perfect crescent just below her shoulders. "Just open a file and start typing. Any old thing."

So I did, discreetly appreciating the shape of her denim-clad behind.

"Now stop."

I stared out the window at the rain. She said, "Now start typing again."

After a few minutes of this, she went out into the business newsroom and worked on a spare computer. Then she came back and sat cross-legged on the floor, looking up at me. She pursed her lips, moving her mouth to the side and up. "This is really interesting. See the processor lights?" She pointed to the box on the floor. "They blink when you're not doing anything. So I looked in back, at the network interface card's activity light. Packets of data are being sent out when they shouldn't be…"

"So I'm being spied on?"

"I'd say. It's pretty sophisticated snooping, though. I called up the task manager a few minutes ago…"

"Don't know nothing about no science, Faith."

I got a smile out of her. She adjusted her black oval glasses. "The task manager, Mister Economics Columnist, should show any spyware that's running." She smiled with one side of her mouth. "If you know where to look. Now they can name it something innocuous, but I couldn't find anything. But I'm pretty sure we've got a cracker. Somebody who's broken through our security." She rubbed her small hands together. "Takes me back to my cracking and hacking days. Want me to take it down? Re-route them to a porn site? Send them a virus?"

I shrugged. It might be useful to let them think I was as clueless about this as I was about the rest of the situation. I asked her to let me think about it.

"I'd guess it's just you," she said. "I have to check and make sure it's not a general breach, but it looks like they are targeting you. Why would anybody be snooping on the business columnist?" she said, rising to go. "No offense."

"None taken. Thanks, Faith. You'll have a job long after I am living under a bridge."

"I actually gave notice today. I'm going to a startup. May as well get off the Titanic."

I told her I was sorry to see her go, knowing she was too young to miss the good times of newspapering, wondering if she even reads the paper, if someone of her generation has had her brain so rewired by constant electronic distractions as to be like me at all. She broke my reverie.

"You write at home, too," she said.

"I own a Mac. Two, actually."

"Don't sound superior. Assume that's been cracked, as well."

I held out my Blackberry and asked her if it was safe.

"My God, that ought to be in a museum. It's so not safe. If they can get past our firewalls, they can easily snoop wirelessly. They can also track it." She bites her lower lip. "I can get you one of the new Blackjacks they have downstairs."

"I thought those were just for the bigwigs."

"They'll never miss it. And I can put an encryption program into a Blackjack."

The newspaper is failing and they don't know how many expensive cellphones are sitting around.

"Want your old number?"

I think about this and tell her to keep my old number on the Blackberry and give me a new one on the encrypted cellphone.

I ask, "Can they crack that, as you put it?"

She gave that little half-of-the-mouth smile. "Not the way I do it."

I sit on the bus, trying not to stare at the bearded lady. The driver announces Pike Place Market and the monorail and I think about the blonde. Suicide blonde—who sang that song? She ran into me as I walked toward the elevator that day in Troy's office tower—that much I'm sure of. She is tall but willowy, hardly the type who could toss Troy the gym rat off a balcony. Maybe she had help. Maybe he looked away at the wrong moment. Amber is checking the license tag on the blonde's gray Ford. I still haven't seen her face up close.

So far, I don't know anything else except she was standing outside my building. Maybe I am the next to die—she bungled the assassination, so Stu and Bill were understandably upset last night out on Mercer Island. But I'm still alive—foolishly comforted by the bright lights inside the bus—and they were looking for something, going into Troy's old house. They were looking for something in my notes. I can't figure it out and I am running out of time. Two weeks to November 11th.

Chapter Twenty-four

The rain eases into a steady mist as I walk down the hill to First Avenue. It gives haloes to the street lamps. I stop in a little convenience store and buy a throwaway cell phone. I read somewhere the world has four billion cell phones; now I have one more. Out on the street, I find it actually works and I call Amber's pager. *Free Press* police reporters still carry pagers, as well as cell phones, don't ask me why. They are barely used now. Amber hasn't returned her pager, even though she is off the cops beat. In five minutes she calls me back.

"What are you wearing?"

"A big smile for you," I say. "Is the line safe?"

"I'm at a pay phone. What about you? Did you buy the drug-dealer cell like I suggested?"

I told her I had, and quickly brought her up to date on my day's dead ends.

"I have good and bad news. If I sound distant, it's because I don't want to catch Ebola from this phone mouthpiece. The good news is, I snuck back to Seattle early and pulled a missing person's report on one Heather Brady. She's a runaway from Denison, Texas. Seventeen years old. Long story short, she was in Seattle for about a year, but got back in touch with her parents three months ago. She would call them twice a week. They'd send her money, hoping they could lure her back home. She said she had enrolled in community college and was finishing her GED. But a month ago, the calls stopped. Her dad flew up here and filed the report, which the cops promptly shelved. What's another runaway in Seattle?"

"And this one's named Heather Brady?"

"Heather Jo Brady, five-feet-five, one hundred pounds, brown hair, looks pretty from the photo on the report. Homecoming queen-type."

"Any connection to Megan or Ryan?"

"Not in the report."

"But it did have the parents' phone number?"

"Got it. I'm on that."

"So she disappeared about the same time as Megan Nyberg."

"Exactly," Amber says.

"So what's the bad news?"

"The car tab from your blonde. Comes back registered to a used-car place out on Aurora. I drove by, and it's a real business. So either you wrote it down wrong, or somebody's going to a lot of trouble to conceal their identity."

"Or the car lot is fronting for somebody, like the Feds."

Amber doesn't answer.

I scan the street for the fifth or sixth time in that minute, seeing nothing out of place. "I wrote it down right."

"When do I get to see you?"

I tell her later. I need to run an errand first. Wiping the mist off my face, I walk up the hill to the newspaper, to retrieve my briefcase.

◇◇◇

At home, I change into black jeans, black T-shirt, and a black rain slicker with a hood. Underneath, the black nylon shoulder rig wraps comfortably under both my armpits and stretches across my back. Inside the nylon holster on the left side, the revolver sits with the barrel pointed down and the grip right in line with the movement of my right arm. It is secured with a snap, which can be undone with one move of my hand. I pour out a dozen extra bullets from a cardboard box and slip them in my coat pocket.

I stand in front of the mirror with the rain slicker open. The gun is not visible. I have slipped it on easily, with not a millisecond of moral or ethical second thoughts. It is a momentous step, opening another door that I'd rather avoid. At least this time I'm the one turning the knob. I do not feel tough or invulnerable. I feel sick and corroded, from the moment of Troy's death, and I am the one dropping, too, dropping down a hole into an alien world without oxygen. The revolver is an accessory here. Still, I feel the revolver weight against my side. I stand there a long time watching myself, avoiding my reflected eyes. If I were like Jill, I would be afraid Pam's face would appear to me. I reach in and touch the pistol's grip, securely strapped into the holster, then I drop my arm.

Outside it's dry and the homeless guy, George, is on duty, sitting on his crate. A young man and woman walk by, cuddling against each other. He asks them for money and they ignore him. I nod to George, reach for my wallet, and prepare to take out a couple of bucks, then stop. I peel off two twenties and hand them to him.

"What the…?" His head jerks up in surprise. "Thank you."

I ask him to do me a favor.

Melinda Hines lives in West Seattle. She's an assistant professor at the U-Dub who teaches and writes on 18th century English literature. Samuel Johnson is her hero. She's forty-six, medium-tall, and has auburn hair that falls straight to her shoulders. I met her last year as she was going through a nasty divorce—but are there any other kinds? Melinda is a life-long newspaper reader—reads it all the way through every day—and knew me through my column. She liked a friend who could hold a conversation about books, appreciate dry, ironic humor, and one night, after a bottle of wine, she stopped me at the door and kissed me. She has given me the best compliment: that I brought out the sexy side she never knew she had, that I was someone she never thought she would have in her life.

Everybody has his theory about the death of newspapers. Melinda Hines is no different, but hers is extravagant, wildly conspiratorial, and alluring. She calls it her Grand Unified Theory to Keep America Stupid, or, simply, "my conspiracy theory." As in, I'll tell her some fresh bad news and she'll say, "Well, you know my conspiracy theory…"

It goes like this: Newspapers consolidated and largely became owned by large companies that must deliver unsustainable profit margins to Wall Street. So they already have pressures to cut back. But they also have business before Congress, such as changing the law to allow ownership of newspapers and television stations in the same market. So they don't want to really dig for dirt anymore. And the financial industry that controls the government already has them "by the balls," she says, professorially. So they keep dumbing down the coverage, eliminating investigative reporting, silencing the best columnists—"except you, so far"—and playing up silly things, especially entertainment news. It helps keep the public constantly distracted, more and more ignorant about the government and the world. She says, "Do you think it's any coincidence that the war in Iraq was waged on lies during the exact same time that newspapers began their tailspin?" And, "Technology is making illiteracy powerful."

It makes more sense than many of the ideas trotted out by high-priced consultants.

She has been in Oxford for three months, lecturing, and sending me a letter a week. I've been checking on her condo twice a week, making sure the plants on her balcony are watered. That's usually not a taxing job in Seattle. Melinda is a techno-Luddite and proud of it. Don't look for her class syllabus on the Internet. She refuses to use email for personal correspondence—being convinced that it is killing both the language and the art of letter writing. The university makes her use it at work.

I walk four blocks to my old Toyota, climb in, and lock the door. I sit in the dark car feeling the weight of the gun under my left arm. A concealed firearms permit is in my wallet, a souvenir of a year ago when I was writing columns that caused death-threats from an anonymous anti-tax reader in Spokane. He never came over the mountains to get me, but I still have the permit. After five minutes of watching, I start the car and drive toward the West Seattle bridge.

The bridge soars high over the Duwamish River, Harbor Island, and the port. I have to admit it: I am less comfortable with heights every year I get older, so I just watch the road. Traffic is light and in minutes I am driving along Harbor Avenue, looking back at downtown across a dark Elliott Bay. I pull into the park where the water taxis dock and choose a deserted part of the lot. A half-dozen cars are parked close to the walking path, facing the light show from across the water. I turn out my lights and sit. No one else pulls into the parking lot in the next ten minutes. I turn on the lights and drive out.

Next I turn up California Street and drive around the neighborhood for a while. Headlights pass and turn. None seem to be sticking or lingering. It's late enough that the sidewalks are deserted and the pleasant, postwar houses are lit with cheery, warm lights. Finally I pull into a little park. It has only a few spaces for cars and none are taken. I again wait for a few minutes, then step out and lock the car. I walk uphill carrying the briefcase past hedges and flowerbeds, then turn into an alley. What do I look like? Just a guy who got off the bus after working late. I go a hundred yards and step quickly into the space provided by a brick garage jutting out unevenly. No dogs bark. I can hear only the wind and a light rain begins. I pull up my hood, wait, and listen.

Five minutes go by and I walk again, keeping close to the fence line, until I come to a sidewalk that runs downhill between hedges and fences. You wouldn't know it was here unless you were one of the neighborhood walkers. A shadow suddenly materializes ahead and my gut freezes up. The briefcase is in my left hand. I wonder about reaching into the wind-breaker, just to have my hand close. It's an older guy, thinning sandy hair, Patagonia zip-neck jacket with a company logo. We say hello and pass by. I walk faster and turn back to see him keep moving uphill.

Another block and I reach Melinda's third-floor condo. The locks are secure and nothing looks amiss. They don't know about this Melinda because she doesn't use email. I don't turn on the lights until I am in her study. It's an enclosed room, encased like a blast shelter by bookshelves and stacks of newspapers, magazines, academic journals, student papers—some are four feet high. I sit at her desk and turn on the lamp. It has a green shade. A photo of the two of us sits on the desk. I have been bracing myself for her inevitable break with me. The time she concludes that she wants to find a relationship that could lead to marriage, to "a future," whatever that means. I'm surprised her latest letter from England wasn't of the "Dear John" variety. If she used email, her subject line would be something like "re-thinking you and me." Sometimes it scalds me for months. In Melinda's case, it will hurt even as I wish her well. Now I have bigger worries.

I open Pam's Coach briefcase, the leather mournfully soft to the touch, and pull out my copies of the notes turned over to the Feds. I go through them page-by-page, line-by-line. I make four pages of handwritten notes in a fresh reporter's notebook. Just a few reminders about my interviews with Troy Hardesty. Still nothing that creates an "oh, shit!" moment of recognition.

When I am finished, I slide the notes back into the briefcase. I put the fresh reporter's notebook in my slicker pocket. From the kitchen I retrieve a plastic garbage bag and drop the briefcase inside. I double-bag it, then fold all this into a neat rectangle. Out on Melinda's balcony, the soil in her pots is moist. It's starting to rain heavily. I unlatch a heavy plastic storage bin she uses for gardening tools and pack my rectangle at the bottom. Somehow I feel as if I am interring Pam. I don't count the minutes I hold tightly onto the cold metal of the balcony, far beyond the time when my hands have started to ache.

Chapter Twenty-five

"Hello, Writerman."

Rachel raises her face and I kiss her without hesitation. I love the way Rachel kisses, as if the muscles in her mouth were made for it. She takes my hands.

I feel warm looking at her. I can't help it. She's like a well-made cocktail. "I didn't know if you'd cut class for me."

"That's what substitute teachers are for." Then the music is gone from her voice. "I'm worried about you."

The last thing I had done before going home the previous night was to stop at a 24-hour Kinko's and pay cash to use their computer. I signed up for a Gmail account. The Feds couldn't track me that quickly—we're talking about the government here. I had sent Rachel a message: "Please meet me where we first kissed. Urgent." This morning I had arrived at the paper early and banged out my Sunday column, a report card on how the governor was handling the recession. I can write outrage. I can write heartbreak. But I had written the thing I wasn't feeling: cool analysis, and I had filed it by eleven. Faith had given me the Samsung Blackjack, newly encrypted. Then I had driven out to Ballard, past the locks and Ray's Boathouse, to the park. I had scoped it out for thirty minutes before Rachel might arrive. Then I had walked up the slight incline from the water, across the parking lot, and into the tunnel.

Now it is three p.m. and we stand in a small tunnel that carries a hiking trail from Golden Gardens Park under the Burlington Northern Santa Fe railroad tracks.

"We're taking a terrible chance by meeting," she says.

"Am I in that much trouble?" I try to say it light, like a joke. She says nothing and lets my hands fall away like regrets.

The tunnel is just long enough to go under the double tracks of the main line, and it is wide and filled with light. Outside a low cloud cover shelters the sky. Puget Sound is dark blue, the color of Rachel's eyes, and three sailboats cut through the water half a mile or more from the shore. Across the water, the Olympic Mountains are jagged and purple. It's far too beautiful an afternoon to harbor the sinister, so I am on edge. Still, something about her eases me. What is it about a blue-eyed brunette, contrasts that work so well together?

"Why no suit?" she asks.

"Casual Friday." My suits aren't cut large enough to conceal the gun, so under the black windbreaker, I am in khakis and a blue shirt.

"You hate casual Fridays, and I love you in a suit." She glances both ways.

To allay Rachel's fears—and mine—I position her so she is on the outer edge of the tunnel, facing toward the woods and the neighborhood to the east. I am inside and can go west, toward the parking lot and the shore. We're close enough to talk, but at a 90-degree angle from each other. I tell her if anyone suspicious approaches, just walk away and I will, too. It seemed like a clever plan this morning. Now it seems a little silly. So far, the park is nearly deserted—a few dog-walkers close to the water. No one is on the trail. We take our positions.

I hear her voice from my side. "I asked you not to contact me."

"Rachel, what happens on 11/11?"

"I don't know."

"Rachel…"

"I don't know!" I glance around to see the back of her head. She runs a hand through her thick, curly dark hair. "I don't know! Dad dictated that part of the note to me! He was trying to keep you out of trouble."

"It's too late." She turns in and reaches for me, shaking her head in concern. I gently turn her back to watch her side of the approach.

"I went to see a hedge-fund guy named Troy Hardesty for a routine interview. The next thing I knew he was falling out of his office onto Fourth Avenue. He mentions eleven/eleven in our conversation—asked me if I'd ever heard of it. Later that night, a bag lady on the street yells it at me. 'Eleven/eleven.' She says, 'You'll get yours.' I found it tattooed on the leg of a dead man. He just happened to be the boyfriend of this girl who's missing, Megan Nyberg. Then I get your note. Eleven/eleven, again."

A hundred yards away, a black Lab drags a woman to a minivan. They get inside and in a moment the car starts up and backs out. I wait for Rachel to say something, to make some sense of it. When she's silent, I continue.

"After Troy's death, I got picked up by federal agents. They flashed badges but never showed me their credentials again. They took me to an unmarked building in SoDo, asked what I knew about Troy, then they let me go." I instinctively look down at the scar on the top of my hand. "A couple of days later, they kick down my door. They burn my hand with a cigarette and show me a National Security Letter. It demands all my notes and emails regarding Troy, Megan Nyberg, the boyfriend Ryan Meyers and someone else, Heather Brady. Do you know those names?"

"Only Megan, from TV."

"This guy's a hedge fund boss, and they're teenagers. Both girls are missing and Ryan's dead. The paper gives up the notes without a fight. I can't believe it. The *Seattle Free Press*!"

"Please let this go!"

I curse and lower my voice. "It's too late, Rachel. These agents are killers…"

"What do you mean, killers?"

"I need to know what happens on eleven/eleven. We've only got thirteen days." Jill would have said that's a bad omen in itself.

I catch my wandering mind. "I learned that Troy Hardesty had his house on the market. He told the Realtor that he wanted to be on the other side of the Cascades by the second week in November. We're back to eleven/eleven, and none of it sounds good."

I hear a train whistle in the far distance and look around to see if Rachel is still there. She is looking back mournfully.

"We could just run away." Her lips make a sad smile. "It wouldn't be awful."

"It would be wonderful, but you deserve way better than me. Soon-to-be unemployed journalist."

"I know you think I'm just acting like a doormat. I'm not. I know you better than you think. Being with you felt right, righter than anything in my life. I just can't let go of this vision I have about us. I went to a fortune teller a year ago..."

"I know."

"She told me I would fall in love with a writer and he would be a righter of wrongs, too."

"I know."

She steps to face me and takes my hands. She has lovely hands, pale with long, sculpted fingers. She could be a hand model.

"And he would be a very worldly man who would scare me a little. But he'd be just what I needed. I like to tell that story. But I would have had this vision without the fortuneteller. I had it that day you kissed me, right here."

I look at her and my chest constricts. Is this what they mean by heartache? In the long moment, I know I'll miss her forever. I know I'll look back and ache and wish I had done differently, been a different man. It passes and I place her hands at her side brusquely. I never had a sixth sense. I do have an essential intuition necessary for journalists and cops. I can tell when someone is lying to me.

"Goddammit, Rachel, lives are at risk here." I advance on her and her loving face suddenly shows fear. "I know you're lying to me. Your father invested in Hardesty's hedge fund. Don't you get it? I've got blood on my hands! Somebody's going to pay! I want the truth!"

She says my name over and over, denying she knows anything, retreating as I match her step for step. A part of me, deep inside the bastard, is watching that she doesn't trip.

"Tell me!"

She starts crying. She looks behind her, to see an avenue of retreat. But I take her shoulders and make her face me. Then she whispers, just audible above the noise of the wind.

"Dad was in the CIA."

Chapter Twenty-six

I had only met Craig Summers once before the encounter at Pike Place Market. Rachel had taken me to meet her parents for dinner. The "meet the parents" thing had set off my worry meter, but I had enjoyed the evening. Summers didn't live at all like the stereotypical Seattle tech mogul. He and his wife owned a Victorian painted lady on Queen Anne Hill. It was beautifully restored and tastefully furnished, but honestly, too, as if real people lived there. The parents were nice people. I should have expected no less considering their daughter.

Now, as we sit in my car, Rachel lays it out for me. The real Craig Summers bio was somewhat different than what appeared in the newspaper. In fact, he went through the University of Washington in three years on a full academic scholarship. Then he joined the Central Intelligence Agency, where he worked for a decade. When he became the chief executive of his first company, Praetorian Systems, it was a CIA front.

True, it sold new software for tracking ships by commercial satellite—but the technology came out of government labs, not Craig Summers' brain. It was "sold" to the U.S. Navy and allied navies at first, giving the agency a way to launder some money at the same time. But it gave Summers and his team credibility as defense contractors, and soon less-friendly governments came calling, sometimes covertly. The idea wasn't to sell the software, but to identify international arms merchants, offer virus-ridden software code to less-friendly governments, and find domestic double agents. It was a late Cold War enterprise. Once the Berlin Wall fell, Summers indeed made money from the sale of Praetorian—but it was his separation fee from the CIA.

Rachel claims she knew none of this until she was in college.

"I hated him when I found out," she says. "I was in my student rebel days and had read about CIA abuses. When I grew up a little more, I came to believe he was serving the country. Then I got mad all over again after 9/11, when I read about the secret CIA prisons, rendition. The black sites. Dad was genuinely angry about it, too. He was horrified. He said he had never done anything like that, that it violated the agency's own rules. I believe him. He's a good man."

It is hard to imagine Rachel of the calm dark blue eyes rebelling against anything, but we never really know anyone, do we? "And Moonglow Systems, that was a scam too?" I ask. It was Summers' next company and biggest success.

"Dad was never in a scam," Rachel says with heat in her voice. "And, no. Moonglow was all his. He's a very good executive. He understood the possibilities of the Internet very early. He built that company."

"With a nice nest egg from the CIA." Maybe Craig Summers invested some of it with Troy Hardesty because Hardesty was involved with the CIA, too. Maybe that's why Troy's hedge fund survived the recession so well. Maybe her dad stayed on as a consultant with the agency. When I say this to Rachel she flares at me.

"I don't know anything about that! I've never even heard this man's name before you told me about this. How do you know he and Dad knew each other?"

I scan the parking lot in the rearview mirror, seeing nothing amiss. "So the guys who roughed me up are CIA. I need to keep you out of this," I say. "Your note said he knew bad people. Did you write that?"

She shakes her head. "My part was the missing you terribly line. And that you were making a mistake, with us."

"And 11/11—written as a date. You don't know." I sigh heavily.

She stares ahead and says nothing. I don't think she knows. The sun breaks through the light cloud cover and suddenly the sound has a brilliant white V running across it. It lasts for long moments of silence.

"You said you have blood on your hands," Rachel finally says. "What do you mean?"

Now it's my turn to clam up. All I dare tell her is what I finally say. "It's better, it's safer, that you don't know."

"Those were almost exactly the words dad used, the day he just lost it about you. He said, 'Oh, my God, I'm going to have blood on my hands.' I don't think I've ever seen him more upset."

I ask her when this was.

"The Sunday after you dumped me."

"So he was already pissed at me."

"I hadn't told him," she says.

"So what set him off?"

"I don't know. He was reading the paper. Maybe he was upset about this Troy Hardesty's suicide."

"But we didn't report it. Neither did the *Times*."

"Wait," she says. "He was reading the business section."

That was the day my first column on Olympic International appeared. My mouth is suddenly sandpaper. A giant container ship pushes south toward port. The sun has gone away.

Rachel takes my hand again. Her hand is cold and I instinctively cover it with my other hand to warm it.

"Why can't you let this go?"

"Too much has happened," I say. "All I can do now is tell the story. That's the only way I can make things right."

"Why can't you just live a happy life?" she demands. "Aren't you afraid?"

I tell her that I'm terrified.

"I was afraid to come here today," she says. "But I'm not afraid any more. It's too bad you are."

"There's just a lot…" I let my voice trail off.

"You're afraid you'll fall in love with me."

Maybe so. Maybe so. I put my hand against her soft, thick curls. The feeling lacerates me inside.

Chapter Twenty-seven

I drive fast back downtown. The Ballard Bridge is down and I sail past the masts of the fishing fleet without interruption. At home, I change into my navy pinstriped suit and slip on a red rep tie. I need sartorial armor. I slide the revolver into the briefcase I am now carrying, an old brown leather briefcase that my ex-wife had given me years ago. It still looks good. When I walk out of the building, George is sitting on his plastic crate, pedestrians walking by and ignoring him.

"All clear, el-tee." He smiles.

"I was no officer."

"Sure. Old first sergeants can always tell."

I walk north on First Avenue and then climb the hill. Why did that shake me up? The agents seemed to have their own reality of my time in the Army, too. I had never even told George I had been in the service.

I check my watch and double-time it to the transit tunnel entrance on Third Avenue, in the old Washington Mutual Tower, then sprint down the flights of stairs. I catch my breath as I watch the buses and light-rail trains roll through. The tunnel is well-lit and clean, but it still smells of diesel fumes and I vaguely feel shut in. I think about Amber's claustrophobia attack in the closet. My eyes scan for trouble even though my brain realizes I won't see it coming. The wide platforms are crowded with people headed home from work. I am looking for only one.

Of the many reams of corporate fluff that come my way, few are of any use. But I remembered reading an article in the Olympic International newsletter about employees "doing their part to make Seattle America's greenest city." Somehow one detail stuck with me: Heidi Benson, director of corporate communications, always rode the Sound Transit 554 bus to her home in the east-side suburbs. Yesterday's piece of fluff is today's critical intelligence.

I wait forty-five minutes, lingering close to the wall and hidden by the clots of commuters. It is ten minutes after six when I see Heidi stalking down the platform toward an eastbound 554 that has just arrived. Heidi has strawberry blond hair worn in a pageboy and a face with fair, slightly freckled skin. She wears a black slacks suit that accentuates her long legs, and she moves as if her cone of personal space extends ten feet in every direction. If she could smile and unwind, scrape off some makeup, she might be considered pretty. I will never get that smile, particularly today. She stands beside the blue-and-white bus, examining some papers before stuffing them into her briefcase. Then she checks her Blackberry and looks at the ceiling, apparently not getting a signal. Other buses pull away with noisy roars. The 554 starts to fill up. Then she steps aboard.

I walk quickly to the back door and follow her inside. She doesn't see me and sits by the window. I slide next to her, settling into the cushy Sound Transit seat. It takes a full three minutes for her to realize who is sitting next to her, and by this time the bus is rolling. My heart rate is up in the triple digits, but I keep my face calm and immobile.

"What are you...?" She lets the question hang. Then she says my name with the same inflection she would use for a venereal disease. "What a coincidence seeing you here." She cranes her neck, seeing if there are any seats she can flee to.

"Actually, I wanted to talk to you."

"Then make an appointment. In the meantime, I wish you'd move."

She is cooler than I thought she'd be, given her outburst over the first Olympic column. But I can see her gripping her briefcase so tightly that her already white skin is nearly translucent.

"Please move."

"I like it here."

"Then I will." She starts to stand but is pushed back in her seat as the bus blasts out of the transit tunnel and starts its way east.

"Don't you want to know why I'm here?" I say it in a conversational tone, smiling at her as if we were ordinary seat-mates on the commute home.

"I don't want to know," she hisses. "I want you to move."

"We're set to go with a story on Olympic Defense Systems. The CIA connection." I say this in the same tone of voice but slow it down for emphasis. I watch her body go rigid. "We know everything, Heidi."

She stares ahead and I can almost see her eyes start to fill with tears. They suddenly dry up like a desert lake. "You're bluffing."

"You know I'm not."

"Now you listen to me!" She turns to the side and nearly leans over me. She stabs her finger toward my face. "This little ambush tactic is not going to work. I don't know who you think you are. We've dealt with your publisher. This has been settled. The *Free Press* is not publishing anything."

She becomes aware of the people watching her and slowly settles back in her seat, nervously running her left hand through her hair. It's nice hair. What a waste. Her phrasing is interesting: *"We've dealt with your publisher."* I wait to respond until we are halfway across Lake Washington. The bus sits so high on the floating bridge that it seems as if we are hydroplaning across the dark water. If we went off the road no barrier could save us. No exits would work. The water would be fatally cold. I make myself avoid looking.

"It's too bad the way they always cut the flacks out of the real deal," I say. "So I'm trying to help you do your job. The fact is, the four days of stories are already set to go. They've been edited and lawyered. And I mean lawyered to death. We've got the CIA connection nailed. The same with Troy Hardesty and Animal

Spirits." Her face winces as if I have slapped her. "We're already bullet-proof. I've tried to give you a chance to be more open…"

She starts to speak but nothing comes out of her mouth.

"But you've stonewalled us. So this is your last chance. We always want to be fair and accurate. From the number of documents and sources we have, I know we're being accurate. But I told the editors I wanted to make one more try. It's only in your interest to have the company's voice in these stories. To respond to the issues that they raise. And, Heidi, nobody deals with the Sterling family when the integrity of their newspaper is involved."

Brave talk but I pull it off. She pulls her slim frame as close to the window as possible. Her eyes are glassy. I wonder how much of this information she is even privy to. I know I haven't put the puzzle together. But her reaction tells me I am on the right path.

Finally, she gives a raspy, "What do you want?"

"I want an interview with Pete Montgomery."

"That's impossible. He's the chief executive officer."

"That's the point. If Steve Ballmer and Howard Schultz talk to me, I think Pete can, too."

"I'll call our lawyers." Her voice gains a little steel.

"You certainly can. But I have a deadline."

She sighs.

"And I want to visit the ODS headquarters."

"In D.C.? That's out of the question."

"I hear there's a facility in Arizona. That will do."

She refuses to make eye contact. I put my hand on her shoulder and she shivers.

"Don't dick me around, Heidi." I am smiling and my voice is almost a whisper. "This story will run with or without you. You know we'll do it. We've done it before."

Then I stand and walk to the back of the bus where I find an empty seat. I watch her motionless head until the bus takes the exit for the Eastgate Park and Ride station. She makes it a point to take the front door so she doesn't have to see me. Out on the asphalt, she walks toward her car checking behind her to make sure I am not following.

"She's quite a bitch, isn't she?"

I turn to the man sitting next to me. He's slender, with high cheekbones, olive-brown skin and dressed in regulation Friday casual. I'd guess he's on the downside of forty.

"She can be," I say. "How do you know her?"

"I worked for her until today. They laid me off."

"Sorry."

"You're the columnist. You're taller than your photograph in the newspaper." He says this without humor.

The bus is moving again and I decide to ride to one more stop before heading back to Seattle. Disgruntled former employees can be useful, although you have to account for their biases.

"So what did you do?"

"I was in charge of communications liaison between corporate and ODS." He says the initials with a vague British accent. I feel my lower back tighten.

"An interesting subsidiary." I try to keep my voice neutral. I have on my wide-open, talk-to-me reporter's face.

"More than that." He smiles. "Did you dig deeper, as I told you to?"

I almost visibly shiver. The mysterious emailer. "I'm trying," I say. "I don't understand the connections. The CIA, Troy Hardesty, Animal Spirits...eleven/eleven."

He grips my arm painfully, his slight frame deceiving.

"Not here." He releases my arm. Then he reaches into his jacket, retrieves a business card, and writes an address on the back of it with his left hand.

"Come see me at my house tomorrow at ten. The wife and kids are going early." He hands me the card. I give him mine. He quickly slides it into his shirt pocket.

"In the meantime, I think it would be a good idea for you to move, and get off the bus before Issaquah."

I call Amber and she says she can't come over tonight. Maybe I imagine something in her voice, distance, a pulling back.

Normally, it would give me relief—another bit of transitional fun. She got the best of me, and I the best of her. But this night her absence gnaws at me. The bed looks impossibly large.

For the first time in days, I go to the Conspiracy Grrl Web site, knowing I am probably being tracked. The screen shows "error 404." The site is down. Even my Conspiracy Grrl has abandoned me tonight.

Chapter Twenty-eight

Saturday, October 30th

I have lit a fuse. It's attached to my cell phone. I watch it sitting there on the nightstand, attached to the charger cord, as I wake during the night. Heidi Benson won't let our encounter sit through the weekend. The only question is whether she and her big boss will think I'm bluffing. The Blackjack stays silent. I think about what Rachel said; her father's reaction to my Olympic column. That's how I got into this. And I wish I could claim to be the most prescient journalist on the planet, but the truth is that I picked the topic at random. I had made a list of companies we weren't covering intensely because of the staff reductions. Olympic came up. I started asking questions. Now people are dead and missing and eleven/eleven. The street erupts with the sound of loud drunks at closing time. Then I only hear the occasional train whistle until I fall into a deep sleep.

I rise early, with no woman in bed to make coffee for. So I dress, walk down the street to Starbucks, then climb in the car and drive. Before I leave the curb, I study the business card: Olympic International Corp. James Mandir, Corporate Communications Business Partner. It has no mention of Olympic Defense Systems. On the back is his address, written in a neat, draftsmanlike hand. I check it against my worn street map in the car. There's no way I'll use Mapquest and give my minders a chance to see where I'm going. On the atlas page, the address looks like it sits amid a spaghetti splatter of streets. I leave the page open on the passenger seat as I let the car amble through downtown, then out to Magnolia, where I park and watch.

While the fit, well-off Maggies walk and jog past, I let my paranoia run wild. I check the car for a tracking device: in the glove box, under the seats and dash. I climb out and get on my knees, looking for anything amiss on the underside or the bumper. The sky is partly cloudy—their satellites can see me. I stand and brush myself off as a young woman pushes her stroller by: *You are odd*, her look says, *you don't fit in here*. That's true enough. I start the car again and take the long way back across Interbay Yard and around the backside of Queen Anne Hill, through the sleepy Saturday campus of Seattle Pacific University, down Westlake past the yacht brokers, before finally reaching the freeway and driving east.

I'm not being followed.

Across the lake, the car starts the long climb that will take me into the Cascade foothills. The mountains are jagged purple. It was a cool morning in the city, and I can feel it grow colder when I touch the car window. The interstate soars and sags as the wall of tall evergreens grows denser. The land undulates upward, showing hill upon hill, revealing sudden valleys. The signs promise I am near Lake Sammamish State Park, but then it's time to exit. I have never been an east-sider. I am a city kid. But I can remember when there was nothing out here, just the highway to Snoqualmie Falls. My parents would take Jill and me there during the few calm periods in our family life. Now it's suburbia, with a new parkway that gives way to new streets. It's all calm and pleasant and would drive me insane.

I go through the same drill again, just driving and checking. I have given myself plenty of room to arrive on time. Finally, I make three turns and swing around a crescent street where Mandir's address sits in neat black letters on a gray house with white trim. It's a long, pleasant split-level with wide windows and a two-car garage that seems to overwhelm the rest of the house. Tall evergreens and aspen with their last gold stand behind the place and it's surrounded by a perfect lawn and hedges. I pull into the driveway, to the side with the closed garage door. The other garage door sits open, presumably from the departure of his wife and children. The house has a red front door atop a short white staircase at the end of a flagstone walk. I scan the rearview mirrors one more time, wondering if my notepad will spook him. I decide to take it, grabbing an extra pen. I leave the gun in the car.

Outside, it is preternaturally quiet. I can't hear even a distant leaf blower or lawn mower. The nearest houses look neatly uninhabited. The doorbell sounds deep within the house. James Mandir. I should have stopped at Kinko's and used a computer to do a Google search. I don't remember reading his name in the story about the flawed night-vision goggles. It will have to wait. I am here to listen to him. I ring the doorbell again.

The window glass seems slightly reflective. I can't see anything inside, just the image of puffy autumn clouds passing quickly overhead. After the third time of ringing the doorbell and waiting, I grow edgy. Maybe this is a trap. But a slow scan around me shows nothing amiss. Not a car on the street. One white minivan parked in the driveway of the second house to the west. No humans. Maybe he just got cold feet and stood me up.

Perhaps he's working in the garage. I walk down the wooden stairs again. They are sturdy and make no sound. The open door is nearest to the flagstone walk. It's wide enough to accommodate a Hummer. Inside, I can see a silver BMW in the other bay. It's a neat garage; no clutter of lawn mower, fertilizer spreader and long-unused children's toys. The concrete floor is spotless and the lights are off. I stand on the side of the opening and call.

"Mr. Mandir?"

No answer.

I slowly step inside, my eyes drawn to the partly open white door across the bay that must lead into the house. You would reach the door by walking up a concrete step and James Mandir is sitting on it, looking at me.

But he's not really looking at anything. He's dead. He's lean-ing against the doorjamb, his head bent at a quizzical angle, as if he's about to ask a question. His mouth is curiously white. A large pool of blood surrounds his feet like a stain under an old car. In the dimness of the garage, it looks like several quarts of transmission fluid, except where it reaches up to his hands and wrists and then it's brighter red. It's come from three long, deep slashes into his wrists—two on the left arm, one on the right. The slashes are deep and parallel to the arm, certain to reach deep and get the arteries. A box cutter, blade extended, sits in the blood just below his right hand.

He wrote left-handed.

I approach slowly, almost floating. A strange calm envelops me. I call his name but it's obvious that he's long dead. Maybe his ghost is here floating with me. Frank Sinatra said that if he wanted to kill himself, he would climb in a bathtub and slash his wrists while listening to Sarah Vaughn on the record player. I don't know if it's a true story. That's one of those stories that's too good to check, or so goes the old joke in my business. I don't hear Sarah Vaughn. I don't hear a damned thing.

I break my stare-down with those dead eyes and see his mouth more clearly. Something is in it. It's white, folded. A straw? My spinal cord turns suddenly cold and the feeling radiates out into my ribs. The blood slick is now one footstep away from me. I finally do a belated three-sixty around the garage—nothing. The lights are off but the neatness of the place makes it easy to scope out. I bend down and look under the BMW. I'm alone. Behind me, the outside world looks normal, but it's as if I am watching it on a movie screen. Every muscle in my body wants to turn and run back through that door.

His mouth. The object is too short and thick to be a straw. It's a folded piece of paper. I make my itchy muscles stay and step closer. I edge over to his left, which is somehow higher ground on the concrete floor. The blood hasn't pooled here. I make a fist and use it to lean against the doorjamb—am I unconsciously trying not to leave fingerprints? It's a move that comes too easily.

I will worry about that later. I lean in closer...closer...the blood now an inch from the tip of my shoe. My hand brushes the edge of the paper but it stays firmly in his teeth. I look behind me at the movie screen. Nobody is looking in. I touch Mandir's cheek. It's cold.

Once again I lean forward, using the doorjamb to steady myself. I go lower and to the side until my abdominal muscles are aching. I reach as if I'm manipulating a robot arm, except I can feel the thick paper in my fingers and I pull.

I lean against the BMW and unfold the paper. It is curiously without any moisture, any saliva—just neatly rolled into a small tube.

It's a business card. My business card. I stare at it then turn it over. The neat script in black ink stares back at me: "Eleven/eleven, asshole." The old editor in me notices the comma. A grammatically correct killer.

I walk out to the car, numb but somehow unsurprised. Now it's my move. *Your move, asshole.*

My feet carry me back to the car, where I lean heavily against the fender and dial 911.

Chapter Twenty-nine

The house phone is ringing when I bolt the door inside my loft a little after one. I think it might be the cops. It's Heidi Benson.

"Mr. Montgomery wants to meet with you."

I just let her hang. I'm in no mood to feel grateful.

"Today."

"What time?" My pulse rate jacks up.

"Can you be here in an hour?" She asks. "Of course, you can. You live right downtown. Check in with the guard in the lobby and ask for me." The line goes dead and I wonder how she knows where I live.

There's time to take a quick shower to get the death off me and change into a suit. I keep James Mandir's eyes out of my mind's vision. The sheriff's deputies were very nice. It's amazing how a press card can still be a get-out-of-jail-free card—especially when they don't know how many dead bodies are trailing me around. Especially when they don't know my business card was found in his mouth. I kept my story simple: Mandir lost his job and wanted to talk to me. No, I didn't know what about. I also didn't mention the discrepancy between seeing him favor his left hand and that the box cutter lay near his right.

"He did himself the right way," one of the deputies said. "Lots of fools slash diagonal, like in the movies." Well, somebody did it the right way.

I check the time and call the managing editor at home. He doesn't seem happy to hear from me. I apologize for calling on the weekend. Could one big story save a newspaper? I'm not naïve enough to believe that, especially when the Sterling and Forrest heirs want to cash out. But I have a big story. I lay it out for him calmly, with the foundation being Olympic Defense Systems, a history of contracting problems, a secret link to the CIA, and now a suspicious suicide. It's less a settled story than a line of inquiry, I know, but this is how many great exposés begin: with questions.

Sometimes I move too fast. The biggest question is who killed James Mandir—and I know the answer: the same people who killed Hardesty and Ryan Meyers. There was no clear connection with Olympic until Rachel told me her father's reaction when he read my first column on the company. Now this federal assassination squad has killed an employee who wanted to talk. Did the blonde do it? She had to have help. And why the hell am I going to talk to Pete Montgomery? They won't kill me in their downtown tower. They think I know something. Otherwise, they would have killed me already. All this is far in the background of my brain as I talk to the M.E. There's no time for doubt. I talk the story up as confidently as I can, and prepare for his questions about public records, lawsuits, documents, sources. He can't block me with the National Security Letter because he doesn't know that Olympic International is involved.

He just says, "It's too late."

"What do you mean it's too late? I've got an exclusive interview with Pete Montgomery in thirty minutes."

He says my name. "You're going to be tapped on Monday."

"Tapped." That's their management jargon for being told to take a buy-out or be laid off. I sit down, feeling as if all the organs inside me have disappeared, replaced by air.

"I'm sorry. You're a high-cost employee. You make one of the top salaries in the newsroom."

"How many other columnists?"

He's silent. So, none. Just me. I've suspected this might be coming since the day of the big announcement, hell, since the day Maggie Sterling died. The credibility I built up over the years, the reader following. I was the first to call the big recession, the first to see that Washington Mutual would go down. It didn't matter. Why am I in a near state of shock now?

He says, "I'm really sorry, man."

I muster enough saliva in my mouth to speak again and ask about the story.

"That's not going anywhere," the M.E. says.

I just sit staring at my tie. After half a minute of silence, he goes on, "James Sterling personally said, 'no more Olympic stories.' I had to fight like hell to get your second column in."

"Why?" The exclamation covers a world of questions in my life that moment.

"I've got to go," he says. "Come by my office on Monday. We'll talk about what comes next. I know readers will want to have a goodbye column. The severance will be decent, not terrible. Look, I'm trying to save the newspaper, get the newsroom down to a staffing level where the consultants say it might attract a buyer. But it probably won't happen in this environment, so I'll be joining you in the unemployment li…"

I hang up. Before me is the nook where I write from home. Above the desk is my ego wall, with awards and photos from a quarter century of newspapering. I look impossibly young in some of the photos. The awards include some for stories I barely remember—I only remember the hard work, the all-nighters, the sense of justification when they appeared on the front page. All gone. So many good people have lost their jobs in the past few years, and more than a few have never been able to get back to their old earnings power. Why should I have been special? But my eye goes to a photo of four men in suits, smiling and clinking glasses. It was taken years ago. One of the four is me. The other three went on to lead major newspapers. I became a columnist. I never knew how to go along to get along.

I still don't. I stand and grab my notebook. Then I'm not sure I want the information inside to go with me to this interview—you never know. So I stash it in a file drawer with a hundred other identical reporter's notebooks, and pick up a new one to make notes from Pete Montgomery. I also take my small tape recorder. Heidi will be recording, so I don't want any arguments over the accuracy of quotes. I don't have anywhere close to the whole story put together, but there's a start—and Olympic is scared enough to grant a weekend interview.

◇◇◇

George is sitting in front of the building when I step out of the elevator into the lobby. He sees me through the glass entrance and casually but unmistakably crooks his arm at a ninety-degree angle and makes a fist.

"Freeze," it says. Infantry hand signals. The old first sergeant then drops his arm and wraps his left forefinger over his right forearm: "Enemy." He signals two fingers—two of them—and points to the south.

I immediately turn and walk quickly to the back door, toward the recycling bins. I step into the alley and Stu is fifteen steps away, maybe closer. His face is set in hatred. Suddenly I feel so goddamned tired and beaten, but something inside makes my body run at him. He's surprised to see me coming toward him and starts reaching inside his coat. But by that time I've hit him head-on with a body block that would be a technical foul in any contact sport. He hits the ground hard and I run toward the street, expecting any second to feel a bullet in my back.

Instead I see a yellow play gun. It's attached to Bill's hand and pointed at me.

The darts are very fast and hit me in the gut, cutting into the shirt. The worst cramp I've ever imagined convulses my abdomen and spreads from there. My arms are uselessly out at my sides and my legs are frozen, the muscles twirling backwards. My mind is somewhere else, where everything hurts a lot, so I can barely see it as the old cobblestones come up hard and fast.

I do a face plant in the middle of the alley.

"Roll his ass over…get his coat off…"

I hear them talking above me but I can't move. My middle still feels like it's been folded in on itself.

"Get his sleeve up." Fabric comes up on my skin.

"Can you hit a vein?"

"Yeah."

One of them has a syringe in his hand. So this is how it will end for me.

Not very creative when you think about their previous work. But, the end.

I try to fight back but my arms and legs don't work. They are abstractions, divorced from the commands of my brain. I try to pray but I just see the faces of the people I have failed, Jill, Pam, Rachel, now Amber…so many. I never doubted that I'd go to hell.

Chapter Thirty

Hell, as it turns out, is a cold place.

At first, the cold is all I am conscious of. And the dark—impossibly black. The black of perdition. It would terrify me except that my body is shaking uncontrollably, my legs and arms, even my belly. Arms won't move beyond the trembling. My skin is nothing but a scrimshaw of goosebumps so large they hurt. My jaw aches from a constant, cold-induced tremor; I hear my teeth chatter like a child's toy dentures. When I force myself to stop, the silence is as frightening as the dark. The cold has seeped deep inside my bones, which ache with a fathomless intensity. It's a chill so pervasive I can't remember my past or my name. My head has a large weight attached to it, causing my neck to throb in pain. I try to lift my head and it falls backwards again, sending a freezing ache into the tendons of my neck and shoulders.

Then I fall back down the well of unconsciousness.

Chapter Thirty-one

"Wake up, asshole."

A hand slaps my face hard. I awake to the sting rippling out into the nerves of my left cheek. My eyes are nearly blinded by the light. My body won't move. I slowly focus on Bill, the slimmer of the two agents. He kneels before me, his moonlike face inches from mine.

"He's awake."

He backs away and I can see his partner, Stu, standing behind him, his arms crossed. They are both dressed in jeans and jackets. I am still shivering hard from the cold. Slowly, the world returns.

We are in a long gray room that probably measures twelve feet wide and twenty feet long. The walls are gray cinderblocks. A long gray institutional table sits in the middle, a darker piece of rubber running around the edge of the top. Two gray chairs are placed beneath it. Four tall gray lockers are in the far corner. A gray door holds down the opposite corner. It has a small reflective window in it. My arms and legs are cuffed to a heavy metal chair. I catalog all this so I don't start screaming. Moving my head still hurts, so I just try to take it all in with my eyes. Above me are hanging banks of fluorescent lights. The floor is concrete and has a drain in the middle.

It's never good to be shackled in a room with a drain in the middle of the floor.

I'm completely naked, one with the chair. It seems as if it was built for it—locked down to the floor with bolts. My arms are held straight down and handcuffed to loops in the metal of the chair. My legs are similarly shackled. There's little room to move. Between the handcuffs and the welded attachment of the chair is only one link of steel chain. The metal burns me with transmitted cold. A wide leather strap circles my chest and goes behind the chair back. Little scars sit prominently at my solar plexus. The Taser hit. My butt hurts from sitting on the metal seat—how many hours? How many days? My first insane thought is that I have a column due on Monday. Then: I missed my interview with Pete Montgomery.

Bill pulls up one of the chairs and places it directly in front of me, chair-back facing me. He straddles it and stares at me. Stu picks up the other chair and positions himself at my right, just at the outside of my peripheral vision. My left cheek and eye are throbbing with pain. I'm shaking from the cold again.

"You're in violation of a National Security Letter. You have no rights. Let's get that out of the way right now, because I don't have time for your games." Bill sounds very reasonable, his pastor-like face kind and reassuring.

"You can be held incommunicado forever if we choose," he goes on, as if laying out the Bible study class for the next several Sundays. "We can put you in stress positions. We can put you in a box. Are you claustrophobic? We'll find out. Maybe you'll find out."

Stu's large hand covers the side of my face and turns my head toward him. My neck muscles spasm in pain. "We can beat you and kick you all we want," he says. "We can stick your ass on a jet and take you to Syria where they really mean business. By comparison, we're nice guys."

"I'm cold." I hear my voice for the first time.

"You like that? We can make it colder." Stu pushes my head back into the straight-ahead position. "We can stick you in a coffin and bury you for a day with just enough air to breathe, if you're careful. God, I wish we could. But we don't have time."

"Where's Megan?" Bill folds his arms atop the back of the chair and watches my face.

Megan. My mind slowly comes out of the deep freeze. Of all the pieces I have: Troy's murder, the CIA connection, whatever funny business is going on in Olympic Defense Systems—it always comes back to the missing girl. And from his question, they believe I know where she is. I'm too cold to think it through in my head, to be clever. I try.

I shrug. Then, "She's in a safe place." I can barely talk because my teeth keep chattering. "And the plan is to go public if I don't check in within twenty-four hours."

Bill smiles slightly. He looks like an amused lizard. "You're a really bad liar." But he had hesitated just a second. His eyes had flitted to Stu before he talked. He's not sure that I'm bluffing.

"She knows more than you think," I continue. "We have it all down. Eleven-eleven, asshole." His eyes flicker. "And we have it in sworn affidavits. It's going to be published, no matter what."

"You're not even going to be working for that fish wrap," Stu says, "if you ever get free again."

"Doesn't matter," I say, gathering strength as I keep spinning the yarn. "There are other reporters and other news organizations involved. Do you think I'd just leave it to myself? Or to the cowards who are my bosses." I make myself laugh. "And we know about you two: your little death squad. Pretty soon the world will know. You bastards killed Pam and you're going to pay."

Bill's jaw tightens and he stands, throwing the chair theatrically against the wall. The noise is shattering, amplified by the concrete and cinder blocks of the room. Stu stands, too. Bill strides out the door and closes it behind him. Stu hits some kind of lever out of my line of sight. The chair back collapses and I fall back. My abdominal muscles turn in painful knots. Another metal-on-metal sound, as if the chair is locked into a new position. My body is bent so my lower legs are still aimed at the floor but the rest of me is nearly horizontal. Then my feet go up and my lower body is tilted high. The chair is meant to do this. I stare up at Stu's immobile face and the overhead lights. Then the door opens and Bill walks in more slowly.

He's carrying a clear plastic gallon jug.

He tosses what looks like a black hand-towel to his partner. He puts his face close to mine, his breath smelling of peppermint.

"Did you ever do this as a military intelligence officer?"

"I was an Army journalist." My voice in unsteady with the upwelling terror inside me.

"Sure."

Bill speaks out of my line of sight. "You were a trained interrogator. What would you do?"

The blood in my veins feels like it's turning to ice. "I know torture doesn't work. Very inefficient…"

"Army pussy," Stu says. "I've read your jacket. You were also trained for black ops. You were a trained killer." His heavy-jawed face is two inches from mine, like a drill sergeant's.

"Take off these handcuffs and find out."

He stares at me. "I'd love to. But I don't have time. You don't get it. There's no time."

"Don't do this." My teeth start chattering again. "You're breaking the law. You took an oath…"

He studies me, amused. Then, "You are going to tell us." He mutters it to himself.

Suddenly, I feel a hand on my forehead pushing my head farther back. The force rams my skull so hard I hear the chair shake and shafts of pain shoot down into my shoulder blades and little lightning bursts come into the edges of my eyes. I try to resist but my head stays at the unnatural angle. My arms and legs struggle vainly against the shackles. I start to panic even before Stu drops the towel onto my nose and roughly pinches my nostrils. The fabric is scratchy. My eyes are covered next. As if I want to see.

"I think he'll talk."

"I bet he will."

I feel the towel fall across my mouth and chin. Then it's pulled tight.

"Think he went through SERE?" It's Bill's voice.

It's the military's Survival, Evasion, Resistance and Escape training. I'm doing a damned poor job at it right now.

"We're gonna find out." Stu chuckles. Then his breath at my ear: "There's no code word, asshole. This is the real deal. Maybe you'll live through the first few minutes and then," his voice rises painfully, "we're going to ask you again, where the fuck is Megan!"

It's already hard to breathe. The towel sucks into my mouth as I draw air. I fight the instinct to hyperventilate...*I am okay, I have all the oxygen I need right here*...try to put my mind somewhere else. Some place that is not looking forward to the first few minutes or even this moment. I start to run through the women in my life. This, I tell myself, will stop the tachycardia that's so pronounced as to be felt in my eardrums.

Leslie. Linda. Sharon. Susan. Mary Beth No. 2 was a great kisser.

The towel punches against my lips and I feel its wetness. Then I inhale, but there's hardly any air. I keep counting. Deb: for us, it was always full on—rock-my-world sex and soul baring—I was a fool to let her go. Kathy, Wendy...Patty who loved for me to brush her hair...Tess who looked so sexy when she would put on one of my dress shirts...Rachel with the luminous hair and eyes. Amber..."

Then a deluge....feels like one... And another. The towel leaks water into my mouth but no air. My throat closes off and I gag. I struggle to move my head but it's locked in place. Suffocation quickly begins to overtake me. The last coherent thought I have is a wish that I had taken a deeper breath.

What's left are primal feeling and sounds: The slopping of water off my face and onto my frozen chest. My wrists cracking repeatedly against the restraints and the sound of metal being jerked hard and fruitlessly. Gagging...head won't turn...gagging...air, God give me air...but there's none. Lungs burn. My nose is cemented shut. A high keening coming from somewhere deep inside my head. Lungs... More water past my tongue... My entire throat is seized up...stomach acid meeting water... can't breathe, can't...

"Stop. Stop now."

The water stops and the towel is relaxed. I make a great, greedy inhalation and immediately start coughing and gagging again.

After a couple of minutes the towel comes completely off my face and the chair is readjusted so I am sitting up again. I look upon the suicide blonde. She closes the door behind her and walks into the room. I cough violently and struggle to keep from vomiting. But I can breathe again.

"You two, back off."

Bill retrieves his tossed chair and sits, arms folded. Stu leans against the far wall.

Up close, she's beautiful. Hair the color of harvest wheat is parted on one side and falls to her ears, thick in front and very cropped in back. It is the same color as her eyebrows. She has large pale eyes, high cheekbones, very red lips against a peaches-and-cream complexion. She wears a navy suit with a knee-high skirt and slingback, open-toed medium-high heels. Even freezing, I appreciate her well-carved ankles.

When she sits across from me, the skirt rides up on her thighs.

"We don't have to do this," she says, looking at me sympathetically. "The columnist doesn't want to put the country in danger any more than any of us would." She looks at Bill. "Turn up the heat in here and get him the blanket." To me, "It's going to be all right. I'm sorry things happened this way."

So she is the good cop in a room full of bad ones. I'll take it. Momentarily, Bill returns with a blanket and she directs him to drape it around me. My heart rate slows down and I gradually stop coughing and trembling. The temperature in the room grows noticeably warmer. She uses the edges of the blanket to dry my chest and legs, then wraps it tight against my shoulders. Her hands push back my wet hair and gently dry my face. Her finger gingerly touches my left cheekbone and I wince. "Sorry," she says.

As she has settled in the chair, it's impossible to avoid seeing that she's not wearing underwear. She smiles and puts a warm hand on my thigh. "Nice to be appreciated," she whispers. And my recently tortured body rebounds quickly, appreciating. "Very nice…"

"You're enjoying this way too much, Laura." Bill leans against the wall and shakes his head.

"You can leave," she says.

"We'll stay," Stu says.

"Suit yourselves. Now focus on me." She caresses my face, aims my eyes at her. "I'm going to explain what's happening and why it's essential for you to help, and then we can get you out of here and back to a normal life."

It sounds so wonderful that I want to believe her, this pantiless angel sitting before me. She inches her chair closer. Our knees touch.

"Megan is so beautiful," she says, putting a hand on each of my thighs. "I was never pretty in high school."

"I can't believe that."

"I'm gonna barf," Stu says.

"It's true. I was a nerd. A late bloomer. Like you."

I say nothing more. She gently strokes the tops of my thighs. "Warmer now? You must have felt like a nerd, at the U-Dub, one of a handful of all those thousands of students, who was in ROTC. Definitely not cool back then. But it was the only way you could get through college. And the Army loved your scores, off the charts...."

"You've got me mistaken for somebody else..." My throat is still feeling shut down, but the rest of me starts to react to the warmth of the blanket and her touch on my legs. And I do react.

"Army Intelligence." She says it like a lover. "I always admired the smart ones."

"Fucking oxymoron, we used to say in the Corps." This from Bill, who seems an unlikely former Marine.

"Ignore them. They never liked officers, much less journalists. You're with me." Laura rubs my chest and my muscles ache and try to relax.

My mind doesn't. "You killed Troy Hardesty. You're the one who pushed past me that day outside his office." Her eyes lose their seduction fix for just a moment. She is surprised that I saw her there. "Why kill Troy?"

The corners of her mouth turn up slightly. "I just do a job. I know you did things in the Army you can't talk about."

"I was an Army journalist…"

"I know." She smiles at me, tracing a line with her fingernail down to my navel. "Afghanistan, 1982. You still have your old Combat Magnum. The guys in your unit preferred them to the nines. Isn't it funny that with your background, you might have married Rachel Summers? Considering her father's history? All in the family, right?"

"Rachel doesn't know anything."

"I know." She starts stroking my penis with her left hand. Not that it needed encouragement. "Oh, you like that. I like it, too."

She says my name as if we'd been together for years. "All you need to do is help us. Take us to Megan." The stroking keeps up and I am breathing heavily. My brain has been through a sieve and I try to concentrate. Why does she want to know about Megan? Why not about what Troy told me?

Then I look down again in time to see the object in her right hand. It is bright silver and looks about six inches long. Maybe it's a hat pin or maybe it's some kind of cocktail swizzle. My pelvis instinctively jerks back but there's no give in the chair. Through all her gentle ministrations the shackles have never been loosened.

"I know you want to talk to me." Up to now, her touch has kept me erect, even with my eyes locked on the pin in her right hand. It glistens in the reflected light. "No, no, baby…" She pulls her left thumb and forefinger tightly around the base of my penis. "Don't go soft now. I want you full of blood for me." She keeps me almost painfully hard.

She runs the head of the pin along the top of my left thigh. I see it penetrate the skin as I feel a sharp burning. My leg jerks upward.

"Funny little nerve network there," Laura says. She raises the pin to her mouth and silently sucks the blood off. "Pain and pleasure, right?"

Her left hand has me securely. She lowers the pin and rubs the long edge against the shaft. It's cool compared with the warmth of her hand.

"I love cocks. So hard and yet so soft and vulnerable. So sensitive." She readjusts her right hand, like someone about to eat with one chopstick. At first, the sharp edge of the pin just adds to the sensation. Then, pain. I see her run the tip of the pin against my penis, hard enough to leave a little red trail of worried capillaries. It's deep enough to make me cry aloud.

"This is so unnecessary. But I tried." Laura turns to Bill. "Get some towels because he's going to bleed like hell. I don't want any of it on my shoes." All the gentleness is gone from her voice but her left hand keeps its hold around my penis. Bill walks to the door and opens it. He stops as if he's hit something and backs into the room. The movement only catches my attention for a moment. I return to staring at the silver lance at my groin, when I hear:

"Get your hands off that, bitch. It belongs to me."

Chapter Thirty-two

Bill keeps backing up, revealing a tall redhead crouched in a combat shooting stance and holding a black semiautomatic.

Amber.

"Oh." She holds out an open black wallet, containing a gold badge and two windows for credentials. "FBI."

She quickly repockets it and returns to a two-handed grip on the gun. The door is in the propped-open position. She leaves it that way and moves into the room. "Back up. Against the wall."

She sweeps the room with the barrel, her movements economical, almost a dance step, alighting her aim on Stu. "If you reach inside your jacket, big boy, I'll kill you. I don't care if you're trying to get a cough drop." He relaxes his arm. "Everybody. Arms straight out. Make a 'T.' Do it now."

They reluctantly comply. Amber wears a businesslike black pants suit. She sounds different, too.

"Stand up slowly, bitch. And drop your little toy. I can see it." The pin hits the floor and rolls toward the drain. "Arms out! Very slowly. Back up to the sound of my voice." Amber does a quick search, then pushes Laura forward. "Now, go get their weapons. Take them by the barrel and do it very slowly. Hold each one out by the barrel, your arms straight out, so I can see it. If you don't, I'll kill you."

Laura walks over to the men and does as instructed. Amber tells her to put them on the table and she does. Next she orders Stu and Bill to lie face down on the floor.

"Unshackle him."

Laura gets a set of keys from the table and unlocks my legs, then my arms. Amber orders her to the floor with the men, face down and arms straight out. The room's smells, sweat, something else, are distinct now. I can't tell if they're coming from them or me. Amber walks to the table and unloads the guns, dropping out the magazines, ejecting rounds from the chambers, and locking them open. She tosses the guns through the open door. All this takes less than ten seconds and she has her gun back in both hands, an authoritative presence.

"Keep those arms out!" She backs up to the lockers and opens one, then the other. She brings my wallet, keys, my cell phone, and clothes. Or what's left of my clothes. My suit jacket is gone. I liked that suit. I dress as quickly as I can. Every muscle feels foreign. Every one aches.

"You're making a big mistake, G-girl," Laura mutters.

Amber ignores her and takes my arm. "Can you stand?"

I nod and start up, only to nearly pitch over. I grab the top of the other chair and steady myself. "Just give me a minute." My legs are asleep. They burn as the blood flows normally again.

"Ready?"

We step into the hallway and she closes the door, locking it from the outside. She moves with supreme confidence and no wasted motions. This is the cub reporter who totally took me in.

"Where's your backup?" I ask.

"No backup."

"What…?"

"No time to explain."

The semi-auto disappears behind her back and she has both hands free. For a few steps, she steadies me before I can do it on my own. My walk is uncertain but her voice is quiet and insistent. "Go. Go."

We walk down the same hallway that I had seen on my first visit here. It's the anonymous building in SoDo. Two bundles lie against the wall. As I get closer, I see they are uniformed officers, face down, and handcuffed. Amber grabs my hand and hurries us through a heavy door and gate to the outside. It's daylight. The air tastes like Eden.

Chapter Thirty-three

Sunday, October 31st

We drive in silence through the city. It's been raining and the sun is starting to come out, bathing the mass of towers in a magical glow, alternately golden and purple. The air smells of rain and seawater. It must be Sunday because the streets are empty around the office district, while people congregate at Westlake Park with Macy's and Nordstrom bags. It is a normal, wonderful, alive world. Amber drives the speed limit.

I ask her to turn on the heat. Wearing only my scuffed white dress shirt and suit trousers, I feel the chill through the windows.

As the car climbs Queen Anne Hill I study her face. It's set in an unreadable mask. My legs ache and my face throbs and I'm giddy to be saved and I'm pissed off. I want to erupt with questions. But I don't. She makes several turns, coming too close to Pam's house, and then we're in the parking lot of the old high school. It's been turned into condos, and they have spectacular views of the Space Needle, Elliott Bay and downtown. My car is sitting in a space.

"I had your friend, George, drive it up here. The keys should be under the visor. What did they ask you back there?"

I tell her: It was all about Megan. "I had bluffed and bullied one of the most powerful CEOs in the Northwest into granting an interview—so I assumed Olympic had called down these dogs on me. But they didn't ask anything about Olympic."

Amber changes the subject. "I packed a bag for you. It's in the back. I found your working notebook—you should have hidden it better. Still, took me time. I almost lost my favorite part of your anatomy." She strokes me. I push her hand away. "You've got your wallet, but don't even think of using a debit or credit card…"

"Wait, wait, wait!"

She undoes her seatbelt and turns to face me. "What?"

"I have to…"

"You have to disappear," she says. Her face softens. "Oh." She lightly touches my cheek. "I wish I had ice." She pulls a packet of Wet Wipes from her console and gently strokes my forehead and cheeks. I remember falling on that face now, as well as getting a rough slap, and I involuntarily recoil from the touch. "Just another minute," she says. "There, better."

"Amber, I can't just disappear. What are you talking about? I need to know what's happened."

She becomes agitated again. "We don't have a whole lot of time here. What happened is everything has turned to shit and the only way to keep you safe is to get you out of here."

"You're FBI? Where are the other agents? Why didn't you arrest them?"

"It's complicated."

"I can understand complicated. What? The FBI's afraid of the CIA?"

"They're not CIA. They're private contractors, mercenaries. William Blankley and Morton "Stu" Farmer, former Marine recon. Laura Monahan, former Blackwater. They called her "Gitmo Laurie." Enjoyed enhanced interrogation way too much. They all work for a company you've never heard of called Praetorian."

I suck in a deep breath of air. Craig Summers' CIA front company—the one that was supposed to have been dissolved.

I tell this to Amber as she fidgets. "They're not CIA anymore," she says. "And they're not about surveillance, or just about surveillance."

"What are they about?"

She doesn't give me a straight answer. "I didn't expect to run across them here."

I study my wrists. They are bruised and cut from where I struggled against the handcuffs.

"Laura killed Troy," I say. "I saw her that day, heading toward his office before he hit the street. She rammed her shoulder into me, like she was in a hurry…"

"Or a girl with an attitude," Amber says, "who was going to take Troy out for talking to a member of the press."

"No, she seemed surprised when I mentioned it."

"Troy pointed you toward Olympic Defense, right?"

I nod. But he did it in passing, to show he was the smartest guy in the room. I didn't come to Troy's office with the agenda to find a secretive defense unit. I just wanted to shoot the shit, add some depth to a column I was doing on a major local company. Troy never mentioned Praetorian. He did ask about eleven/eleven, but not like someone who really knew what it meant.

"Why can't you arrest them?"

"Because that's not the way the world works. And I'm on my own right now. I don't know who to trust on my own team. I need to find a lifeline. If you stay, you'll be killed." She reaches down and pops the trunk. "I have a suitcase for you. Inside is an envelope with five thousand dollars in hundreds and small bills. It's the best I can do. You can't use your credit cards. You can't fly."

"What about my gun?"

"No."

"Oh, yeah, the pen is mightier than the sword."

"That revolver is too heavy," she says. "Too difficult to conceal." She reaches across me and opens the glove box. She hands me a dark triangle of fabric. It takes me a minute to realize it's a holster. I pull out a small revolver with a black graphite skin. The hammer is enclosed by a cowling and the barrel is short but thick, adding to the gun's compact but menacing look. It's the lightest gun I've ever held.

"Smith & Wesson 340PD Airlite," she says. "Scandium alloy frame. Titanium barrel. Twelve ounces. The holster's designed to stay in your pocket if you have to draw it. Here's one Speedloader as a backup. I want it back."

She hands me the circular device. It consists of a black plastic circle with five bullets hanging from it and a metal catch on top. Drop them into the cylinder of the revolver, twist the catch on top, let the cartridges fall in, snap the cylinder back in, and you're done. The name says it all. The Speedloader is about the same weight as the gun.

I study the pistol. Open the cylinder, which is fully loaded with five rounds. "Will this work? I like my Combat Magnum."

"It has stopping power, believe me. Special government-issue bullets, .357 magnum. Just don't run out." Her voice is businesslike, knowledgeable. This is the same woman who feigned helplessness against the dogs in Ryan Meyers' apartment.

She reholsters the revolver.

Still I make no move to get out of the car and she's forced to sit with me as a light rain taps on the windshield and the panorama below us becomes runny and insubstantial.

I ask, "So all that stuff about walking into the lobby of the *Chicago Tribune* building with your first reporter's notebook. That was all bullshit."

"I wish it had been true."

"Is your name even Amber?"

"Yes." She gives me a sad smile and brushes back my hair. "It's not like you never kept a secret from a woman you made love to. Anyway, I told you I was older than I looked." She uses both hands to pull back her hair. "I didn't plan what happened. With us."

I make no attempt to move.

"This is about Megan's disappearance and it's about something going on in Olympic International," she says. "The two are connected. I just don't know how. That's why we need to work together."

"Work together!" I slam a hand on the door's armrest and let out a string of obscenities. "That begins with trust. Like telling me about this connection. The paper's going to lay me off anyway!" I hear myself babbling. I keep it up. "Nobody seemed to give a damn about Olympic until I started writing about it. Just Conspiracy Grrl…"

I am watching her face and expect to see a reflex of interest. Instead she stares at her lap and my stomach drops out. "Oh, hell. You were Conspiracy Grrl…"

"I was trying to get you started."

I shake my head. Part of me still feels as if I am being waterboarded again. I take a deep breath. "The passion page was a nice touch."

Her mouth parts in a half-smile. "I knew your reputation. Thought it might help get your interest. Now you need to get going."

"Who is Mister EU? Another agent?"

"He's you, silly."

"EU?"

"Emotionally unavailable." She leans over and kisses me passionately. I hold her as tight as life.

"Now," she says, "you've got to get the story and get it out there so people know what's going on. I've packed a bag for you and swept it for any listening or tracking devices. It's clean. So be careful what else you might gather along the way." Then she gives me a precise set of instructions.

"I can't do that." The ice is back in my bloodstream. My chest constricts.

"You will do just that," she says. "Why are you shaking?"

"I can't do it!"

◇◇◇

But I do.

Chapter Thirty-four

B-matter.

In my line of work, the term "B-matter" has an elastic meaning. It can be copy that's written in advance—say, for a notable person's obituary—to be topped by the "A-matter." It can also be information that's less important to the news story—stuff that can be trimmed if there's not enough space. Or B-matter can simply be background on a story, whether you use it yourself or pass it along to another writer. It might never make the finished article. It's just there. It happened. But it's an orphan. No editor ever went to the mat over B-matter.

Here is some of mine: My sister Jill was always a strange girl. Bookish and withdrawn as a child, unhappy about her beauty as a young woman, prone to terrible tantrums over seemingly small things. Only when I got older did I realize that she was reacting to what would now be called a dysfunctional family: alcoholic mother, a dad who was too old to be a hippy but wanted to try, until he found his calling as a crackpot who believed he had a legal right to refuse to pay income taxes. He found many like-minded souls who agreed. Unfortunately, one who didn't was a federal judge. Fights at home and flights from creditors and ever-present shame. I did my best to protect her.

It was only during college when her mind became a haunted house. She had to drop out. She became afraid of everything. Panphobia, they called it. By this time I was in the Army and could no longer shelter her. Grammy, my grandmother on my mother's side, had enough money to try to help. Jill would slip in and out of normality—taking part-time jobs and lovers, then falling apart over seemingly trivial things and clinging to a single room.

Jill was hospitalized. She went through a platoon of therapists. She ended up on disability at age twenty-five, living in a little apartment in the U District that had a view of the ship canal. She had her books and music and view. She rarely left this sanctuary. When Prozac came along, she seemed to get better. But the improvements were always temporary, tentative. When I worked for the *Free Press* the first time, it wasn't unusual to get her calls, sometimes magically fluent, often raving. I was dear and I was the enemy.

The only thing Jill wasn't afraid of was the water. She loved swimming as a child and teenager. She was very good—working as a lifeguard during good summers. In college, she became an ocean kayaker—a Puget Sound and Lake Washington kayaker. She likened it to cross-country skiing—as opposed to the high-adrenaline whitewater variety, like downhill skiing. Here, she was fearless and it always seemed to give her the peace that eluded her on land. She returned to it again and again. By the time I took the job back east, Jill seemed to have reached as much equilibrium as was possible, and I gave the kayak credit.

That's what made what happened so unbelievable.

That night, I arrive at the main downtown ferry terminal in plenty of time to make the 10:30 sailing for Bremerton. I use my credit card for the last time to buy a ticket, which I place on the dashboard. It is full dark but the sky above the city gives off a washed-out turquoise glow under low clouds. The parking lot is brightly illuminated. Beyond it is the blackness of Elliott Bay and, in the distance, dots of lights from Bainbridge Island.

The lot is hardly full, maybe forty cars spread out into three lanes. Just about the right size crowd. A few pedestrians walk past us to be ready to board. Sailors going back to the Navy base, young couples that enjoyed a weekend in the city, a family with a stroller. People who probably don't read the newspaper. We sit in our cars and wait. I make fists and unclench them, over and over. The big boat emerges out of the dark and slides into the dock. In a few minutes, cars stream off in the opposite direction, headed into downtown.

The ferry has the same green-and-white paint scheme I've seen my entire life. It's anchored securely to the massive terminal. But I can detect a menacing rise and fall of the boat as it holds its position, the water of the bay pushing and pulling the riveted steel. A vague nausea that I've felt for hours becomes more pronounced. I make myself watch the streetlights. A cop with a dog wanders by but he pays me no mind. Other cars line up behind me, to my right and left. Most shut off their lights and engines. I scan the mirrors but see no sign of pursuers.

I am out of the remains of my suit, now wearing a black leather jacket, gray long-sleeved T-shirt, and black jeans. Amber did not pack a varied wardrobe. In the right-hand pocket of the jeans, the Airweight sits in its holster. It's barely noticeable when I stand up and the bulge doesn't look like a revolver. In the passenger seat is the small, black duffel that Amber packed for me, along with the old brown leather briefcase. The briefcase has a Macbook, my old Blackberry, and a number of files from work. In a few minutes, it's time to drive onto the ferry.

The ferry is named the *Hyak*. What an irony, a sick, sick irony. It has five decks standing out of the water and bridges on each end. I follow the car ahead, a new Accord: we slide toward the water as crew members direct us. The car bumps slightly as it crosses the platform that connects the dock to the boat, then I'm inside it, on the long car deck. The confinement tightens my chest. The boat ever so slightly sways and my nerves start to eat through my skin. Why the hell do I live in a city nearly surrounded by water?

I slide the gearshift into park, turn the ignition off and grip the wheel for several moments until the feelings pass. Then I grab the duffel and walk toward the stairs. I leave the keys in the cup holder and the briefcase in the passenger-side floor well. For just a moment I look back: the Toyota is eight years old and paid for, but I never fell in love with it. Then I turn and follow a lanky young man up the narrow, metal stairway.

The main cabin is warm and spacious, far bigger than we need tonight. My quick count shows about sixty people in the room as a voice makes announcements over the PA system and the ferry prepares to sail. Then the big engines rev up and we're moving. The sense of pushing hopelessly against the great waters of the sound. I walk to the restroom, lock the door, and lean my head against the cool wall, just standing there. I fight my gag reflex, remind myself I can breathe.

It takes a long time for the wooziness go away. I finally sit on a long cushioned bench against a wall, staring at the floor, my hands wrapped under my arms for warmth. A column is due in a little more than fifteen hours. But, no. I am due to be "tapped," as the managing editor warned me. Pretty soon, no more columns. I wonder if they would have let me write a farewell. I wonder if they would have let me tell the truth. My stomach gradually settles into a stew of acid, but I have plenty of time to feel better. The crossing takes an hour. I just want to sit here in the cabin, imagining that I am in the banquet room of a third-rate country club or an old American Legion hall on firm ground. I want to, but I can't.

The dead trail me. Now I know the three Praetorian employees are hired killers and torturers. Troy needed to be silenced quickly. But did they take their time with Ryan Meyers? Holding him to the floor as they tightened the belt around his neck? I wonder only a second about the difference between the two. Ryan might have known where Megan is, so he needed to receive their full list of services. He didn't talk—so they worked me over to find out. Where is Megan? Somehow Megan mattered more to them than the tattoo on Ryan's leg. They must have seen it. Without the information they believe Megan possesses, "eleven/eleven" means nothing. Two numbers. And it's not as if they could have removed the tat easily; messing with it would only have raised suspicions. So they left it. Ryan had information about Megan; it was his death warrant. I don't know why Troy had to die.

I zip up the leather jacket and lever myself up from the seat. A sturdy door opens against my push, leading out onto the upper deck. It's deserted in the cold, wet wind. The blast helps my stomach, does nothing to help my mind. The black water spreads out around us, churning from the distant engines that leave a shadowy white wake. It's cold enough to kill, even in late October. Looking back, Seattle looks like a dream city, an open jewel box of tall prisms with lighted diamonds inside. I push back against the damp metal of the cabin wall. A young woman and her son dart past. He wants to look over the side. I zip my jacket higher against the cold and pull my head down into the collar. Then I walk to the rail and force myself to stare over the side.

In a few minutes, I make my way to the forward cabin. On a busy morning or afternoon, it could comfortably hold fifty commuters. Now it's nearly deserted. I push through the door to the forward deck, push against the wind and it finally opens, and I watch the sea come at us, the arms of tree thick land at a far distance on both sides. I think about my sister, sick with guilt. I stare into the undulations of the water, pulling off my leather jacket to find some relief against the sweat that has engulfed me.

I leave the jacket off as Bremerton hoves into view and I put on a snug, black ball cap that Amber had given me. It has a small Phoenix Suns logo. I hate ball caps. As the crew starts to make announcements, I sling my duffel over my shoulder, return to the main cabin, and sit at a table until the right moment comes to join the crowd going down to their cars. Then the big boat bumps into the terminal and the sound of starting car engines fills the crisp night air.

I'm not with them. I walk off with the pedestrians, in the middle of the crowd, just a tall man in a gray T-shirt, carrying a jacket, wearing a ball cap, lugging a duffel. I walk neither fast nor slow, just the right pace to keep with the group. From the walkway I can see the water much more clearly, smashing and gurgling between land and boat. Somehow it has lost its power to frighten me. I did not want to be here. I did not want my happy alignment of the planets destroyed or my life dug up and used against me. I didn't start this. Now I am going to finish it. I'm not feeling terror or grief. I'm not feeling anything except that I am running out of time, trying to claw my way out of an hourglass.

My legs carry me onto the firm land, past the news racks, across the parking area, and out into the night. It's a choice I make, very different from the course Jill chose when she boarded the very same ferry five years ago on a cold night. It was a week before they found her body.

Chapter Thirty-five

Monday, November 1st

At 8:15 a.m., I board an Amtrak Cascades train going south. As the countryside rolls by, the pictures of Megan Nyberg and Heather Brady sit in my lap. I memorize their faces. Megan is already in my head from the constant repetition of television: the straight fair hair that seems to hold every color from gold and honey to the lightest brown as it sweeps down to her shoulders. It is a limited rainbow, but more than enough for any man to find irresistible. Perfect crescents of brows set off large blue eyes hardly innocent. Her smile is wide. If she smiled at you, it would make your whole day. Heather's smile looks more uncertain and shy. Her brown hair is lush and thick, falling across and down a red cheerleader sweater. Her nose is a little long, her chin has a small, pale mole on the left edge, and her smile too crooked to be considered classically beautiful. But she's very attractive, or was. Something in her smile reminds me of someone. It's a fleeting recognition and I don't want to think about women in my life.

I try to read the Tacoma newspaper. It's a shell of its former self and I am through it in ten minutes. Most of it is dutiful reading—there's little that's compelling or interesting among the stories. Bland. Safe. I guess that's the intention of the bosses, but it has nothing in it that I would pay to read. I am the only person in the car reading a newspaper.

Still in wi-fi range, I check several papers online, including the *Wall Street Journal*. I'm a news junkie. No news is out concerning Olympic International. Its stock price has settled around $35. Maybe the takeover has fallen through. Maybe I was wrong about it.

The day is starting at the *Seattle Free Press*: the clerks dropping newspapers before the closed doors of the editors with glass offices, the early reporting staff straggling in, phones ringing, the section chiefs preparing for the morning news meeting. One thing is sure: my column won't be on the business department's budget for Tuesday.

Even the scenery won't let me alone. The train takes a siding at Centralia to wait for a passing freight train, and along the tracks line up long buildings bearing the logo and name of Olympic International. The name shouts out from the tall structure that is the centerpiece of the plant. They've seen better days. The paint is fading and part of one building's roof is gone. The place looks deserted, the parking lot and truck loading dock empty.

I know this much: I am rusty. It has been years since I was a reporter.

The train trundles over the Willamette River bridge and into the historic red brick station on time at eleven. I check my bag at the baggage counter and walk out front to wait for the light rail train. Portland is beautiful and compact, but to me it always feels small and stifling. That's a prejudice from growing up in Seattle, I guess. But the MAX Green Line train shows up almost instantly—Seattle should be so lucky to have such a system. The train is new and crowded. It takes me down the transit mall to the busy center city.

I stop by a luggage shop, then check into my favorite hotel, a lovingly restored monument on Broadway. It's filled with memories from weekend trips here with two different lovers over the years. I'll pay cash for one night—but I have to be careful how I handle it. Terrorists and drug dealers pay cash—cash attracts attention. So I say that I was a victim of identity theft, how it makes me prefer cash. I can be a good actor. But I have to take a chance and let them run my credit card for "incidentals." Up in the room, I break down the small brick of federal money Amber packed for me: plenty of twenties, then hundreds. Some of it goes in the newly purchased money belt, a little in my wallet. Other bills are stuffed into the pairs of socks she packed.

Thirty minutes later, I walk back outside. The day is clear and cool. A short walk and I pick up the MAX train to Portland State University.

At noon, just as Amber promised, I see Megan Nyberg.

The woman lingers uneasily near a half-circle of benches that look like concrete pallets. She's medium-height, petite, angel face. She drops a backpack on the bench and looks around.

I say, "Are you Tori?"

She turns and looks me over uneasily. Her movements are of a bird about to take flight. And I am not the columnist in the suit and tie. I'm not even what Amber may have promised her. I'm just a guy in jeans and a leather jacket, topped by a ball cap. Stubble is coming in on my face, per Amber's orders. On the other hand, I look like every third guy walking down a street in the Northwest. I introduce myself to Megan Nyberg's older sister.

"Are you with the FBI?," she demands. "I want to see your identification."

"Let's sit down."

I sit on the cool concrete. She takes a step back.

"Agent Burke asked me to meet you. Let me see your identification."

I knew this was coming, but I hoped it wouldn't come so soon. So I tell her who I am and hand her a business card.

It's a lousy handoff. The card flutters to the sidewalk and she's already running away. I chase her, giving her a safe distance but keeping up. I call her name.

"I'm working with Amber Burke. It's okay for you to talk to me."

She turns on me and stands with her fists clenched. "You people in the media will stop at nothing! You think she's already dead. You just want to see our tears!"

I want to say, I'm not in the media—I'm in the *press*. It would make no difference to her. So I just let her rage. I get it. We're eight feet apart but at least she's stopped and is interacting with me.

"I wish there were a different way," I say in as soft a voice as the city noise will allow. "I respect your privacy. I only want to find your sister and we're running out of time." She stares at me. "I'm just a business columnist. I'm not a police reporter. I just want to help find your sister."

I'm also lying. I want to find Megan, but I also want the story. Those are the breaks. Tori turns away, crumples onto the damp grass, and sits with her knees folded, arms around them, rocking back and forth. "Why can't you people just leave us alone."

I let her sit like that for a few moments and then gently sit next to her. It makes my knees hurt. For a long time neither of us talks. She's not an exact copy of her sister. Her hair is parted on the side and wavy, shoulder length. She's tan, with her skin young enough to take the exposure and still look perfect. Her eyes are big, brown, and knowing.

"The police and the FBI want to make this somehow Megan's fault. They want to make her some kind of junkie or slut. Why did she drop out? Why did she move to Seattle and live with her boyfriend? As if I know! As if any of us knows! I'm sure their badgering caused Ryan's suicide just as much as you people did."

She looks at me as if I have running sores. Yet she sits next to me and vents. "When mom couldn't reach Megan, she knew something was wrong. Ryan didn't know where she was, either. You know what the police did? Nothing. Just another runaway. We'd have to wait. If dad didn't know the deputy mayor, who knows how long we would have had to wait before the police took this seriously."

I ask her when Megan disappeared. October 1st—one month ago. About the same time Heather Brady was last heard from.

"The truth is," Tori says, "I'm three years older and Megan and I are very different. She's dreamy and curious about the world. But mom and dad never pushed her. When she dropped out of high school and moved to Seattle, I wasn't surprised. I knew she'd have an adventure and then get on with life." Her voice sounded suddenly raw.

I let the silence envelop us before I speak. "But you didn't personally talk to the police, right?"

She nods. There was no reason. The parents had handled it. And although Tori came home on weekends, they all thought it would be good if she stayed in school and tried to carry on normally. Nobody in the media feeding frenzy even knew she was here.

"There are some things sisters tell each other."

She looks at me sharply. I keep my voice soothing.

"Like new friends she had made?" I added, "New friends she and Ryan made." I don't want to hit the "sister is a slut" nerve and cause her to walk away. "Anyone named Heather?"

She nods. "She told me about a girl named Heather. She was from Texas, I think."

She pushes her hair out of her face and stares up at the buildings. "I'm so worried about her," she says. "We would talk occasionally, but we were drifting apart. She thought I was judgmental because I disapproved of some of what she was doing."

Now I want to back off. We're making progress, but I don't want to push it too hard. I will ask about her life, about Megan as a young girl—softball stuff. Cool the interview down. I don't want things to get so intense she runs away. Maybe find some common ground between a mongrel like me and a pretty girl from Mercer Island money. Then I can ask if Megan talked about any threats, any stalkers. My body language says I have all the time in the world and there's nothing on my mind but her. My face says, talk to me.

She watches me, then stares at nothing, eyes straight ahead as two cops ride slowly by on bicycles. They don't even look at us.

Tori throws the softball herself. "Why are you a business writer?" She looks at me curiously, like an exotic creature in a zoo. I start talking about wanting to hold power accountable, and how much more power is concentrated in business than in the government, but when all the youth drains out of her face, I shut up.

"That's not what I mean," Tori says. "You said you wrote about business. The FBI agent sent you." She screws up her face in thought, looks past me. "You're not telling me everything."

I lie, of course, telling her that she knows everything I do. That I am just trying to help FBI Special Agent Amber Burke.

"Have you ever seen one of those Tiffany key pendants?" she asks.

I nod. I vaguely recall seeing a newspaper ad and thinking it was a sign that some people still had way too much money.

"The last time I saw Megan, she had one around her neck," Tori says, pantomiming. "And it wasn't the cheap one. It was white gold. Later I checked, and it retails for $1,500."

"I couldn't have afforded that when I was seventeen."

"Neither could Ryan. And you know all about this, so I don't know why you're playing games with me."

"I honestly don't."

Tori mashes her lips together, struggles to get it out. "Megan was in something…deep, I don't know. She'd started seeing someone. Someone other than Ryan."

"Someone who gave $1,500 gifts."

She nods and her eyes grow wide with tears.

"She made me swear to keep it a secret."

Tori shakes her head, anticipating my question. "She never told me his name. Just Mister Big. She was a major *Sex in the City* fan. Mister Big. She was dazzled. An older man, I learned that much. Probably married—men are such pigs. A wealthy businessman." She wipes her eyes and draws herself up. "So when you said you were a business writer, I thought you might know."

Chapter Thirty-six

Monday, November 1st to Wednesday, November 3rd

Back at my favorite hotel, I try hard not to jump to conclusions. Megan was with a rich, married man who gave her expensive presents. Troy Hardesty would fit the profile pretty well. If I were jumping. Troy had the money to have it all: multiple houses, sailboat, Maserati, wine cellar, stunning blond wife, Rainier Club membership—and a teenage mistress, perhaps? I knew all the other things from the profile I had written about Troy, one of the hedge fund managers who had not only survived the crash but was profiting from it.

And yet—if I were jumping—Troy wouldn't strike me as the type. He had all the goods. He was a walking *Robb Report*. But he didn't really seem to enjoy it. He struck me as the least sensual of men. He loved the game of making money. And yet, he was dead under mysterious circumstances. He had asked about eleven/eleven and then I had found the numbers tattooed on Ryan's leg. Tori didn't react to my question about the numbers except to plead ignorance. I ignored her answer, as if those numbers didn't really matter, watching her face, finally believing that she didn't know their significance. But, as she said, Megan was into something deep.

Amber answers her cell on the first ring and I give her an update. She tells me the *Free Press* and the *Seattle Times* both have stories online about me disappearing from the Bremerton ferry. I don't want to know more. I just hope it shakes my pursuers.

"What are you going to do next?"

When I tell her, the phone carries a long pause.

"Please don't do that," she says.

"You told me to get the story. I can't get it by hiding out here and surfing the Internet. I'm at a dead end on Megan. I'm going after Olympic."

"There's not enough time."

"So you believe something's going to happen in eleven days."

After a pause, Amber says, "I don't know. Like I told you a long time ago, maybe eleven/eleven is a meme that doesn't mean anything. Maybe it's a report number."

"You don't believe that."

Silence.

"What if there's a terrorist attack planned for November 11th? You're the FBI, for God's sake."

Her voice is calm, explaining that the bureau is an investigative agency that gathers evidence for the Department of Justice. It's all bureaucratic and evasive. Then she reminds me of the agent in Minnesota who brought forward evidence pointing to the 9/11 attack, and how she was ignored.

I say, "You never have told me why you were posing as a reporter."

"I will someday. For now, I need you to stick to the plan we agreed to."

"You said get the story. That's what I'm doing. If you don't like it, clear me to take a flight down there. I can move faster."

"It's not safe."

I soften my voice. "No lifeline yet?"

"No," she says.

"Then I'll do it the hard way."

I hear her give a resigned shrug and she tells me to be careful. I wonder if she misses me.

At a drug store, I buy toiletries, then head back to the hotel. I take a long shower, dress, and go down to the business center. Can't help myself: I read the story on the *Free Press* Web site: "Columnist Missing from Ferry." It's written by Amber Burke, and includes too much information for my taste. "He had been told his job was being eliminated and was despondent." And, "His sister, Jill, committed suicide by jumping from a ferry into Elliott Bay." I'm not really paying attention to the details about my career, my awards, my scoops, the people who said "he filled up a room," was a "star" and "made non-business readers want to read the business section." The publisher and executive editor express their concern. My briefcase and computer were found on the boat. A police officer said it's not unknown for people to just leave their cars on the ferry and turn up later.

I take a quick spin through the *Seattle Times* site. It has an update on the *Free Press* troubles: How a buyer is unlikely to emerge when so many newspapers are in trouble. The mayor bemoans the potential loss of the newspaper but says there's nothing city hall can do. No shit. Plenty of politicians and bureaucrats will join the dance on our grave. One less set of shoes kicking over their rocks to see what's underneath.

My real work is drudgery, but necessary. Three hours on the Securities and Exchange Commission's EDGAR Web site and I have printed out a three-inch thick stack of documents related to Olympic International. I go to the Olympic site and print two of CEO Pete Montgomery's most recent Power Point presentations and speeches to securities analysts. There's another rich, married man who might have an inclination toward teenage girls and an account at Tiffany. It would tie up the connection between Megan and Olympic International, neat as can be. Probably too neatly. I take the paperwork up to my room, then I go down to the bar, where I drink two martinis and eat bar food. I'm famished. The high-ceilinged room is ornate and inviting, and it seems to have a high proportion of attractive, unattached professional women. They don't give me a second look.

I return to the business center and spend another four hours, researching private contracting and national security. From the volume of material—credible stuff, not nut sites—the research I have time to do doesn't even begin to scratch the surface. Still, I find congressional and General Accountability Office reports, declassified Defense Department reports, think-tank papers, stories out of major newspapers and a couple of interesting Web sites run by former military men. I use the search function to go through 300-page reports in PDF form, looking for "Olympic" or "Praetorian." I save useful URLs and email them to myself at my new Gmail account. It's the drudgery of research you save readers from. I print out and add the relevant pages to my growing sheaf of reading material for the train. With luck, the work will save me from all the loose ends that pop out of my psyche when I'm not in the paper, when I'm not getting the daily rush of the news. Upstairs again, I shove a chair against the door, latch it, brush my teeth, put the gun under my pillow near my right hand, fall asleep early, and don't wake up until 7:30 the next morning.

I change into a blue shirt and tan chinos, ones with enough give in the hips and crotch that my lightweight .357 is virtually invisible in the pocket. So is the money belt. Broadway is cool and blustery as I walk to the Portland train station. Amtrak's *Coast Starlight* departs on time, south to Los Angeles, where I can change trains to the *Sunset Limited* for the ride into Arizona. Trains are wonderful. Nobody wants your ID. Nobody recognizes you from Sunday's column. I am nobody. The train takes you places you can't see from a car or an airliner, sometimes they are breathtaking in their beauty, or simply as a reminder that places exist in America that aren't cluttered with houses, strip malls, and cars. And you get to see pieces of the economy. I see one when we leave Portland: An impressive compound of nearly new industrial buildings with Olympic International's logo and the name on the side: Portland Litho and Lamination Plant/ Portland Distribution Center.

Except the buildings look deserted and empty—just like the ones I saw on the train down from Seattle. While we're still in cell range, I find the phone number for the Portland Litho and Lamination Plant of Olympic International and call it. After four rings, there's a click and a new set of rings. "Thank you for calling Olympic International," an automated voice drones. It's the same recording you get if you call the headquarters in Seattle. I dig through the Olympic files because I remember seeing a press release that had mentioned that operation had won a sustainability prize just last month.

I'm a curious guy: that's essential for a good journalist, and its loss is one of the things that has hurt our profession. Lose your curiosity and you're just taking up the oxygen in the news-room. So I call the Portland Chamber of Commerce and after a few dead ends finally get a woman who knows all about this Olympic site: it closed three years ago. I call the chamber up in Centralia and ask the same question: that paper mill closed four years ago—"you people in Seattle ought to get out more," the man says. I keep saying that I'm with the *Seattle Free Press*. It opens doors, always has. But I'm really just with me now. I am a truant, a nobody without the newspaper. It feels strange. Almost as strange as a company whose active facilities are actually closed. The latest annual report lists the Centralia mill among Olympic International's operations.

Just a boring, integrated paper company with a subsidiary in the defense business. A company that's reporting operations on its books that are actually closed. A company the Seattle newspapers haven't covered very completely for years. The train rolls through the peaceful farms of the Willamette Valley, toward the mountains, and I read. I read to get the story, and I read so I don't go crazy with grief over Pam and the gaping absence of Rachel and Amber, Melinda the professor and Melinda my oldest friend, and everything in my old life. I miss a warm body and a warm voice that might miss me. Grief over the deaths of newspapers. Instead, I walk to the bar car and drink a martini, then another. Back at my seat, I make myself read.

Last year, the Special Inspector General for Iraq Reconstruction released a report that showed ODS had over-billed the State Department for $50 million. It has a contract to protect dip-lomats in Iraq, but apparently didn't fully staff and cover its obligations. ODS also over-billed the government for airfare and couldn't account for government equipment it had received. I search through Olympic's SEC documents. By law, it should have to disclose this to shareholders. There it is: Hidden in the fine print deep in the 10-K annual report. The scandals at Blackwater and Halliburton got all the coverage. This has never been in a newspaper.

By the time we arrive in Klamath Falls, I begin to understand Amber's worry over whom to trust. I read Justice Department budget documents related to an advanced electronic surveillance program for the FBI called "Going Dark." It's an advanced program designed to allow the bureau to get control over new technologies. That's what the report says. An old editor of mine would have asked, "What does that mean?" The report is unclear. But when I scan through the pages, I find a list of contractors for the $234 million program, and there's Olympic Defense Systems getting a nice chunk of change. Yet it's not reflected in the Olympic International reports to shareholders or to the SEC. I find this again and again. ODS is bringing in much more revenue than Olympic declares—and its mills and distribution centers sit shuttered. Apparently nobody on Wall Street or at the rating agencies cares as long as the cash comes in.

I fall asleep to the gentle rocking of the train, documents clutched in my lap. The next day passes and I barely notice the view across the bay to San Francisco, the ocean right by the tracks after we leave Santa Barbara, the long slog through the suburbs of L.A. My mind is on the story.

Chapter Thirty-seven

Thursday, November 4th

This is not Europe. We don't have fast trains most places in America. My train doesn't even go to Phoenix anymore, which is the nation's fifth largest city. Instead, it lets me out in the desert in a little crossroads called Maricopa. I begin to wonder if I should have gone all the way to Tucson and taken a bus back, when I hear a woman's voice, asking me if I need a ride. I walk across the dusty, hard ground, feeling the intense sun on my skin. She's somewhere over fifty, sixty pounds overweight, wearing a tight pink pastel T-shirt, and sitting in an ancient Chevy van with the top of the dashboard covered with paperwork of some kind. She's the only taxi service into the city and the fare is $60. I peel off three bills and climb in. The only other passenger is a big guy with an eye-patch and a ball cap that reads, "When I have sex, it's so good the neighbor has a cigarette." He reads a comic book and doesn't talk during the trip.

It's hot.

It's early November and blistering. The sky is an enormous vault of dusty blue without a single cloud. I have never been to Arizona: the land is flat, treeless, brown, everything the Northwest is not. To me it's ugly, but I'm sure they think it's God's country. It's that way everywhere. Don't ask me to be in a tourist frame of mind, anyway. I have a lot of enemies. Time is one. I'm grateful the dash clock is broken. We drive out of the little crossroads and enter a morbid landscape of new, close-spaced, dun-colored houses. They look cheaply built and deserted. Faded sales signs hang limp in the air. She tells me the place has been killed by the real-estate crash. A huge Indian casino whooshes past and then we're on the freeway, doing seventy-five. I keep checking the mirrors. Nobody seems to be following us. We're swallowed up by a city of subdivisions and big-box stores, surrounded by bare mountains. The scenery runs from shabby to breathtaking. There seems to be no zoning.

She lets me out downtown. This is the oddest big city I've ever seen, hugely spread out but with a downtown more modest than Bellevue's. Still, I'm a city kid and step out on the curb beside a skyscraper from the 1970s. Without the van's air conditioning, the heat instantly hits me again. No one is visible on the sidewalk for blocks. In the distance, a low range of blue-brown mountains keep the southern horizon. A light-rail line runs up what looks like the main drag. I walk toward a pub to grab some lunch and see a small men's store. There, I use my federal money to buy a suit, white shirt, dress shoes, tie and belt. Lucky for me I've always been able to buy suits off the rack with minimal alterations. Forty-two long coat. Fits great. I add a natty straw fedora and throw away the ball cap.

The owner is named Barry and he wants to talk. Where am I from? Chicago, I say. He is, too. Good thing I know that city well enough to fake it. After lunch, I use his directions to take a light-rail train half a mile to a dry cleaner that Barry said could do alterations. I offer the woman an extra $200 if she can hem the pants while I wait: a full break and cuffs. Back on the train, I ride north, past skyscrapers and vacant lots until I am in shady blocks. There I get off and check into a motel, and finally unload my purchases and traveling bag heavy with files in a dim room with the air conditioning set on high.

◇◇◇

An hour later I pay the cab to wait. We sit outside a sand-colored three-story office building in Scottsdale. It is both new and drab.

The heat hasn't abated, so I keep the suit jacket off until I step outside and walk toward the front entrance. I grew up poor, so I like to wear suits. I love their design and feel. I love not dressing like every casual Microsoftie in Seattle. And a suit still gets you entree—fewer people will ask questions when you walk in a place where you shouldn't be wearing a suit. My beard is coming in now and I've trimmed it neatly. The straw fedora is on and I keep my head down. No reason to attract undue attention from anybody's security cameras.

The glass entrance doors open with gold handles and give way to a tall atrium with elevators on each side. They have gold doors. Walk straight ahead and it's the entrance to what was once a mortgage company. The name is still on the wall but the interior is dark and a discreet "available" sign is in the window. There's no security desk or, as far as I can tell, camera. No one comes or goes as I wait. But the directory on the nearest wall confirms what I had learned from Olympic's Web site, that the offices of ODS are on the third floor.

I ride up and the elevator door opens with soft bell and a quiet whoosh. The atrium is deserted. An insurance office sits in the main space and behind a spacious reception desk, I see people walk around doing whatever it is they do. The ODS office is located down a hallway painted off-white with dark wooden doors every few feet and a drinking fountain set back in an alcove that also contains the doors to the rest rooms. Nobody is out in the hallway besides me. The carpet is thick and yet I can hear my footsteps. The place smells like icy air. I pass a real-estate attorney, another real-estate attorney, a CPA. I dated a CPA once. She was much more fun than one might have imagined. These offices have large windows beside the entrance doors. I am re-running the lines in my head that I will say when I reach the ODS office and open the door. My stomach is tight. I take note of the door to the exit stairs at the end of the hall. It is fortuitously located near the ODS suite.

But when I get there, it's just a dark door. No window. No gold plate with the company name. Just a suite number. I place my damp hand on the door handle and press it. It doesn't turn. It's locked.

"Nobody's there."

He has crept up on me so silently that I didn't hear anything. I don't like it and my hand drops into my right pocket and finds the butt of the .357. But he looks benign enough. A medium-sized Hispanic man with dark skin and a white shirt with "Oscar" embroidered on the left side. He has a large set of keys dangling from his belt by a red carabiner. Maybe a janitor.

"There's never anybody there."

"Really? I was looking for Olympic Defense Systems. I have an appointment there at two…"

He shrugs. "Whatever. But I've never seen anybody come or go. You tried the door? Locked right? Always is. They don't want it cleaned. Not much to clean. It's the smallest office on the floor. Just one room and a closet. Building manager says, never go inside." He gives me a sly smile and jangles his keys. "I went in once. There's nothing there. Not even a chair. Nothing."

Back at the motel, I start making calls to the East Coast: analysts at defense industry think tanks, my trusted Wall Street research people, a finance professor at Wharton who is an expert on corporate structures. While I wait for return calls, I read the Phoenix paper. It's the typical Gannett piece of crap, full of stories based on one source or press releases, "news you can use," boring features. Stuff that mostly screams "Don't read me." It's a pretty product, with color, graphics, boxes, and assorted doodads. But there's not much worth reading. Too bad Wall Street loved Gannett and every other chain followed its lead. It doesn't surprise me that Olympic Defense Systems would have something down here. It's the kind of town where the press wouldn't ask tough questions. You could get away with anything. What that is, though, I don't know. I've hit another Olympic dead end. There's only one other possibility here, based on my digging through the corporate reports, but it's getting too late to check it out today.

I had a friend years ago who worked with me, then came to Phoenix for a job at this newspaper. His wife wanted sunshine. He completely dropped off the national radar, and he was a fine reporter. I consider calling him, but decide against it. Instead, when I get back to my room I call another old friend and colleague. We've known each other going on thirty years, and we talk every year. His wife answers and we chat. When she hands him the phone, he gives his characteristic greeting.

"Fitz happens!" Then he gives a high cackle that I know is totally out of keeping with his sturdy, six-foot-six body, handsome coffee brown face, and position in the world. I circle slowly around the real reason for my call. Then he says he wants to call me back. He does so in fifteen minutes. It's on a secure line. The kind of communications available to Lt. Col. Tony Fitzgerald of U.S. military intelligence.

Chapter Thirty-eight

Friday, November 5th

At precisely nine a.m., a black Dodge Ram pickup pulls under the portico of the motel. He has driven hours to reach Phoenix from Fort Huachuca, but the truck looks immaculate. I am standing there wearing the same outfit I wore when I walked off the ferry, today enjoying the dry, cool morning. A light cloud cover mutes the previous day's intense sunshine. The truck is an extended-cab job, jacked up so that the door handle is at my eye level. The tinted window rolls down and Fitz is behind the wheel wearing a white polo shirt and jeans. I use the steel rung step to lift myself up into the cab and settle into the passenger seat.

"Turned into a goddamn hippie." He indicates my beard.

"Long story."

Fitz's close-cropped hair is going gray and he's wearing wire-rimmed glasses that give him an unaccustomed professorial look. In my mind's eye, we're both young and wearing green.

"So you want to go to prison?" His voice is a low rumble above the truck's diesel chant. I show him what I had printed out that morning at the motel business center: a page from the state corrections department on the Arizona State Prison Complex-Cortez Peak and a Mapquest route to get there. It's a private prison operated by another subsidiary I had never heard of: Olympic Correctional Services. Fitz studies the map and hums to himself. I look in the back and see a red cooler and a long black duffel. The cooler has ice and water. The shapes inside the duffel feel like firearms.

"You came prepared."

"Always out front," Fitz says. I lean over and check the map. The prison "complex" is more than out in the middle of nowhere. The writer and editor in me itches against the jargon word "complex." What the hell does that mean? Sounds like a psychiatric disorder. I'd have a complex if I were in prison, too. I wish this were my biggest care in the world.

Fitz slips the truck into gear and we roll. Half a mile to the freeway—eight clicks, Fitz would say—then we drive west. It takes a long time for the suburban sprawl to fall away and be replaced by desert.

"So how the hell did you get in with ODS?" He's the kind of driver who looks at you as he steers casually with one hand.

"Another long story."

"Well, I'm not surprised you were supposed to be dead. My friend, you have fallen down the rabbit hole of the hidden defense budget. Everything down looks up and you can't believe your own eyes. The world has changed since you left the Army. Now almost half of national security has been privatized, and it's not just wiring barracks showers that electrocute soldiers. It's everything. And ODS is the best-kept secret of all."

I tell him that's what happens when newspapers cut back on investigative reporting, but he doesn't seem interested.

"Makes no sense for Olympic to be running a private prison." He shakes his large head. "Makes no sense unless it's a black site, in country. They've got terror suspects out there, and nobody knows it. Sons of bitches…"

I make no comment. The floor of the truck is solid under my feet and even with the clouds the sky is an endless vault of light, but I feel as if I am sliding deeper into darkness.

"So, since we're talking about secrets, ever heard of something called Praetorian?"

"That's a secret," he says solemnly. Then, a perfect comedic beat and his cackle laugh fills the cab. "Praetorian started out

CIA. It was a brass-plate operation that claimed to be in the shipping industry but was really involved in satellite surveillance. North Korea. Iran. Iraq. All the places we couldn't go. This was years ago. Then the CIA closed it. Fast-forward to Operation Iraqi Freedom and Praetorian shows up as an ODS outfit."

"They're part of Olympic? You're sure?"

"No doubt. But now it's not about high-tech shit. It's bad-asses, mercenaries. I ran across them in Iraq and Afghanistan. Each one making two-hundred K a year when the average grunt getting killed has to put his family on food stamps. Lot of former military. Well trained. Very well equipped. Word was, under the old administration they were running the vice president's special executive assassination squad. You didn't hear that from me."

I tell him about Craig Summers and how I know him. It takes awhile and ends up being a briefing on the whole train mess my life has become since that meeting with Troy Hardesty.

For a long time, Fitz stays silent. He chews on his lower lip and scans the road, subtly checks the mirrors. "Every organization has its assholes. We had ours at Abu Ghraib, and they had orders from DOD—top assholes always get off. But Praetorian is all asshole, all the time. Ask me, I think they're trained killers."

We take an exit off the freeway and turn south, bumping onto a wide dirt road that runs between irrigated fields, some bright green and some brown and fallow. We're in a flat basin marked off by bare, rugged mountains We drive toward the closest range and after ten minutes the agriculture disappears, replaced by scratchy vegetation, some cactus, rough, short bushes.

"The thing is, a lot of these contractors are on hard times," Fitz says. "The new administration and Congress have been a lot tougher. Lots of contracts have been canceled, tasks have been returned to the military where they always should have been. Money's tighter. Don't get me wrong, there's plenty still there. Plenty in black ops, in DARPA"—the Defense Department's research outfit—"but there's less growth in the budget, a lot less. And you know how that affects a business, being a big-time business columnist. When the growth slows down, the shit hits the fan."

"Profit margins shrink."

"Exactly."

"If only they could create their own housing bubble," I joke.

He raises his eyebrows. "They could, with the right political connections—and an event."

"You mean a terrorist attack. New York, Washington…"

"Hell, if I wanted to scare the hell out of Americans I'd set off a suitcase nuke at a shopping mall right here in Phoenix."

"Sometimes you scare the hell out of me, my brother."

The road becomes even less improved, but Fitz barely slows and his shocks are so good we hardly feel the rutted ground beneath. Foothills bend down to meet us, marked by the stands of majestic saguaros. Behind us is a long dust trail. Ahead, empty country with a road curving to the left, seeming to peter out into trackless badlands. I begin to wonder if we've taken a wrong turn.

Suddenly we're on blacktop. It's as if the truck is riding on glass. The road is wide, new, looks barely used. A dry creek passes beneath a bridge of clean, unscarred concrete. Craggy low buttes and mountains with fantastic shapes surround us, but the only sign of man is this perfect, empty road. Fitz pulls off. I can see him watching the rearview mirror, checking to see what might be behind us as the dust dissipates. I crane my neck. Nothing.

"Anybody asks, we're geologists," he says. "From the university."

We drive another ten minutes and a long, low set of buildings appears on our left. They're colored the same brown as the desert floor: two- and three-story structures that look like they run almost a mile up against a mountain. As we get closer, the guard towers and double sets of concertina-topped security fences become apparent. A blacktop perimeter road runs between the fences but has no vehicles patrolling it. We slow as a sign proclaims "Arizona State Prison Complex—Cortez Peak." Another wide, new asphalt road connects with ours. The road goes fifty feet before it is hemmed in on both sides by the security fences.

Another hundred feet and it jigs through concrete barriers and comes to a gray guard tower. The second story of the tower has large tinted windows with blue trim. The structure is shaded by an awning and surrounded by a low railing. I see no vehicles and no people.

"Let me see your printout," Fitz says as he cruises past doing an even thirty miles an hour. "Built in 1999. Total inmate population, 3,750…Mandatory literacy, special ed, GED preparation, vocational services…The site supports its own wells, water and wastewater treatment plants…The complex maintains six kitchens that can produce 12,450 inmate meals per day and a laundry capable of washing 53,000 pounds of clothes and linen each week." He tosses it back. "Kiss my big, black ass. We travel half a mile, and pull off. He reaches into the back and picks through several U.S. Geological Survey maps, ones with such precision that they show power lines and abandoned mines. He pulls one out.

"This map is from 2005 and there's no prison on here."

He indicates with a thick finger. I lean over to look and he's right, the spot is empty. Nothing was built in 1999. He leaves the map open. I look around, relieved once again to have the .357 in my pocket, but we're alone. From this distance, the prison nearly blends into the side of the mountain.

"Let's take another look," Fitz says, and the truck drops heavily into gear. He slowly makes his way another half a mile, scanning to his left. Then he spins the wheel and we bump off the perfect road into the desert. My insides tighten. On the road, escape seemed easier. Now we're more exposed. The truck shimmies and bobs across the ground and the sound of rocks and scrub can be heard beneath the floor. Fitz goes slow. He doesn't want to raise dust. I keep watch but it's hard to see much. The spindly desert trees, if you call them that, are about at eye level. Good camouflage, I hope. Fitz spins the wheel and drives on the edge of a dry creek. We go uphill. The prison is completely out of sight. He drives maybe another five hundred yards and shuts off the engine. We're facing a mountain.

He reaches behind him and unzips the duffel. He produces what looks like a weapon out of a science-fiction movie.

"Ever seen one of these?"

Part of it looks like a tricked out M-16 with a folding stock and pistol handle, but the barrel is big and protrudes from a thick housing ahead of the trigger guard and magazine. It's sleek and black, about two-and-a-half feet long. I've never seen anything like it.

"Franchi SPAS-15," he goes on. "Shotgun. Little Italian sweetheart. Help you win friends and influence people. Here's the position for manual pump action. And this for semi-auto. Push and hold this button." He goes through a quick tutorial and hands me the weapon. "Think you can handle it?"

I nod and take it, keeping the barrel up as I swing the stock out and lock it into position. It's very lightweight.

"Holy shit!" I exclaim as the long, iconic weapon comes out of the duffel and into Fitz's hands. It's an antique. It's very deadly. "That's a BAR."

"Yes it is." He strokes it, smiles fondly. "Browning Automatic Rifle. This is a great state to be a gun collector in. It's almost mandatory here." The BAR was a mainstay of the military in World War II, a very badass infantry weapon that fires thirty ought-six ammunition, full-auto if you wish. It has the tough but elegant design of the zenith of American industrial power. I definitely feel as if I am back in the days at Fort Monmouth and other posts where "boys with their toys" meant guns, even among the outsider intel guys. It's an odd feeling; somebody else's life—not mine. Fitz brings a bandoleer belt of magazines for the BAR, hands me an extra magazine for the shotgun, and I agree to hump a daypack with water. We step out. I chamber a round into the shotgun and we hike into the dry wilderness.

"Just remember…"

"I know," I say, brandishing the high-tech toy, "geologists from the university."

"Never know what varmints you might find out here." He laughs with anticipation.

The desert is quieter than anything I have ever experienced. The silence leaves a vacuum in my brain. A small lizard scurries out of our way and it sounds like a freight train by comparison. The land is also lush in a strange way, with many varieties of spare but lovely plant life. You have to pay attention, but there's no time. I scan the landscape for humans, the sky for sensors or helicopters. I leave it to Fitz to make our trail.

He aims toward a low arm of the mountain, a rocky hogback, and we walk toward it across the hard, parched ground. My black running shoes turn ochre from the dust. It becomes rocky as we climb and before long my legs are hurting and I'm out of breath. I feel sweat run down my back and thank God the cloud cover is still in place. He still looks like he's a twenty-two-year-old lieutenant. As I recall, the BAR weighs nearly twenty pounds. It takes us forty-five minutes to reach the top of the ridge. The view is panoramic, reaching far enough that I can see the perfect rectangles of farm fields we left behind miles before.

Below us the vast prison is empty.

Chapter Thirty-nine

The prison backs up to the hogback and its outer buildings form an inverse U, shielding the large interior space from the outside. It's supposed to look that way. When we had approached from the road, they looked like massive prison buildings, with small windows and dun-colored walls. Now I can see they are fake. Two arms of the U are just tilt-up walls with windows in them. The third leg of the U is a long set of barracks or dorms with doors that open straight out into the yard, and on one part of the rooftop is a freshly-painted helipad with a door that goes down into the structure—hardly the maximum security prison "complex" advertised on the state Web site. The yard is huge—four football fields, at least, and it looks like the back lot of an old Hollywood movie studio.

It contains a street lined with commercial buildings and houses. There are streetlamps, parking meters, a mailbox, newspaper racks. If you stood down there, you might think for a moment you were in a small New Urbanist town center. Closer to us is a range with silhouette targets still in place. Next to it is a tactical range like the cops use, with barricades and false fronts where targets can pop up, giving the officer only a couple of seconds to decide whether it's friendly or hostile. Somehow I don't think any police officers have been here.

In fact, nobody's there. The huge compound looks deserted. No people, no vehicles. Fitz pulls out a pair of Steiner binoculars and scans it. The guard towers are empty. The perimeter road is clear. It's another Olympic International property that's deserted, but it looks a hell of a lot more menacing than a closed paper mill.

"I'm gonna look around," he says, and side-steps his way down the rocky ridge disappearing around a boulder formation.

I stand there and catch the barest breeze. It makes the stiff desert scrub rattle in the silence. Then I go down on my haunches, lay down the gun, and take out my notebook. I sketch the prison complex as best I can, making note of the landmarks, especially the firearms ranges. I use the cell phone to take some bad photos. At that moment, I wish I had the gadgets of a "mojo"—a video cam, a still camera, that would be nice right now. But a twenty-two-year-old mojo with no sense of what he or she knows or needs to learn, with no mentor or good editor, accustomed to writing single-source stories off press releases… well, he or she would never have gotten this far.

"They're gone."

I nearly jump out of my skin—there's a lazy journalist cliché, but it's just what it feels like. Off to my left is a thin man with scruffy puffs of white hair protruding from a cap. His face is as red-brown, permanently sun-scorched, and as rutted and grooved as the desert. It's a face that looks as if two tectonic plates have collided on it: pinched from the eyes down, but with a wide, high forehead with a dozen deep wrinkles. He's wearing hiking boots, khaki shorts, and a soiled Harley Davidson wifebeater. He has an amiable voice. He also has a handgun trained on me.

My skin stays detached and my heart rate is so high I can feel it in my ears, but for some reason my tic of a pinching eyelid has gone away. The shotgun is black and beautiful and an impossible distance away from my hand.

"I wouldn't do that, if I were you." He reads my mind.

All I can do is ask questions. "Where did they go?"

"That's a pretty piece you got," he says, using the revolver as a helpful pointer, indicating the Franchi. "Looks like the kind of ordnance they were using."

"So you watched them?"

"I'd sneak up, just like you. Had to be real careful, 'cause they'd send out patrols with dogs, helicopters. But nobody knows this mountain better than me."

"Then it'd be a pity to leave your chunky salsa all over it."

Fitz Happens.

The scruffy man immediately drops the pistol. It's a miracle it doesn't go off. "Holy shit, man…" He speaks in a whisper.

Fitz has flanked us and trains the mean-looking automatic rifle on the man's mid-section. It looks menacingly long from this angle, the barrel huge, like a hand-held howitzer. He walks closer and orders me to get the revolver. I grab it and my shot-gun and stand.

Fitz doesn't lower the barrel. "So who the fuck are you?"

He sits cross-legged on the ground and tells us. His name is Rusty Grayson and he's lived for almost thirty years in a little hamlet south of us, a place he went when he came home from 'Nam and wanted to be away from the world. He says he's a desert rat and nobody knows these mountains better than he does. I tell him my name and newspaper, so everything's ethical—he knows he's talking to a journalist now. He says he didn't realize reporters were so well armed. I take notes while Fitz stands, the BAR resting in the crook of his arm.

Rusty says the prison was built two years ago and immediately "they" showed up. He never knew who they were: a hundred or more men at a time, dressed in camo, looked military but nobody saluted. They'd spend a month down in the compound training, then they'd be replaced by a new group. "Urban warfare," he says. "That's what it had to be. They had weapons looked like what you have." He indicates the Franchi.

"And other badass shit. Looks state of the art. All kinds of sidearms. Armored vehicles. They'd practice clearing houses, taking out snipers, crowd control, what looked like protecting a VIP from bad guys, quick evac. They did some police stuff, like arresting each other, arresting large groups. But most of it was kill-zone city, y'know? Live-fire exercises. Night firing with tracers and that laser-guided shit. It was fun as hell to watch. I'd take station up here and they never found me. I figured they was headed to Eye-rack or Afghanistan. But like I say, something never seemed right. They looked military, but not, you catch my drift. Hell, reporters never been in the military—no offense. Anyway, had to be some super-secret shit, pretending this was a prison and all. You want my two cents? Mercenaries. For what it's worth. The older you get, the less people want to hear what you say. And you've finally got a lot to say. Anyway…"

"You said they're gone."

"They are," he says. I offer him water and he guzzles it. "Pulled out three weeks ago and nobody's been around until you two. Not even a caretaker down there. But I figured they had electronic surveillance, so I didn't go in. I coulda cut through those fences, no problem, but I didn't. This place scared the shit outta me."

◇◇◇

Fitz threads his way back to the freeway in an ebullient mood, mostly telling stories about me from the Army. They called me the PVLT—permanent virgin lieutenant—because I couldn't get a date.

"You should have stayed in the Army," he says. "You missed the 'we came, we saw, we kicked their ass' days."

"And how many times have you been to Iraq?"

"That came later. A charlie foxtrot from on high." A cluster-fuck. "Anyway, you had to go off to right all the wrongs in the world, become the big-time columnist."

"Yeah, some big-time columnist. I'm probably out of a job. Can't get anybody who'll pick up what I write. Maybe I'll reenlist."

"We're desperate, but not that desperate." He cackles with a high screech. "Anyway, you think you got a story now?"

"I'm getting there. It's interesting that everything I see connected with this story has no people, except for the assassination team that was after my ass. Two paper mills that are supposed to be open are closed. ODS's office out in the suburbs turns out to be a broom closet without even a nameplate on the door. Now, the prison complex that's not really a prison, but it's deserted."

He makes his rumbling "mmmmmm" sound. "That empty training site back there? They've deployed those people somewhere."

"What are you getting at?"

"Like I told you, the early years of the Bush administration were really good for the private contractors. Then things got tougher. With the deficit and the new administration, hell, finally more pushback from the brass—the gravy train has slowed down. And it'll keep slowing down, contracts keep drying up, unless there's an event."

The sun breaks through making the cab warm but my legs go cold. "Event?"

"Think about it," Fitz says. "What happened after 9/11? The whole country goes ape shit. The contractors make billions. What happens if there's another event? Maybe that's your eleven/eleven. And these Praetorian assfucks are deployed and ready to go as a paramilitary force to restore order. It happened with Blackwater after Hurricane Katrina. It wouldn't surprise me if there are much bigger contingency plans out there. Maybe a contract has already been let. Top secret, of course."

"Can I quote you?"

"On background. Call me a high-ranking intelligence officer."

"You're a light colonel."

"Heavy enough to order around where your butt used to rank. Call me what you want, but leave my name out. I know these contingency contracts exist for homeland security, even for operating detention facilities if there's major civil unrest in the homeland. 'Homeland,' my ass. Sounds like Nazi Germany. It's a permanent state of war, baby, a permanent state of fear. And I can't even imagine how much money they'll make."

It's not long before we're swallowed up by the city and a long traffic jam, which we mostly endure in silence. Finally, he swings the truck under the motel portico and I prepare to get out. We exchange a firm handshake, but he pulls me over and gives me a quick hug.

"Take care of yourself."

"Do my best," I say.

"What are you going to do?"

"All I know how. Write the story. What are you going to do?"

"I'll work it from my end. Who knows what's already set. Your girlfriend's daddy, the spook, seems to know something. It's going down."

"I've got to get back to the Northwest in a hurry," I say. "Can't wait for the bus or train. But my FBI friend told me not to fly."

Without a pause, he says, "I can fix that. You sure that cell phone's secure?" I nod. He says, "Then I'll be in touch later today."

I climb down, wishing I could borrow the high-tech shotgun. The truck is coated in dust.

He says my last name. "You were a good soldier, you know."

"I would never have been accepted by you West Point snobs." I smile at him.

"You still got that chip on your shoulder, but you know that's bullshit. Your only problem was you were too sentimental." Wrinkles furrow his dark skin. "You'd better think about that if you meet up with your killer threesome again. Yucatan, baby." He laughs his long, infectious cackle.

I close the door and watch him swing quickly through the parking lot and disappear.

YUCATAN: An old military slang acronym: "You're Under Certain Annihilation, Throw a Nuke."

I wonder if the young guys even use it anymore.

Chapter Forty

Briefs.

Editors love briefs, short stories that can run anywhere from two or three sentences to a handful of paragraphs. "Just brief it," an editor will say. They've convinced themselves—always citing somewhat murky research—that readers love them, too. When used properly, briefs have their place, especially in a society with a terminally shrinking attention span. Unfortunately, like everything in the newspaper business except excellence, they've been done to extreme. Often the most important stories in the paper are briefed. This is certainly true in the Phoenix paper—boring stuff gets relatively long treatment with jumps. Two grafs are done for something really compelling—I keep thinking, "Tell me more"—but they don't. They often don't even put the "where" in the brief, beyond the name of the town. I wonder what's going on that never even makes the paper.

I started out as a young reporter writing briefs and obits. I can still do them.

Early Saturday morning, I check out of the hotel and take a long cab ride to a civil aviation airport in the far north of the city. There I meet Fitz's friend Bud. He doesn't give me his last name and I don't ask. He's retired military and he's willing to give me a lift to Portland.

We fly in a Cessna 350 Corvallis, sleek and showroom new. The comfy cockpit looks like what you'd find in a sports car, with the control sticks coming out of the doors. Normally, I am a nervous flier on a big jetliner, much less a single-engine propeller plane.

Somehow this time it doesn't bother me, even as we encounter the up- and down-drafts crossing the mountains. Bud's not a talker. By late afternoon, I have checked back into my favorite hotel and given them my credit-card for "incidentals."

◇◇◇

Government documents are waiting in my Gmail account, some sent by Amber, a declassified Pentagon inspector general report sent by Fitz. Both mention a Homeland Security program from 2003 called "Project 10/11." It would have awarded no-bid contracts for private paramilitary forces to "assist" the military and law enforcement in the event of a new 9/11.

All the biggies were there: KBR, Blackwater, and one that never received publicity, Praetorian. The program was canceled after criticism over no-bid security contracts in the aftermath of Hurricane Katrina.

So maybe that's what eleven/eleven is, just a new way to make money. People get killed over money all the time. But the contractors are getting squeezed now, by the recession, by the current White House. All my instincts tell me eleven/eleven is a D-Day for Praetorian, maybe for an entire shadow government.

A month ago I wouldn't even have replied to an emailer who stated such a scenario.

◇◇◇

I check Olympic's stock price again. It ended the week at a dull, steady $35.25.

◇◇◇

Now the risk becomes overgathering. It's something that can afflict everybody from a cub reporter to a veteran—even a has-been columnist relearning the reporting trade. Overgathering sounds like the opposite of the one-source story, but it can result in the reporter being overwhelmed and producing a murky, overly long story.

It's time to write, do it with authority and command of the material. I'm a columnist, and in an ideal world I would turn my notes over to the crack I-Team at the *Free Press* and be happy with a co-byline. There's no time, and the team may not even be on the payroll any longer. It's up to me.

I have enough now for the story, if not for *the* story—the killer series that will answer all questions.

What I have will shake trees, cause more things to fall out, bring phone calls and emails with new angles and information. This will be a news story, not an opinion column. It will do more. It will rock Olympic International's fraudulent and murderous world. It will not be what journalists call a "thumbsucker" on the issue of privatizing national security. Those have been done, and done well. Nobody seemed to notice. No, I will write what one of my editors used to call a "hard news, put-'em-in-jail' story"—and I hope somebody will notice and care.

I think of a lede and start writing. No newspapers now. No books to distract myself. No Web news sites. I so love to read that I'll read the Kleenex box if that's all that's in a bathroom. I will read nutritional labels in the kitchen. But for now I will allow myself no distractions.

I do not have Megan Nyberg. I do not know what eleven/eleven means. The Praetorian thugs who chained me down didn't seem to give a damn about Olympic Defense Systems. They wanted to know where Megan was.

They would have asked about my knowledge of ODS eventually. After all, they slit open the wrists of James Mandir before he could tell me more. But it wasn't their priority. They wanted to know where Megan was. And I told them she was safe.

Megan can hurt them.

I plan the structure of the story and write more. Every fact is multiple-sourced. When the business center gets busy, I go to an Internet café or a Kinko's. I try not to spend too much time worrying about where the hell I will get it published.

The *Free Press* is out. "We've dealt with your publisher," Heidi Benson had said with a chilling authority. Indeed, Olympic has powerful connections with business leaders and politicians; it will do everything it can to stop this story.

Everybody I knew back east has retired or been laid off. I send queries to Huffington Post and Talking Points Memo, realizing I am not enough of a celebrity to get the attention of the former, not an Ivy graduate to merit consideration by the latter. A quarter century in the working press means nothing. To get the attention of the news aggregator blogs, I will probably have to be published in a real newspaper first.

I can set up my own blog, or have Amber restart Conspiracy Grrl, but we would attract maybe a hundred readers. I focus on writing. My right hand aches from typing and stress. I am horny as hell.

I call Heidi Benson in the afternoon. Having a list of sources' home and cell numbers is a wonderful thing. She's so taken aback by hearing my voice that she falls into a momentary fugue state of candor, admitting that Praetorian is a unit of Olympic Defense Systems.

She quickly recovers, refusing to comment, making threats of lawsuits, saying I am "the worst journalist in Seattle" and "it's too fucking bad you turned up alive." I want to ask: From the ferry, or from your company's death squad?

I say, "Praetorian waterboards innocent people."

The pause is so long that I think she has hung up. Then, "Nobody will publish your pathetic lies," and the line goes dead.

I have a working draft by Sunday night. It is datelined CORTEZ PEAK, ARIZ., and opens with an anecdotal lede, describing the fake prison. The nut graf says that Olympic International, far from being a boring natural resources company, is really a shell for as much as $20 billion in black-ops private defense dollars. And it's most controversial secret subsidiary is a paramilitary unit called Praetorian that is prepared to respond to emergencies in the United States, including the sealing off of cities because of civil unrest or terrorist attack.

One military intelligence source says Praetorian has been hired and trained for this event because some policymakers question the reliability of American troops to carry out such orders.

I have an email exchange with a reliable, long-time source. He works for a government agency. When we've talked on the phone, I kid him that he's really a spook. He laughs.

Now he's more cynical than the most burned-out newspaperman. "The coup has already taken place. The big banks, the transnational corporations and, sure, the defense contractors own the government. The rich and the powerful get what they want. They can sway public opinion, get around the law. They can operate Praetorian in plain sight. Think what the name means—Praetorian…

"In my years of experience in developing countries, we are by far THE most corrupt country in the world. Nigeria and Indonesia are nothing compared to DeeCee."

I polish the story. It's a complicated topic—like life, and exactly the kind of thing newspapers avoid nowadays. So I work, feverish and precise, to use the written word as well as I know how, to explain, to unravel, to cut to the truth. I email copies to Amber and myself.

Amber said get the story and I did. I just don't know where to get it published. My money is low. Now I'm nobody in the national media. I'm only known and respected in Seattle, and there I'm rapidly becoming a former somebody, with no column, no newspaper. I'm running out of options. Amber said get the story and I did. Now I can only hope she has her lifeline.

Then I go down to the bar and have two martinis and dinner. Sunday nights are always the most desolate. Desolation breeds regrets. I fall asleep and dream of working in a newsroom. Then I move into another dream where I am drowning. After I scream myself awake, I pick up the phone and make a call. We talk for three hours.

Chapter Forty-one

Monday, November 8th

It is full dark when the train pulls into Seattle. Every glimpse of the city looks as dear as a long-lost love. The last, slow pull into King Street Station seems as if it takes hours. I shake my right leg and shift the small black duffel bag. I have discarded some of the old clothes to make room for the files I printed out on the trip. Still, my mind is easy. Home is just a short walk from the station and I won't have to make the walk alone. My suit looks good and my tie is tightly knotted, all the way she likes it. The train car is full: couples, college kids, techy types, off-season tourists. The train comes to a complete halt by Safeco Field, then in five minutes creeps into a siding at the south end of the station. The platforms look empty.

The cold snaps at me before I even step off the car. It feels fine, especially after the desert. After a quick scan of the area, I step into the middle of a crowd of maybe a hundred people as we walk along the concrete platform. It smells like rain but the weather is dry. Beyond the platform's overhang, the sky looks moody with pleated clouds reflecting the city lights. The historic brick station adds to the darkness, except for the warm lights glowing from the large doors that lead inside the waiting room. Rachel stands at the door along with a company of strangers waiting to greet the travelers. Her dark, curly hair falls down to a black sweater and she holds a coat over one arm. I want to fly to her, just like in the movies. But I make myself stay inside the clutch of travelers, checking my surroundings. No Stu, Bill or Laura. My insides relax. I can't suppress a wide smile.

For ten seconds.

Rachel doesn't wave. She doesn't smile. She just stands there, almost braced at attention, staring at me, her eyes wide. I am maybe fifteen feet from the door when she silently mouths a single word.

Run.

I hesitate for a second, not wanting to believe it. Then I turn against the crowd and walk south quickly, past one railroad car, then another. I thread my way around the maintenance crew talking to the conductor and engineer. When I get to the locomotive it's idling loudly and I look back. Bobbing above the people leaving the train is the prominent head of Morton "Stu" Farmer, former Marine recon. I curse under my breath. In the next seconds, the platform clears enough that Laura and Bill appear, all in their official dark suits, all headed for me. I've played this scene before and I'll never play it again.

Now I sprint full out, cross in front of the locomotive and run back toward the station. Stop, look and listen. No—I can't stop, but I make sure there are no other trains coming. A string of high-level Amtrak cars sit on another track but they're not moving. I double back and run along the other side of them, wishing I didn't have the duffel, knowing I can't lose it. The station now sits on the other side of the railroad cars, to the west. A concrete wall prevents any break to the east; it's at least twenty-five feet high and supports the edge of Fourth Avenue South. I move north toward the dark.

Realities confront me. Away from the passenger spurs, the train tracks are built for heavy freight trains. They have thick, rocky ballast and heavy, high rails. They sit on a raised roadbed to ensure easy drainage. It's great for trains and treacherous for a running man. I find this out the hard way as I trip and nearly go down, catching myself but still losing precious seconds to escape.

The second problem is that King Street Station sits snug against a sharp rise in Seattle's topography. Beyond the terminal, downtown rises on a hill. Maybe a hundred yards north of the station, the two main-line tracks disappear into a tunnel that runs under it. Without going back to the station, there's no other way out. So I run as fast as I can toward the thirty-foot-high half-circle tunnel portal. The train cars that had sheltered me fall behind, but nobody else seems to notice me. The Jackson Street bridge passes high overhead with the sounds of cars and safety. Then another bridge that carries Main Street over the tracks. There's no time to look back. It's all I can do to keep from falling. I reach the portal and slip inside, momentarily leaning against the wall.

Stu appears at the end of the Amtrak cars and stands looking south, toward the stadiums, with his hands on his hips. Laura and Bill join him. I move deeper into the darkness of the tunnel. The wall is concrete: rough, cold, and damp to the touch. There are no cameras or alarms that I can see. The tunnel is more than 100 years old and runs a mile. I don't want to run that mile. My hand finds the butt of the .357 in its pocket holster. I leave it there as the three look around and confer. Rachel is not with them.

Then Bill says something but all I can make out is "tunnel," and he heads my way. Somehow the wind shifts so I can clearly hear his orders: "Go around the other end, to Alaskan Way!" Stu and Laura run back toward the depot. Bill breaks into a slow trot but nearly smashes his churchy face on the rails. He regains his footing and walks toward me. I'm already moving, hoping like hell a train doesn't come.

The last ambient light from the outside fades. The tunnel has no lights. The tops of the rails conduct the outside glow the longest, then even that disappears. I try moving in the center of one of the railroad tracks. It's flat and stable. Until it curves slightly and I nearly fall again. So I move over to the wall and run my hand along it as I make my way along the uneven terrain where the roadbed falls off toward the ground close to the edge. The space smells of diesel fumes and emptiness. It gives no hint of the roof or far wall. Who knows what I might find in here? There might be an alcove that opens up and lets me into a homeless camp nobody's ever heard of, or at least some maintenance room for the railroad. But the wall stays smooth and faithfully engineered close to the edge of the tracks, and I calculate there's enough room for one man to survive if he stands as flat against it as possible when a train is passing.

I move as fast as I can in complete darkness. My shoes make too much noise on the gravel ballast of the tracks. Rocks get kicked against the wall. I stop and listen: the walls hum and a sound like muffled wind is barely audible. No footsteps behind me. I heft up the duffel and keep moving. Just a mile. How fast can I walk a mile in darkness?

A train whistle wafts into the tunnel. There's no way of telling where it's coming from. I push down the spike of panic and walk faster. Then I'm making good time, catching a rhythm, feeling the edges of the ties under my feet but not tripping. Step, tie, step, tie.

I spot a blue light and walk toward it. It marks some kind of sensor for the tracks, but in this gloom it might as well be a lighthouse. I step out on the tracks—maybe that will keep Bill from seeing my silhouette against it. Stop—no sound of walking behind me. But I can hear the rumble of a locomotive engine, growing closer. By the time I pass the blue light and move back to my trusty path by the wall, a whistle sounds much closer. It might as well be Gabriel blowing his horn.

Then the tunnel walls in front of me are bathed in bright yellow-white light.

That's when I see it. I don't know if it was part of the original tunnel or added in the ensuing years. I don't give a damn. It's a slight setback in the concrete behind the bulge of a pillar—there's no more than two feet of extra space, but I'll take it. I duck in front of the pillar as my forward vision is temporarily lost to the bright stars of locomotive headlamps. I don't want the engineer to see me and call the cops. My body is pressed tightly against the concrete as the engines thunder past doing an easy speed. The horn doesn't sound; maybe I am invisible. The ground shakes and the noise is nearly unbearable. I cough against the fumes.

But the locomotive lights become my ally: I turn to look back down the tunnel they are now illuminating.

No one is behind me.

Now all I have to do is keep from falling backward into the train as the freight cars trundle by. Metal hits against metal and a screeching sound comes every few seconds.

The next sensation comes beyond surprise: in that sensory zone where noise and nearby movement are so overpowering that awareness is lost. My right knee gives way and I fall to the ground, then I feel a strong grip around my neck.

I'm nearly face down on the rocks and Bill is on my back and in control. He's got good moves—a classic foot in the back of the knee to drop me, then he puts me in a choke hold, where the pressure of his arm is starting to cut off the oxygen to my brain. I outweigh him and I'm taller, but I feel the deadly strength in his arm around my throat and I'm so stunned that I can't even fight back. The gun in my pocket might as well be on the moon.

"It's all over, motherfucker!" he yells above the din of the passing railcars. I am vaguely aware of a gun barrel at my left temple. He presses on my neck and I see light at the edges of my eyes.

"Don't pass out on me yet!" His mouth is so close to my ear I can feel his breath.

"I liked killing your whore girlfriend," he yells. "I want you to know that before you die. It was your fault that I had to do it, but I enjoyed it! I woke her up. Know that? You were both asleep. I went to her side of the bed and touched her shoulder." He repeats himself over the noise. Out of my peripheral vision I can see the wheels of the train go by, their flanges heavy and sharp on the rails. They screech, steel meeting steel. "She had this sleepy-eyed look, your bitch girlfriend." He eases the pressure. I gulp in diesel-tainted oxygen. My forearms and hands are able to gain some precious purchase on the ground beneath me.

"Don't pass out on me! I want you to know how she died. She died afraid! She saw me right there over her with a gun in her face and she was about to scream. She was raising up, starting to scream and turning toward you for help. And that's when I did the bitch—right in the back of the head…"

And that's right when I use every bit of oxygen left in my brain to force up my arms and swing slightly to the right. Some crazy grace has turned fear and anger into purpose. The weight atop me disappears instantly, effortlessly.

Bill screams and his gun discharges harmlessly against the concrete wall, just a pair of piercing sounds and a spark in the distance. But by that time he is under the train. The huge wheels don't even register the fragile human body they are grinding apart.

Chapter Forty-two

After the train passes, I slowly get to my feet and lean against the wall. Whether it's because I am getting nearer to the end of the tunnel or my eyes have adjusted, I can see more clearly: the shiny tops of the rails, the murky edges of the concrete. The oxygen slowly returns to my brain, making the train fumes stronger than ever. I hold the wall, letting the scarred, cold surface calm me. It's a long time before I stop shaking and begin to breathe normally. Awhile longer and my hearing returns. Then I sweep the dust off my clothes, find the duffel, and continue walking toward the north portal. Another fifty steps and I can see it, a crescent of city light against the darkness.

I have made my choice. Going back the other way means another dangerous walk through a mile of darkness and then, perhaps, questions from cops at the station. Going forward might be worse. Stu and Laura will be there. They might have backup, with all the weaponry that would make Fitz envious, and all I have is the small revolver, five rounds in the chamber, and another five reloads—if I get that far. But there's an advantage in being underestimated. Bill made that mistake and gave me the edge I needed. Now I count on it again. I walk to a quarter mile of the end of the tunnel and lay an ambush.

The sound of shoes crunching on gravel reaches me even before I see them. Stu and Laura enter the tunnel's portal walking down the middle of the tracks. Laura's blond halo disappears as they leave the outside light. Stu has a flashlight, but he's aiming it at the ground. Their hands are otherwise empty. It's amazing: I have given them every reason to believe I am slow and witless. That I am weak. Now they walk down the middle of the railroad tracks expecting to meet up with Bill, who will tell them, mission accomplished. The last thing they expect is for me not only to be alive, but in a comfortable shooting position, concealed in the darkness.

The .357 is out of my pocket now, slipping silently and easily from its holster. It is the lightest gun I have ever held and I have never fired it. I wish I had taken time to go to a range in Phoenix, even squeeze off a few with Fitz when we were in the desert. But I was always afraid of using ammunition I might need later. And, as always, there was no time. But Fitz, who loved the pistol, gave me some advice about how to fire it. I make use of that now, as I hold it two-handed and spread my elbows wider than if I were shooting the heavy Combat Magnum. Both of their silhouettes are clear and black against the city light emitted by portal. The trigger gets as warm as my finger. I let them walk closer.

Years ago, in that other life, I was taught that most firefights take place within fifty feet. I wait until they are half that distance before I make the final alignment of my sights, aiming for the torso. I exhale and smoothly pull the trigger.

The revolver explodes twice in quick succession, echoing eerily through the tunnel. The gun kicks very hard but my wide-armed stance controls it. Instantly, Stu goes off his feet, a dark, viscous shadow flying out from behind his body, then he falls straight back and down as if a wall had become animate and run into him at fifty miles an hour.

"Bill! No!"

Laura screams this and I have already traversed to her silhouette. She thinks her colleague following me through the tunnel has accidentally fired on them. It's a fatal mistake. The first round spins her like a rag doll. The second puts her on the hard rail roadbed.

Ten seconds have passed.

I rise and walk quickly to Stu. He's on his back with a pair of holes in his white shirt and no pulse. I go through his pockets and retrieve what I hope are the keys to the black SUV. His flashlight lies with its head atop one of the rails, spotlighting the face of an attractive woman with short blond hair.

Three feet away, Laura is on her side, her arms splayed out. Blood is coming out of the side of her mouth and her eyes follow me dully. I keep the revolver trained on her. One round is left in its five-shot cylinder. I pat her down and find the mass of a semi-auto in a holster on her back, still in place. Her pulse is weak and thready.

"You can't stop it."

She says this as clearly as if she were still talking to me the day I was chained to the waterboard chair. I kneel down on my haunches, brushing her hair out of her face with involuntary tenderness.

"Stop what?" I nearly shout it. My ears are still ringing from the gunfire.

But she's gone now, her eyes milky marbles in the glare of the flashlight.

The black SUV is parked on Alaskan Way, fifty feet from the tunnel portal near the Port of Seattle office. Traffic is light and the bay beyond is blue-black, nearly invisible. I walk quickly from the tracks, across a low railing, and to the sidewalk. I cross the four lanes of the street and approach the SUV from behind. Someone is sitting in the back seat.

Tamping down the rage that has followed me from the tunnel, I walk calmly along the sidewalk, wishing I had reloaded. One live round is left in the .357. It's back in the holster in my right pocket. As I stride along, just a normal gait, just like anybody going down the sidewalk, my hand rests on the gun. Through the tinted windows, I can only see a shadow, sitting on the driver's side rear seat. He seems to be looking forward.

Backup.

This is where a sane man would walk the other way, catch the 99 bus that would take me to Pioneer Square and home. Yet I walk toward the vehicle. "You can't stop it," Laura had said. They know what "it" is. The man sitting in the SUV will know.

Now I move quickly, quicker than he can check the side mirrors and react. In an instant, my hand is on the cold doorknob. I rip the door open and lean in, putting the gun barrel an inch from his nose.

"No!" It is Rachel who screams. She draws back against the opposite door in a fetal position.

"What's going on? Where are the FBI agents?" she demands.

"In the tunnel. And they're not FBI agents."

I put her in the front seat, put Stu's key in the ignition, and drive.

She must see a wild look in my eyes. She keeps quiet, glances at me in brief bursts, seeking recognition. I watch her out of the corner of my eye, something in me not trusting her, even though she was the one who alerted me to the danger at the station, even though her body language was stiff with fear. Still, she was sitting unrestrained in the SUV—nothing keeping her from summoning help when Stu and Laura went to get me. She obviously had suspicions about them—why else would she have mouthed the word "run"? My bloodstream, bones, muscles are all animated by mistrust now.

After we have gone several blocks, she starts to talk quickly. The three caught her in the parking lot, showed their identification, demanded to know what she was doing at the station. She told them—it was just instinct. Deference to authority. Stupid, sure. But they said they were federal agents. Maybe they were there to protect me. She blurted it out: I was arriving tonight. They walked her in to the station to meet the Portland train, Stu keeping a tight grip on her upper arm. She points to it, rubs it.

"Something about the way he was holding me made me realize they were there to hurt you…"

We drive past the businesses on First Avenue. I don't notice the clever marquee of the week at the Lusty Lady. Rachel talks in a quiet voice. She had been careful driving to meet me, taken all the precautions I had given her.

"But you stayed in this SUV. Nobody kept you here. Why?"

Her voice grows steely. "I can't tell you anything that you'll believe. You've decided now you don't trust me."

I want to hope she's telling the truth. A hundred things could have gone wrong, setting them back on my track, including my own carelessness. She's either a part of this—call it what it is: *plot*—or she's in danger. She sent me a note warning me off eleven/eleven. She claims she doesn't know what it means. Her father does. But maybe he thought he was doing the right thing by keeping me from Praetorian. Maybe he thought eleven/eleven was another drill, and my digging into it would just bring lethal trouble my way. But he's the one who ran the original Praetorian. A man trained to conceal and deceive. I don't have time to sort it all out.

I let her lean across and caress my face. Later I might wish I had been less out of my mind, wish I had debriefed her more. But that would be later.

"You're hurt."

For the first time I notice the throbbing in my left cheek. Where I was knocked to the hard ground by Bill.

"I like your beard," she says.

"Do you trust your father?"

"How can you ask such a thing." Her voice turns hot. "Of course, I do."

"Well, maybe you shouldn't."

"I'm starting to wonder if I should trust you."

I let that hang in the stuffy air of the cab as we glide down the street into the train station parking lot. No police cars, no conspicuously unmarked vehicles, no officers with shotguns and dogs looking for the man who ran down the railroad tunnel. The lot is half-full and I slide into the empty spot next to Rachel's Honda.

"You need to leave," I say. "Where can you go?"

"What are you talking about? What have you gotten into?"

"They'll kill you." I say it simply and she shudders. "Where can you go?"

She purses her lips and stares at me. "We have a condo in Vancouver. Is that good enough?"

"That's a start. Go tonight."

"But…"

"Rachel, you've got to go."

"Then come with me."

"I can't. I have to get the story."

"The story!" She pounds her fists on the dashboard. "Are you insane? If they'll try to kill me, they will kill you! You're not even employed anymore—you told me yourself. I asked you if you'd be willing to just have a happy life, and you told me yes…" She starts to cry, but the anger retakes her. "This is just another way for you to keep me at a distance."

"This is not about you and me."

She shakes her head slowly. "Damn you to hell."

"Go! Tonight!" I shout it and she screams a worse obscenity back at me, storms from the SUV, unlocks her car, and gets inside. In seconds, the tail lights glow red and she burns out of the parking lot.

I drive the SUV up Madison, past First Hill into the Central District. All of Seattle's glamour falls away in the Seedy. I park it on a desolate side street, use my tie to wipe down the places I touched, and leave it with the keys in the driver's door. With any luck, it will be stolen by the morning. Four blocks take me to a bus stop and the chill sea air slowly chips away the calm, edgeless rage that overtook me in the tunnel. In ten minutes, I catch the nearly empty bus back to Pioneer Square. Pam is dead, and now the people who killed her, and probably Troy Hardesty and Ryan Meyers, are dead. I acted with murderous clarity. If vengeance is sweet, why do I taste only bile in my mouth?

Chapter Forty-three

I get off the bus at Pioneer Square. A girl is standing at the curb and reluctantly lets me get past her. Otherwise, the park, so leafy just two months ago, is bare and nearly deserted. The spire of the Smith Tower stands out stark white with its blue light at the top. Across the street, the bare bulbs of the Merchants Café sign beams out as if it's 1910. A small group of autumn tourists passes speaking Russian.

Closer to me, a homeless man hunches on one wooden bench, his net worth in several large garbage bags. I buy a *Free Press* from the news rack, go to an empty bench, and let myself down slowly. My knee hurts from where Bill drop-kicked me. Someday maybe I'll have time to wonder why he had such a personal, visceral hatred of me, while his colleagues were just professional killers. Maybe a newspaper misspelled his name when he was in high-school band. My face throbs. Mostly I feel this huge emptiness in my middle and pressure against my eyes. Like I need a good cry but the tears won't come. The newspaper feels strange to the touch. Someday historians might look back and say it was a perfect "delivery device" for information. Now it's just headed to the dustbin of history. They're starting to run historic photos—not a good sign for the paper's future. I guess that a buyer hasn't been found.

"You looking for a date, mister?"

It's the girl from the bus stop. She's medium-sized, with shoulder-length brown hair, wearing only a bright blue blouse and jeans against the cold. Her eyes are shiny and wide—she's doped out of her mind. I tell her I don't need a date.

All the time I was so alone in my twenties—when I went literally years at a time without a date, just a date, just taking a woman for a drink or dinner and talking—all that time, I never went to a prostitute. Maybe it's a generational thing. I know my father went to them. Maybe it's a class thing. In the Army, the enlisted guys spent plenty of money at the massage parlors off base. Maybe it's a kink thing. Whatever, I never did. I figured if I had to pay for it, I might as well be dead. When I was on the I-Team in Texas, we used prostitutes as sources for the stories about unsolved murders and drug cartels. Sometimes they were reliable, often not. They were usually women supporting a drug habit. Often they were also supporting one or more children.

"I fuck for money," she says. "I'll suck your cock for ten dollars."

Deflation hits the hookers—that would be a column, if I still had a column. She stands in front of me, swaying from side to side. I set the newspaper down.

"No, thanks. You're too pretty anyway," I say gallantly. "You're probably a cop."

"I'm no cop." She smiles and lifts the flimsy shirt. She's not wearing a wire or a bra. I look at her face. She's definitely under-age. But there's something else. Something about the smile. And something about the voice. She has a small, pale mole on the left edge of her chin. I feel the sudden rush of revelation.

I say, "Heather."

She tries to back away but I grip her firmly by the wrist. I pull her down to the bench. Her skin is icebox cold.

"How the hell do you know my name? Nobody knows my name. I say my name is Samantha."

"Like the character in *Sex in the City*. You and Megan loved the show." I've never even seen one episode, but my guess is on target. Now she stares at me. I let go of her wrist.

"You know Megan…?"

I take off my suit coat and drape it over her shoulders. It will at least take away the chill. More will be required to get the skating-rink glare out of her eyes.

"I know about Megan. I need to find her, to keep her safe."

"I don't know. They were after her. Both of us. I got away. Lived on the streets. Maybe you're one of them."

"I'm a friend. You're safe now."

She's too high to run. She adds, "Please let me suck your cock. God, I need money."

"We've got to find Megan. She's in trouble."

"We're both in fucking trouble!" At least momentarily, she snaps out of the high. She looks at me like I'm an idiot. "They were going to kill us. That's why we went to Ryan. He wanted to call the cops."

"Did Ryan call the cops?"

She shakes her head.

"Megan thought the cops, um, would be in on it. So we stayed with Ryan awhile…"

I ask her when and she laughs hysterically.

"Ryan loved Megan. He was devoted to her, would have done anything for her. Very old-fashioned, kinda. Megan wanted to play."

"With older men?"

"I wasn't always a crack ho, you know…"

"I didn't say you were. You're very attractive…"

"I partied with the big guys. Movers…shakers…" She does wavy movements with her arms, first to the right, then, to the left. "Um, Megan got me in. We were tight. Shit, we had fun. Got me on cocaine. I mean really good stuff. All these big shots, so proper and moral back home, but when we were there…"

"Where?"

She shrugs. "Jack and the beanstalk. Little red riding hood." She laughs again. "We flew…" She makes wings with her arms and whoops loudly. I drape my suit coat around her small shoulders again. She stares at the flashing lights the toy store across the street.

"Do you know where Megan is?"

"Look dawg, we had to get out, understand?"

"Why?"

She stares ahead, then buries her face in her hands. "I don't remember things. Shit. They were going to kill us. God, I miss those parties."

She sees a man walking north on First Avenue, a potential john.

"Heather."

She turns back to me. "Do you know me from Texas?"

"Remember, you were going to tell me about what happened to Megan?"

"She went with him. She thought she'd be safe." Her face screws up in a knowing little-girl mask. "But I didn't trust him."

"Who was he?"

"I never knew. He looked kinda like you." She giggles and shakes. "They never told us their names. That was a rule. But they sure liked that young virgin pussy…" She shakes her head sadly. "They wouldn't like me now."

"He gave her the pendant."

"Yeah," she says wistfully. "Wasn't it beautiful? They always hooked up. It was like she belonged specially to him. He didn't like me as much. He liked blondes. Are you going to let me suck your cock now?"

"Did he mention eleven/eleven?"

Her eyes turn clear and wary.

"How do you know about that?"

I watch her closely, ready to tackle her if she tries to run. This is the same woman who had screamed "eleven/eleven" at me that night in the rain, and then had disappeared. Until now. She had said, "You'll get yours." I tell her this slowly, holding her hands. They are dry from the cold. Somehow this takes away the sense of threat. "You scared me," I say.

"I'm sorry," she says. "Sometimes I'm mean now."

I ask her what she meant: eleven/eleven. I describe the tattoo on Ryan's leg. What's eleven/eleven?

"I don't remember…" Her brow is knotted beyond her years. "But it's bad." More gears try to catch inside her head. "See, we heard it. Eleven/eleven. We weren't supposed to. Somehow… shit, dawg…gotta remember. They brought us back same as always. But something was different. The way they were looking at us. We knew it was because we overheard something we weren't supposed to. Megan heard more than I did."

I ask her again what eleven/eleven means. My voice is too harsh and she draws back.

"I can't remember!" Then, "It scared us, so after we got back, we went to Ryan."

"These big shots brought you back?"

"Yeah, in the float plane, same as always."

"And they let you go?"

"Yeah, but then they called Megan on her cell and wanted to meet us. But it's not the weekend. You know? It wasn't the usual time we go with them."

"So you didn't go."

She shakes her head. "But Megan thought they were watching us. My memory…" She pushes her hands up in a gesture of futility, the bats escaping her belfry. "They thought we knew more than we did. Megan said they'd kill us."

I just sit with her. The air coming off the sound grows warmer.

"Megan decided that only Mister Big could protect her. So she called him and he picked her up."

"What happened next?"

"We never saw her again. That's when Ryan got the tat. Eleven/eleven. He didn't even know what it meant, except somehow it took her away from him."

"He thought it was a clue."

"I guess. He was out of his mind over her. But he didn't do drugs. I had to go find a fix. Ended up with this other guy… god, I'm fucked up. Is Megan okay?"

I tell her I'm going to call a friend and I speed-dial Amber.

Chapter Forty-four

It's 10:45 before I get home. Someone has stacked the newspapers neatly in front of my door. It unlocks flawlessly and the inside of my loft looks exactly as I left it. Amber has taken Heather to a safe place. Maybe when she dries out she'll remember more. Amber told me she had been laid off from the paper. I told her I was sorry—she was a good newspaperwoman. I gave her back the Airweight .357 and told her how I had used it. Amber looked like the most beautiful creature ever to walk the earth. I will not let myself wonder what she thinks or feels for me, will not do an autopsy about our meeting in person again after so many days—it was a reunion that could be nothing more than professional, given the circumstances. I will not let her have that power over me. It was one reason why I preferred to see more than one woman at the same time—if one kicked me to the curb, it wouldn't destroy me. Now I can only rely on will. The story is all that matters.

I drop my duffel on the bedroom floor, strip out of the suit I bought in Phoenix, take a hot shower, and change into jeans and a sweat shirt. I retrieve my new MacBook Pro from under the bed and download the story from the file I sent to my Gmail account. Amber said she loves the story. But my email shows no takers for it.

There is little on my home answering machine but one message from the cops asking me to call them, that I have been reported missing from the ferry, and another one, frantic, from

Melinda Stewart. Nothing else. I always told myself that the acclaim I received over the years, all the speaking engagements, all the friends and invitations to dinner parties and cocktails—it would all stop the moment I was no longer a columnist for the *Seattle Free Press*. It hurts to know how right I was. The machine didn't even hold a message of concern from any of the other editors in the newsroom.

It's about the time when the last edition has pretty much been put to bed. Only a skeleton crew will be left in the newsroom. I call Melinda and she immediately starts crying uncontrollably.

I can't tell her everything. There's not enough time and she might still be in danger. So I give her the bare-bones account— "short-cut it for me," a gruff old editor used to tell me—and I describe the story I have produced.

"My God…"

"I can't get it published," I say. "Nobody will even respond to me. Nobody will run it."

She says, "I'll run it."

◇◇◇

I go to the paper to walk her to my place. Seattle's a pretty safe city, but I don't want Melinda walking through Pioneer Square at this time of night. As I walk up the hill, I see the big neon sign proclaiming the newspaper's name in the same font that appears on the front-page flag. Steam boils out of a manhole in the middle of the street. Rainwater sits in the ruts of the asphalt. I wait outside for her. Nobody will know me at this time of night.

Then I see Zimmer, the maintenance supervisor. But he's seen me first, and then we are face-to-face. His complexion drains to a graveyard gray and he stares at me. He looks like he's seen a ghost. I nod to him. He just stares. His large brow gleams with sudden sweat and his neck tendons pulse. Then he hurries past me, down the hill.

Melinda Stewart comes out of the employee entrance, wearing a turtleneck sweater and a long coat. She runs to me and covers my face with kisses. She holds me so tightly my ribs are about to break. Oh, my god, it feels good to be held. We walk back to my place in silence, where I have a bottle of wine and a hot pizza waiting. Then we get down to business. She sits at my desk before the MacBook. I pull up a chair beside her and keep quiet. Melinda puts on her glasses and gives the story a long first read, saying nothing. It takes her thirty minutes and two slices of extra pepperoni. She has never edited me before, but I've watched her work. She's one of the best in the newsroom. One of the best in the business. Wickedly smart. Wise in the craft and in handling writers. I know I won't be flying without a net.

That's a good thing. Highly sensitive stories such as this would normally go through a dozen editors and probably be lawyered, as well. That's the care that distinguishes us, at our best, from most blogs. But there's no time. No time and no support. So Melinda and I will do it together, just us, with the skills we've built over long careers and the trust of a friendship nearly as long.

When she says, "This is good," I know I've earned it.

But we're only getting started. We go section by section, then graf by graf. She asks great questions, gently encouraging me to make improvements—my way, not the way she might do it if she were the writer. She helps me see a couple of holes and plug them. We go through documents and sourcing, slowly and carefully, as she challenges each assertion.

By 3:30 the energy we both generated to work over the story is fading. The wine bottle is empty. "It's a great story," she says, and kisses me. But it's a friendship kiss, nothing more. And I don't push it. The sexual vibe between us has been fading for a long time. Maybe it's menopause. I'm so grateful for her friendship. She agrees it must run for Wednesday's newspaper, November 10th.

I call a cab and walk her to the curb. "How can you get this in the paper? Olympic will cut it off at the publisher's office. The M.E. will never go for it."

"I'm not going to ask him. I'm the night news editor," she says simply. "I'm just going to put it in."

"They'll fire you."

She smiles sadly. "We're all going to be out of work soon enough. Nobody's going to buy the newspaper. That's the skinny I've heard from very good sources. They're going to close it. Let's go down fighting."

Chapter Forty-five

Tuesday, November 9th

I sleep late without dreams. Then I shower, dress, and take the bus to West Seattle. It's cool and rainy, my weather. Melinda Hines' condo looks fine and her plants are thriving. The plastic container on the balcony looks untouched, except for the fine layer of moisture on the lid. I pull it off, remove the garden tools, and lift out the plastic bag. Inside, the Coach briefcase is dry and smooth. The files are undisturbed. I've gathered so much information since I hid it, I doubt these papers will be any use.

Still, they're copies of what I gave the Praetorian crew, and as I go through the last checks of my story I'll want every document at the ready. This is a story that will get you sued. And if Melinda succeeds in sneaking it into the paper, the *Free Press* may not even stand behind me. My only hope is that the reaction to the story will be so explosive, the newspaper won't have a choice. For a few moments, I linger on the balcony, looking across Elliott Bay at the city. Downtown looks more beautiful than any postcard.

Back in my loft, I spend the afternoon triple-checking every sentence. My normally neat desk is trashed with files, documents, printouts. So is the floor in a four-foot semi-circle around it.

Who, what, where, when, why.

I still don't have the "why." Olympic International has been profitable all through the recession. Not spectacular—its margins actually trailed its peers in some quarters—but respectable. But the paper trail makes clear that most of the money hasn't come from its timber or paper operations. It's come from defense—and much of that money was never accounted as such in the company's reports, much less in Pete Montgomery's conference calls with analysts or PowerPoint presentations. Olympic has kept enough of its old businesses alive to provide camouflage, but it's essentially become a massive defense contractor. Before Animal Spirits LLC ever took a stake in Olympic, it had been taken over by Praetorian.

Why? Why hide the sources of money? And could you conceal it from the ratings agencies, the accountants, regulators—well, history shows you could, as long as you made or beat your quarterly earnings estimates by Wall Street. Olympic did that. And it was a dull company headquartered way off in the Pacific Northwest. Not covered by either Seattle newspaper.

Why? One why becomes clear as I tabulate all of the ODS and Praetorian defense revenue. It outstrips the revenue reported by all of Olympic. It's nice to have black ops money flowing in—maybe an inspector general will stop by, probably not. If you get a slap on the wrist, it probably won't lead to federal prosecution, especially if your board is politically connected. A fine here and there is a cost of doing business. And none of it has been reported in that disappearing mainstream media. Meanwhile, the difference between the real revenue and the reported revenue was $200 billion last year. The personal motive is powerful enough: Imagine the secret bonuses for the executives "in the loop."

Why? Perhaps also to conceal the size and missions of Praetorian. The unit began by providing protection for American diplomats, then for entire U.S. installations in Afghanistan. Imagine that: Praetorian guards protecting American soldiers. Now it has become something much more. Fitz is a student of history. He knows that in the Roman Empire, the Praetorian

Guard, the emperor's personal army, became powerful enough to dictate who the emperor would be. There's been a bureaucratic fight going on in recent years between the military and the contractors, and the contractors were starting to lose—lose money and influence.

That could change with an "event."

At that moment, a siren's loud wail fills First Avenue.

I am back in my dense city of narrow streets where the sirens echo loudly off the walls of the buildings. They barely penetrate my focus. I am strangely detached from the killings I did not twenty-four hours before. No remorse. No anxiety. No satisfaction. I want the story clean and tight, to email to Melinda. That way, she can in-put it into the newspaper's CCI editing and composing system later tonight. By that time, the bosses and most of the newsroom will have gone home and can't see it. I ask her once again if she really wants to do this. She says she does.

Another run through the story. So much I wish I had: the killer ambush interview with Pete Montgomery, the first-person account from a whistleblower Praetorian employee, where and when "the event" might happen. What is eleven/eleven? But I can only write the facts I have and hope they are enough.

Then it's done. I spell-check it. I make a notation at the bottom of the text:

--30--

It's the old style that marked the end of a story. I've heard various versions of its origination, maybe as a telegraph code. It is so old school. Melinda will get it and laugh. I do, too, as I press the key that sends her the story.

That's why I barely react to the tapping on my door. It is a quarter before five and full dark outside.

I'm not expecting company, so I carry the Combat Magnum with me as I cross into the living room. The revolver is straight down my right arm, slightly concealed behind my leg as I open the door.

Standing there is Karl Zimmer.

He's wearing his standard maintenance uniform. His big hands are empty and the prominent planes that define his high cheekbones look red raw. He just stares at me, like he did the other day. He struggles to speak.

"After I did this thing," he begins. "Afterward…my mother appeared to me. She shamed me…"

He taps his head and gives a knowing look. "I live alone. Too much time on my hands. Crazy Old Zimmer, I know that's what people say…"

"They say I'm crazy, too." I smile. He doesn't.

"My mother. She demanded to know how I could do such a thing. And she came back, night after night." His jaw strained, as if carrying an unimaginable weight.

He says, "My mother has been dead for fifteen years. She believed in signs, don't you get it? When you came back, when I saw you there, after they said you were dead… I knew I couldn't live with this any longer…"

I invite him inside and we talk for an hour.

◇◇◇

Amber answers her cell on the first ring.

"How's your lifeline?" I ask.

"It's good. Strong. I'm going to have some interesting news for you. Good news."

"Same here." While Zimmer sits in the other room, I give her the details that moments before made me feel as if I had been kicked in the stomach. "Maybe you could talk to our friends at Seattle PD and get a search warrant."

Amber sucks in a breath. "I can do that."

"Don't be in a hurry," I say. "Meet me around eleven p.m."

I am selfish. The story must run prominently in tomorrow's paper. Even this can't get in the way.

"Amber, now I know why the FBI sent you to the *Free Press*."

She only asks me to take care of myself.

Chapter Forty-six

Deadline.

I find that my employee identification card works fine. The guard nods; he must not read the paper. Indeed, I am technically still on the payroll. Paychecks have fallen into my bank account regularly since I walked off the ferry. It would be nice to believe it could last, but I know better.

Instead of taking the employee elevator, I go through a door that leads me into the soaring lobby of the Free Press Building. Even though it's closed after 5:30 p.m., the ornate Art Deco lights are kept burning. I am alone and my shoes click loudly as I walk across the polished marble floor. I kneel down and rub the bronze plaque over Bob McClung's final resting place for luck. It is shiny from being rubbed. The front doors and elevator doors glow golden. The eight Pulitzer Prizes sit in the unpretentious wall cases. I stand and take it all in. Tonight I wear my favorite navy pinstripe suit with a blue polka dot tie that Melinda gave me years ago. I will miss my suits. I will miss this building. This… everything. I press a well-worn button and the elevator opens instantly. The car moves up steadily, past the ghost newsroom of the third floor, and opens on the bright space of the fifth floor.

The newsroom is nearly empty. One cops reporter is left. She's in a corner and doesn't notice me. I see some heads above cubicles in sports. Melinda is sitting on the rim, the circular copy desk. I pull up a chair.

"Hal is copy editing it," she says. "Then I'll slot it." She plans to replace a *New York Times* thumbsucker on healthcare reform with my story.

Hal Pettee is the best copy editor in the building. He has a full head of white hair and a mountainous body when he sits down, which is almost always. He has had that white hair for all the years I've known him. He looks up at me over his bifocals. "Not bad," he says. This is effusive praise from Hal.

So I wait. It is 10:45. Melinda has already sent the night page-one designer home. The front page is essentially done—put to bed—unless late news breaks. If it does, the breaking story can be put in place of one of those already designed on the front page, the metro section front, and one page of briefs inside. These and sports are the last to go before the presses can start for the state edition at eleven p.m.

Melinda shows me the new page on the CCI system: My story is in the lede position, stripped across the page on top of a centerpiece about funding for the ferry system. A chill runs from my shoulders down my back.

But we have one disagreement. Melinda has my column logo running with the story. I say I'd rather have a byline. It's a reported story, not an opinion piece.

"But you're the columnist," she says. "It's who you are. And it will get more readers."

"Melinda," Hal says, "Lock and load."

She presses the reload button on the CCI menu and the page flows back in to fill the computer screen. My story is there. The headline says: Olympic International, With Hidden Billions, Builds Private Army.

She reads through once more quickly, puts her hand on my knee. "Good?"

I nod. "Let's put it on the streets."

Who will tell the people? We will. Whether the people are paying attention anymore is another matter.

Melinda presses the keyboard button that "releases" the page. Two decades ago, an editor would have been in the "back shop," the composing room where printers laid out pages with strips of computer-generated stories and headlines on photographic paper. They would glue it down with a waxy substance that allowed for columns and headlines to be moved, pulled up, shifted. Then the final page was signed off on by an editor and sent to a large phototypesetter machine that took its picture, part of a long process that ended up on the press. The printers were often gruff, working much as their forebearers had done with "hot type"—the Linotype machines which had given newspaper jargon so many gifts: pigs, slugs, the hell box. The printers had better news judgment that many a young editor.

Even with the "cold type" that followed it, editors had to know how to measure headlines and type; everybody had a metal pica pole on his desk. Melinda still has a pica pole, but it's an objet d'art, not a work implement. Now the printers are gone, and all this work is performed by computers using sophisticated software from Denmark, controlled by designers and editors in the newsroom. When a page is "released," the system automatically sets it up for the pressroom. It will also, at 12:01 Pacific Standard Time, automatically go out with the rest of that night's print edition onto the *Free Press* Web site.

Melinda releases the page. The clock is straight up eleven.

She comes out of her chair and hugs me deeply. I wrap my arms around her and say "thank you," stroke her short, soft hair, and run my fingers down to her neck, where they find a cool, slender chain. Years ago, I gave her a piece of jewelry: a chain with a silver hound dog on it. A news hound. She gave me a stuffed animal ferret—I was so good at ferreting out the truth. And she gave me the tie I wear tonight. It is all part of our history, and she wore the news hound for tonight. My fingers playfully sneak under the chain and move toward the front of her throat, then lift it out from her sweater.

But it's not the news hound. It's a white gold key. I drop it and push back.

"It's Tiffany," she says. "You've seen it before." She's smiling and her eyes are lying.

I've never seen it before. I'm about to answer when the elevator bell sounds and Amber steps out, followed by two men in suits and another pair in Seattle Police blue. One of the detectives is my old pal Sgt. Mazolli. The uniformed officers are carrying a pick and a sledgehammer. They linger by the elevator. Amber walks our way. Melinda stiffens.

"Amber."

"Melinda."

She has a badge dangling from around her neck and is wearing a dark blue windbreaker with "FBI" emblazoned on it. "The guard says you're in charge tonight."

"Yes." Melinda tucks the Tiffany key back inside her sweater.

Amber hands her a folded set of papers. "Then I'm serving you with this search warrant."

While they talk, I am digging through the files in my briefcase. I find the old notebook and leaf through it. And I finally understand.

Chapter Forty-seven

Every few seconds, a smashing sound echoes out of the small room, the kind of noise that slams through the ears into the bones. Amber, Melinda, the detectives, and I stand and sit in the Governor's Office. One of the guards had opened it for the cops. It's still just the way it was the day he died. The newspaper that day sits atop his modest wooden desk, now wrapped in plastic to preserve it. His smoking jacket dangles from the coat rack. The 1920s-style lights hang from the ceiling, casting light and shadow.

The bathroom at the far end of the office isn't preserved. Just as Karl Zimmer had told me, the old toilet and sink had been removed. And where the toilet once sat is a recently poured concrete slab, flush with the floor. The slab sits atop a dead space between the floors of the brawny old building. New floor covering was supposed to be installed on top, to make the room look like a storage area. Zimmer never got that far. Now the cops are digging into the slab. One will give a few blows with a large pick, and then the other will step inside to bang with the sledgehammer. It has all come down to this. It's slow going.

Melinda sits in the Governor's desk chair, her eyes dazed. She holds the search warrant in her hands but she hasn't looked at it. She asks me what they're looking for and I don't answer. I look at my hand, where I had held the pendant, and I wonder. Coincidences happen. This is just an ugly one on a night like this. The digging echoes through the room.

The digging goes on for half an hour, then the detectives take off their jackets and take over for the other cops. Their uniform shirts are dark with sweat. Mazolli gives me a vinegary expression and lugs the pick into the bathroom. In a few moments, the heavy blows of steel against concrete begin again. A fine dust begins to drift through the air in the Governor's Office.

"We ain't getting anywhere." This is Mazolli's verdict as he emerges from the bathroom, his face bright red and dripping sweat. My abdomen tightens. "We can bring in a crew tomorrow. Maybe it's just bad information. Wouldn't be the first time that came from a newspaper."

He sees my expression. "Unless the columnist wants to try some manual labor."

I'm already up and stripping off my jacket. "Sure."

He hands me the pick. It's even heavier than it looks. The uniformed cops snicker. I walk into the bathroom nearly dragging the thing. Mazolli leans against the doorjamb.

I know the principle. Use the force of gravity and the weight of the tool to do the work. But just raising it above my shoulders using a two-handed grip is difficult. I aim the first swing into the eight-inch diameter hole that the cops have already made in the middle of the slab. It's a pathetic effort, the pick nearly coming out of my hands. The cops laugh.

I get mad.

Again. Again. After the fourth swing, I find a cadence of sorts, letting the bounce-back from the concrete help move the pick into the air for the next trip down. I stop to loosen my tie, and then I resume. My heart is pounding and I breathe in the dusty air like a runner pacing himself. Again. Again. Shards of concrete fly out of the growing hole and scuttle across the aged tile of the room. I aim for the deepest part of the hole, missing it sometimes, hitting it more and more.

The next strike sounds different, deep and hollow, and the pick doesn't come out. I lean forward on its shaft, breaking out more concrete, and I pull it out to make another try.

Then the smell is in my nostrils. I've smelled it once before in my life. You'd never mistake it. You want to throw up.

"Okay, okay." Mazolli gently grasps my shoulders and backs me into the office. He nods to the officers. "Back at it."

I turn and see that the night cops reporter, Kathy Deane, has joined us.

"I thought you were dead," she whispers to me. Then she sits on the edge of the desk, swinging her legs, reading the search warrant, and making notes in a reporter's notebook. The cops don't pay attention.

"My God, what it that awful smell?" Melinda is by my side, giving me a beseeching look. I just wipe the sweat off my face and shake my head. Amber stares grimly ahead, her arms folded across her chest. More slams of pick and sledgehammer reverberate out of the bathroom. Melinda nearly yells, "What?"

Then the cops stop and silence falls like the concrete dust.

Kathy refolds the warrant and says, "That's Megan Nyberg."

Chapter Forty-eight

When I look back to check Melinda's reaction, she's gone.

I ask and nobody's noticed. Then I am walking quickly through the empty Governor's Library, the red leather chairs misarranged, the big conference table littered with newspapers, and then out into the ghost newsroom. It's deserted.

Adrenaline powers me as I take the flights of stairs to the main newsroom. I rush through it, but she's not there. The computer in her cubicle is turned off. The desk drawer where she keeps her purse is empty. The wall clock says midnight. So I take the elevator down to the lobby and run out into the street, only vaguely aware of the burning pain in my shoulders and back from swinging the pick. The street gleams from a light shower that has passed through, but it's not raining now and Melinda's not on the sidewalk. I jog to the corner and look down the hill. One set of taillights has reached First Avenue and a signal flickers a right turn. The sidewalk is empty. That couldn't have been Melinda's car. She couldn't have moved that fast, wouldn't have been able to park that close to the building.

Returning to the corner, I take another long look each way. Something makes me stare up at the newspaper building. The lights are on in the newsroom, as they should be even at this time of night, and the windows of the Governor's Office are bright. The rest of the tower is dark. Except for several sets of windows on the top floor, shining out into the night. The first of what promises to be many Seattle Police cruisers to visit rounds the corner and parks. Before the cops get out, I go back in the employee entrance. I ask the guard to find Amber and tell her where I'm going.

When the elevator door opens, I see light streaming out of the publisher's office and I hear Melinda's voice, shrill, nearly hysterical.

"You told me you were going to pay her to go away!"

I can't hear the response.

Then, "Why did you get involved with her in the first place?!… I don't care!… Do you know what you've done?"

"He does." I say it as I step from the secretary's office through the threshold into the inner sanctum of James Forrest Sterling.

His eyes flash and he rushes toward me from behind his desk. I give him a hard check with both hands against his shoulders and he falls backward to the Persian rug that sits between his desk and conference table. His glasses fly toward the far wall and he's splayed out on the floor. He's wearing jeans, a white polo shirt and sandals with gray socks.

"Don't hurt him!" Melinda pushes against me, but I stretch out one arm and firmly but gently move her aside.

"I'm not going to hurt him. I don't do business the way his friends do."

He rubs his shoulders, where I shoved him. Then he rubs his beard. His beard. Heather had said Megan went with a man "who looked like me." I have grown a beard, and that night I found Heather I was wearing a suit, the usual outfit of the publisher, as well. Other things Heather said start to gel, too.

"Megan Nyberg came to you for protection." I pull over a chair and sit on the edge of it, facing him but above him.

"So she did." His high voice regains a certain command. "I don't owe you any explanations."

"What about me?" Melinda demands. "Don't you owe me an explanation? You said we were going away tomorrow. Was that a lie, too?"

I stare at her. All I can say is her name.

Melinda says mine back, sadness in her voice. Her face is red from crying. "Jim and I have been together for years. What? You have your playmates. You were never going to really love me. What does it matter to you?" Her voice grows fierce as she reaches the end of the last sentence. All I can say is that now she's implicated in one homicide, maybe more.

I glance at Sterling's large desk, stacked with files. Beside the high-backed desk chair is a large paper shredder.

I cock my head. "Destroying evidence?"

Melinda drops to her knees and puts a sheltering arm around Sterling. "Leave him alone," she pleads. "I let you put your story in. Why do you want to hurt him?"

"Why did you let me put the story in?" I speak quietly.

"Because I knew he'd believe it was the right thing to do, too." She starts sobbing again. "He just isn't thinking. His family has betrayed him, betrayed the newspaper. Then these people got control of him. He's a good man. If I could let you hurt them, then they couldn't hurt him…"

"Shut up, Mel!" Sterling says, grating my ears with his mangling of a lovely name. "What story? What fucking story?"

"The story that's going to put your buddies at Olympic International and Praetorian in jail." I relax in the chair and force my voice into a calm, easy shade. This isn't a confrontation. It's now an interview.

"Are you insane!" He starts to lift himself up off the floor but I raise a hand. I'm taller, bigger, and stronger than he is and he knows it. He sits back on his hands but commands Melinda to stop the presses. For a long time nobody speaks, and in the silence the walls and floor conduct the rumble of the big machines.

"Mel!" His eyes are wide, desperate.

"No." She says it quietly. "I can't. The story is too important. And that you would want to stop it… Oh, Jim, tell me Zimmer didn't kill that young girl."

I say, "Sterling killed her himself. Zimmer just brought her body into the building in an oil drum one weekend. There had been a leak in the toilet in the Governor's office—the plumbing was probably seventy years old, and Zimmer's crew took it out. But they had to replace a lot of the tile and dig down into the space between the floors. Your boyfriend here had him put Megan's body in and pour a new slab over it. She was in a tomb that would never be found, even if the newspaper closed and somebody converted the building to condos. Zimmer did it because it felt he owed the Forrest family. But he couldn't live with it. There's no use, Jim, Zimmer has told us everything."

Melinda is strangely silent. She lets her hands drop from him. Sterling stares at me, blinking fast. "I had to...take care of her, or they would have killed me. You don't understand. If we publish that story, they'll kill us both."

"We're way past that, and I'm surprised your buddy Pete Montgomery didn't tell you about it. But I guess you're out of the loop. Not like Troy."

"Troy." Sterling looks like he wants to spit. "Troy was the one out of the loop."

"Out of the loop of eleven/eleven?"

"Yes." He says it defiantly.

"But you had him killed."

"Not me. Praetorian," he says. "Mission security, they called it. Mission security was paramount. Troy became a liability. All we needed from him was help with the money."

"Hiding it. Laundering it in the capital markets. Making it look copasetic on Wall Street."

"Why the hell do you think Troy's fund did so well the past few years? He was no investment genius."

"Black ops money."

Sterling nods. "He was never a part of the group. He was the bookkeeper as far as we were concerned. Then he started getting too curious. He wasn't reliable. He heard too much."

"Like Megan heard too much."

"I don't know about any of that. I didn't want to know. Don't you understand? Megan was Pete's girlfriend. Sure, she heard more than she should have and she knew it. They were going to dispose of her and her friends. Anybody she might have told. She came to me to protect her. I told her I would. But if Praetorian had known, they might have killed me! So I had to do it and get it disposed of."

It.

I say, "She was more than just Pete's girlfriend. Megan couldn't resist showing her sister the Tiffany key pendant that her prosperous older lover had given her. It looks just like the one you gave Melinda. You were her lover, Jim. She trusted you to protect her, and you murdered her."

Melinda hisses, "Oh, my God." She falls back on her haunches and leans on the edge of the desk.

"Megan was a regular at the parties, at the island." I throw the dice. It's the kind of question that can open a door, or let the guy know you're a fool. I speak it with conviction, adding, "You didn't seem like the type who went for the underage girls, but I guess we don't really know anybody, do we?"

Sterling gazes past me, as if he's reliving it. "The group came to the island to relax. The girls were a big draw. Clean, middle-class, intelligent. A little wild, an eye for wealthy men. Nobody was supposed to be hurt."

"The island?" Melinda asks.

Tyee Island. It is one of some 450 in the San Juans, off the tip of the Washington state mainland. The Sterlings and Forrests have owned Tyee for decades. It's secluded, exclusive. So private as to be nearly secret, even within the company. Even the executive editor has never been there, but Melinda has. So had Troy Hardesty; he mentioned it in passing when I wrote the first column about him. Couldn't resist bragging to me, "I've been to the island," and letting me know he had connections to my publisher. That vital fact had been buried in my old notebook, one of the documents the fake National Security Letter demanded. I had overlooked it before.

Tyee Island. It's where the Governor himself had built a little Bavarian village. One house was supposedly painted in a nursery rhyme theme. Hardly anybody outside the family knows much about the island. But I remember one of the photos of the village that ran in the *Seattle Times* the day it reported on the *Free Press'* impending closing. One showed a house decorated with Jack and the Beanstalk. A detail that Heather, who came to the island as an adventurous virgin, remembered.

"The island is where they cooked up eleven/eleven," I say, working hard to check myself from asking too much, too fast. But I also know Amber will be here soon and then he may not say much. Right now, even though he's on the floor and I put him there, he thinks I'm just another idiot who works for him. Being underestimated can be an advantage—you want it from every source in a confrontation interview.

Sure enough, Sterling can't resist. "It was where the group relaxed. Business wasn't generally talked about. The slip with Megan showed the risks of that."

"The group," I say. "Pete Montgomery, you…" I swallow hard. "Craig Summers."

"Yeah, yeah." He waves his hand. I understand where the cliché phrase "my heart sank" originated.

"You're a pretty good digger."

"Summers," I repeat.

"He's former CIA," Sterling says. "But you know that. He's serving his country just like the rest of us. He's in over his head, but we need a guy like him. We couldn't freeze him out. We couldn't…"

"Kill him?"

Sterling looks like he wants to stand up and take me on. Then he thinks better of it and just shakes his head. "You have no idea what you're dealing with. This isn't just a few guys from the Northwest. It's international. Some of the richest men in the world are in the group. Politicians. You'd be surprised who some of them are. It's been in the planning for years. I was lucky to get in, thanks to my friendship with Pete."

He says it as if he's talking about a smart investment tip picked up at the Washington Athletic Club, which I suppose is how his brain processes it.

"But why didn't you stop me when I wrote about Olympic?"

"Because I knew it would just make you dig deeper. Hell, you might have given it to the *Seattle Times*. But you ended up fucking up the deal."

"Animal Spirits LLC. That was 'the group,' as you call it. Take Olympic private and cash out, before eleven/eleven…" I circle back nonchalantly. "Get rid of the old Olympic assets quietly. Then, when the markets calmed down, take Praetorian public and make a killing." Talk to me. You're the brain here. I'm just the stupid columnist.

"They wanted to pump up the stock price on anticipation of a takeover and then front run it," he says. In other words, illegally sell Olympic stock using information not available to other investors, making a big profit just before the price declined. Declined on, say, the panic following a domestic terrorist attack.

He rocks forward and angrily gesticulates. "There wasn't a lot of time. The group got nervous. Wanted to make sure their profits were locked in, no matter what. The government is divided, at war with itself, don't you see? The patriots against the weak ones, the ones who don't understand the threats we're facing. We didn't know if our friends inside would protect us until…" He stops himself, before going on to lecture me. "We were preparing for the future, the real future in a dangerous world."

"The future where you keep people afraid," I say, "and private contractors like Praetorian are the growth industries. It won't work." I laugh and shake my head. "People are smarter now than they were after September 11th. They've seen the abuses. They won't stand for it…."

"Of course they will!" His voice goes scratchy: tenor and sandpaper. "They'll demand it." He gives me a superior look.

I say, "After an event."

"Exactly." He stares into the design of the rug, realizing he's been trapped.

Only the noise of the presses, very distant, intrudes on the big, gaping silence. I let it hang for a while.

"What happens on eleven/eleven, Jim?"

He shakes his head and forces a laugh. "It's too late."

"Jim." I say his name with enough timbre in my voice that he is forced to look me in the eye. "Eleven/eleven. Everything you've built. Everything your family has built. Think about that. Look at your mother's portrait." He won't. "Look at it!" I shout, and he does.

"She would be ashamed of you."

"I hated her."

"It's going to happen here, isn't it? In Seattle. That's why Troy wanted to be on the other side of the Cascades by November. It's why you're shredding files..."

"Yes!" Sterling bellows it with such force that saliva fouls his beard. He wipes it off and stares defiantly.

Then, "A dirty bomb. Just the kind of thing al Qaeda or North Korea would do."

"Or Praetorian."

He looks around his office. Glances at the portrait of Maggie Forrest Sterling. "They say the damage to the city will be manageable."

The coldness in my body even reaches into my mouth and tongue.

He goes on, "It might not be the same everywhere else. There are at least four other cities. I didn't want to know. I just wanted to make sure my investments were properly hedged. You know, for the aftermath."

Melinda is crying quietly, her head buried in her arms that still rest on the edge of the desk. "What have you done? What have you done?..."

I lean heavily against the chair, wanting something steady in my life. The only other question I have hardly matters now, but I ask it anyway.

"So you were never really trying to find a buyer for the newspaper, because why would it matter? Not much market for a radioactive building. And all those people you laid off in the newsroom. All those lives ruined. It was just because you're another greedy, asshole newspaper publisher."

His expression radiates childish hurt. "I was the only one in the goddamned family trying to save this place! Nobody would buy a newspaper this size with such a big newsroom. We had to make those cuts." He shakes his head and blows out a long breath. "The *Free Press* could be published from Bellevue, anywhere in the suburbs outside the blast radius. We have a great brand. But nobody's buying newspaper companies right now. They have no future."

"And now neither do you." I'm fresh out of pity.

Then I sense Amber beside me. A few second later, the Seattle cops walk past, roughly lifting the publisher from the floor and handcuffing him.

He speaks through clenched teeth. "Do you know who I am?"

Mazolli says, "We know."

Chapter Forty-nine

Wednesday, November 10th

An hour later, two a.m., I sit on the cold bench, staring through the huge glass windows, watching the presses roll. They're running at a very high speed now, rushing to get the city editions out. I can feel the vibration out on the sidewalk. The bronze newsboy keeps me company, forever in a pose to call out the day's headlines.

A few yards away, the big trucks are leaving the loading docks, filled with the day's edition: 301,000 copies. Up the hill, at the front of the building, a dozen law enforcement vehicles are parked and cops come and go. Now I see a bright glare from the same direction. The first television news crew has arrived.

I think of all the newspaper has done for all these years. The Pulitzers. The corruption exposed and wrongs righted. The ordinary people helped. "To the Public Trust," engraved on the tower. Yet the *Seattle Free Press* will be most remembered as the place where the pretty, blond teen, caught in a lurid affair, was murdered and entombed by the publisher.

Until more lethal news arrives.

I have never felt so tired in my life.

"I stopped in the press room. I thought you might want to see." Amber sits next to me, hands me the newspaper. Newsprint has a special fresh, slick feel when it has first come off the presses. Cool, not hot. It feels precious. *The Seattle Free Press*. November

10th. Not just another day. I scan my story, set the paper in my lap, and let my head drop back. Clouds slowly sail overhead but even the mist of the early evening has stopped. The red neon *Free Press* sign looks enormous. Amber says, "It's online and it's already been picked up by AP, HuffPo, Yahoo, Google—with the *Free Press* and you getting credit."

"Shouldn't you be at work, Agent Burke?"

"All the big shots are here now, so they don't need me at the moment. And how about calling me Amber, again. I thought you liked the name."

I admit that I do. "You told me you would have some good news for me. Does it still matter?"

"We're executing a raid on Olympic International here at the start of business this morning. The raid on Olympic Defense Systems in D.C. will happen in four hours. We want to have as many of their employees on-site as possible, to question. Now we're getting an arrest warrant for Pete Montgomery, too." She sighs. "I hope it matters."

"Is he in town?"

"At the moment. We have him under surveillance. We knew these guys were up to something. We had no idea it would be this. You did good. Maybe you'll get a medal someday, in secret of course." She laughs. It's partly the sound of tension being released, but it's a nice sound nonetheless.

"You've got twenty-four hours to save the world." I smile at her. "That always works on TV. In real life, I'd start by looking at Olympic's warehouses down at the port."

"Thanks. We can't evacuate a whole city without panic. We don't even know the location of the other cities with dirty bombs. Maybe we'll break out the waterboards."

I shiver.

"I'm sorry. Things are going to get crazy for me pretty soon. We're going to flood the city with detection gear, so I'm hopeful. We have time. Here, at least. Still, I wish you'd take my Jetta and drive east. You'll have plenty to write about when it's all over."

I don't answer.

We sit and watch the immense presses perform their nightly miracle. It has been my life for so long that I can't imagine another. In cyberspace this second, hundreds of billions of dollars are moving around the world, thousands of bloggers are expressing their opinions, and secret military orders are being encoded and flashed. But I am here, outside the newspaper building, watching the presses thunder. For this moment, which is all I really have, it is enough.

Amber leans against me. Just that.

She lightly runs her fingers down my cheeks. They feel wet. I look at her and see the tears forming in her eyes. She thinks I'm crying, too. But it's just the rain. And the thunder.

--30--

Acknowledgements

Like the columnist, I was blessed for many years to have one of the best jobs in American journalism. The late Bob Peterson gave me my first shot, after looking up and asking if I could spell. Certain other journalists especially graced my career, making me a better writer and editor. Among them: Paul McClung, Joe Finley, Steve Sidlo, Linda Monroe, Mike Casey, Diane Solov, Judi Schultz, John Dougherty, Susan Gilbert, Leah Beth Ward, Meghan Glynn, Melissa Allison, Stella Hopkins, Amber Veverka, Frank Barrows and Cheryl Carpenter. I'm also indebted to David R. Foster and Tom Payne for their assistance on this book. Blame me for inconsistencies, deliberate changes in procedure or descriptions, or errors. Finally, my ongoing gratitude goes to Barbara Peters and Rob Rosenwald of the Poisoned Pen Press, especially this time, for their diligence and inspiration to help me make this special deadline.

To receive a free catalog of Poisoned Pen Press titles, please contact us in one of the following ways:

Phone: 1-800-421-3976
Facsimile: 1-480-949-1707
Email: info@poisonedpenpress.com
Website: www.poisonedpenpress.com

Poisoned Pen Press
6962 E. First Ave. Ste. 103
Scottsdale, AZ 85251